TWISTED DESIRE

Christa Simpson

The Twisted Series
Book 4

BLACK WIDOW
Publishing

TWISTED DESIRE

By Christa Simpson

Print Edition
ISBN 978-0-9919070-8-3

Author: Christa Simpson
http://christasimpson.com

www.twitter.com/_christasimpson
www.pinterest.com/christamsimpson
http://plus.google.com/+ChristaSimpson
www.facebook.com/authorchristasimpson

Cover Design by: Black Widow Publishing
www.blackwidowpublishing.wordpress.com

Black Widow Publishing: August 2014

Printed in the U.S.A.

ACKNOWLEDGEMENTS

I would like to thank Tanya Vought who, out of the goodness of her heart, has spent countless days and nights lending an ear, a hand and a leg. She is one of a kind. I'm lucky to have her as a friend.

To my street team, Christa Simpson's Twisted Sisters; with a special thanks going out to Shana Vernon, Shari Sulser and Dawn Vickers, for their readership and support.

Thanks to Author Sara V. Zook for showing me how to put myself out there and for being a loyal, like-minded friend.

And to each and every blogger who has shared my books, revealed my covers and reviewed my work. I thank you all and anyone I might have missed for everything you've done for me.

Christa Simpson <3 <3

CHAPTER ONE

David H. Gates answers his phone and kicks a booted foot onto his desk. He doesn't care that there's a new client sitting in the seat across from him. She's come to him because he is the best. There is a reason why his face is the one plastered across the town, on the city buses, on every public bench. He has a good advertising plan. But he also has a good reputation. It isn't based on his appearance or on how tidy he keeps his desk. It is because of his impeccable track record.

If you need the dirt on someone, he is the one to get it. Skip tracing, private security, law enforcement. He does it all. Because he can. One might call him a private investigator, but that hardly does his activities justice.

It's true, he doesn't mind getting in a scuffle from time to time, but he thrives on the thrill of the hunt. The police aren't exactly his best friend. He prefers to ride above the law. But even they can't deny that he comes in handy when shit goes down and their hands are tied.

Nobody ties his hands.

After taking his feet down from his desk, he hangs up the phone and picks up a pen. "What did you say your name was again?"

The woman had barged into his office, without a warning. The look on his assistant's face, when the woman took the vacant seat across from him, told him that she was going to be a handful. He had waved Jillian off and let the woman keep her seat. He was used to the handfuls. They were usually his best clients.

"Brandee. Brandee Hawkins." She sticks her hand out for a shake, but he ignores it. "I hear you're the best Rose Arbour has to offer."

He smiles. He can't help it. It is true. "And you need me

because…"

"I think my boyfriend is cheating on me. I know he is."

"If you know he is, then problem solved. Kick him to the curb. I'd be happy to supervise. For a small fee, of course."

Her voice turns snappy. "I'm not looking for a babysitter."

"Then what exactly are you looking for, Ms. Hawkins? Please tell me. Because so far you've done an amazing job of beating around the bush and wasting my valuable time."

The woman huffs, and he holds his satisfaction inside, sticking with the serious raised brow. He watches her bite her tongue, the way they always do when he's their last resort. "I need your help."

"Do tell."

He doesn't notice how Brandee Hawkins is a natural beauty. Her hair is a little limp, her voice a lot rude, and she's more than a little too blonde for his liking. Maybe, if she wasn't constantly frowning, he might have actually checked her out while passing her on the street.

She fidgets under his scrutiny. "My boyfriend runs a little bar downtown. Maybe you've heard of it."

"If it's in this City, then yes, I've heard of it. Please get to the point."

"He owns Riley's Pub. Mitchell Cavanagh is his name."

David nods his head. "I know Cavanagh."

"Oh." She looks surprised.

Is it really that shocking that he knows a business owner who runs a local hotspot not too far down the road from his own small establishment? He makes it his business to know his surroundings and the players in them.

"You were saying?" He wishes she would just spit out the words that practically every woman who comes to see him asks when she is dating a successful businessman.

"I need you to look into him for me. Follow him around. Document his every move when he's not with me. If he is screwing around with this girl, like I know he is, then I need proof. I want the facts. Do you understand what I'm saying?"

He finally nods his head, when he thinks she's done her spiel. "I can get you the evidence you need. But I must ask, before you go spending a boatload of money on this. Have you called him out on it, Ms. Hawkins? That seems to me to be the first step here."

By the expression on her face, you would think he ran over her grandmother's dog. "No!"

Brandee Hawkins is a very dramatic woman. Her voice rises to a shrill pitch. "I never!"

"I see."

When she fumbles for a few more seconds, he decides it's time for him to take over the conversation.

"If it's proof you're looking for, Ms. Hawkins, then David H. Gates is your man."

"That's you?"

"That's me. Now, why don't you get out your cheque book and we'll talk about just how much evidence you would like me to dig up."

The woman writes a number before he even considers proposing one. He glances at the cheque as she hands it over. His eyes open wider, to make sure he's read it correctly.

She gives him a pointed stare. "I want it all. Tell me everything you can about this, Aliah Brooklin, who is tagging onto my man. There's fifty percent up front. I'll give you the other half when you deliver me the goods."

David smiles, but it doesn't reach his eyes. "You mean business."

"You're damn right I do."

"I think we have ourselves a deal, Ms. Hawkins." They shake hands and she stands up. "Jillian, my assistant, will have you sign a few papers before you go."

She makes to leave the room, but he stops her.

"Oh, and Ms. Hawkins?"

"Yes?"

He gives her his most alluring masculine smile. "Have a nice day."

She looks flustered as she leaves the room. He chuckles

to himself, as he kicks his boots back onto his desk. He thinks for a few moments, while listening in on the women's conversation at the front desk. He's curious to know how Jillian knows his new client. He hears how there's no need for introduction and they call each other by first name.

The second Brandee Hawkins leaves the reception desk, he finds himself drifting there to get the particulars. He hands Jillian the fat cheque.

"Can you get this in the bank, please?"

"Sure can. Here are the file opening forms for the Hawkins case. Sounds interesting. And this girl, Aliah, sounds like a real piece of work."

"You don't know her?" He sees the way Jillian acts like she's thinking about it and refuses to make eye contact with him. He catches the unusual twitch in her eye. She definitely knows her.

"Nope. I don't think so."

He lets it go, making a mental note to test her again later. Jillian has been a loyal assistant to him for many years. She has always been forthcoming with information on the locals, where possible. So, why won't she just admit that she knows Miss Aliah Brooklin?

His lips remain unsmiling, his eyes unaffected by her deceit. He was good at hiding emotions from his face. Then again, you would have to have emotions in order for them to outwardly show. As for him, he's convinced he has none. "I don't know why Hawkins doesn't just confront the girl or call the cheating bastard out on it."

Jillian smiles and the worry hiding behind her eyes seems to flutter away, like her blackened eyelashes. "You shouldn't care too much," she says, waving a hand flamboyantly. "Her lack of eagerness to do a little digging on Cavanagh just made you a small fortune."

He turns on a charming smile. "That's only half of it."

"Really? So, what are you going to do to earn it?"

He taps the papers on her desk, ready to take his leave. "I'm going to get started right now. And tonight, I'll pay this Aliah Brooklin a visit."

"Isn't that a little forward? I doubt she'll tell you anything when she realizes who you are."

"I'll be discreet. Have you ever known me to gloat about who I am?"

Jillian smiles gingerly. "Yes. All the time."

"Not tonight." His real smile makes an appearance and slants a little to the left. "Tonight, I'm just Harley."

"Who's Harley?"

"How long have you been working for me?" he teases. "That H in the middle of your pay check. What do you think that stands for?"

Jillian's smiling again, disbelief still marring her attractive features. She tucks a strand of long blonde hair behind her ear. "Your name is Harley?"

"My middle name. My mother used to call me that before my father died, so she wouldn't get us confused."

Jillian nods her head slowly, with a smile so large it seems to stretch across her face, almost unpleasantly. "Well, in that case, have fun tonight, *Harley*." Her voice turns as seductive as her muted beauty. "Don't do anything I wouldn't do."

He turns for the door and gives her a friendly wink over his shoulder. "I wouldn't dream of it."

CHAPTER TWO

Aliah Brooklin has never moaned in one sitting more than she has today. "Oh, yeah. That's the spot... right there."

It feels that good.

"Yes! That feels so good." She feels like the stress of her life comes rolling off her body in waves. "Don't stop." Her voice is low and throaty and borderline breathless.

The man's fingers continue to dig into her skin, massaging away the tension from her muscles.

"Oh, Michael. You're the man."

Aliah rolls up to a sitting position. Michael is in no way alarmed by Aliah's forwardness. She's completely nude, except for the white towel tossed across her lap to cover the bare minimum, which she's only wearing to appease him. Otherwise she'd be happy to tell him where he can stick the rules of his high class establishment.

She's not at all concerned about flaunting her body around Michael when she visits him for her weekly massage. He claims that he likes *the gentlemen*. Funny, he keeps sneaking a peek at her chest whenever he thinks she's not looking. She smiles anyway, not much caring in this moment. He is good at what he does and worth every pretty penny.

Who needs a man when you have Michael?

"Thanks, Michael. You're amazeballs. Same time next week?"

He delivers her a friendly smile; the same one that sometimes makes her wish he was a little less gay. "I'm glad you liked it. Unfortunately, I won't be able to do next week. Vacation." And the way he says it tells her that he is flagrantly taking it up the ass. "I'll be back in a couple of weeks."

"Aww. What am I supposed to do without you?"

"Honey, go find yourself a man. There are plenty of them out there that would be happy to get their hands on you."

Aliah sticks out a pouty lip, not much liking that idea. "I'll see you in a few weeks then, I guess. Because I'm not letting them put their dirty paws on me."

Nope. Aliah Brooklin is not going to find some random dude to help her through her down time. She'll have to suffer. She will have to find other, more productive, things to do with her time.

She quickly redresses and heads home to ready herself for a night on the town. Ever since her best girlfriend Abigail got married and had a baby, their nights out were becoming few and far between. She is really looking forward to tonight. It has been months since their last night out without a kid attached at Abigail's hip.

Abigail is still her best girlfriend. She is her *only* girlfriend, actually. Aliah isn't one to hang out with the ladies. Men are easier to be around. They tend to cut the crap and skip the drama, and she is plenty dramatic for the whole lot of them.

Aliah pulls up to Abigail's house in her yellow BMW and wails on the horn. When no one makes an appearance in the door, Aliah tries again, beeping her car's horn twice. She then holds it down for three long seconds.

Still nothing.

She turns off her car and heads for the front door of Abigail's restored Victorian, soothed by the steady click of her ridiculously tall shoes. Aliah shouldn't be surprised that her friend isn't ready yet. It's a rare occurrence that she be ready on time. But still, Aliah likes to harass her.

Aliah lets herself in the house and quickly realizes that her friend has company.

Shocking!

The young girl sitting on the sofa bears a striking resemblance to someone she knows. Very familiar indeed.

Can't be.

Distracting her from that obvious dilemma, a wet and

wiggly little girl comes pattering toward her, flashing her naked bottom for anyone to see.

"Maya!" Aliah cheers, even though everyone knows she's not particularly fond of kids.

Maya doesn't know any different and takes a running leap into Aliah's arms, soaking her bar clothes. Aliah moans, but quickly replaces her annoyance with a smile. Knowing what little-Maya likes, she throws her up into the air, to hear her giggle.

Edwin and Abigail Santora have made the most beautiful baby girl and she is a sweetheart. *There is just something special about this little one.*

Aliah quickly lowers the kid to the floor and sweeps her hands over her wet shirt, acting like she isn't completely horrified. Then she looks over to her friend, who appears down the hallway with a beautiful baby bump encompassing her middle.

"Woman!" Aliah shouts. "Why aren't you ready yet? You can't go out looking all sweet and romantic when I look like this!" She points toward her own excessive cleavage and lifts a five inch stiletto from the floor.

Abigail sweeps the hair from her face with a sudsy, wet hand, and then dries it on the towel hanging over her shoulder. "Ally, don't you remember? I told you I couldn't do it tonight. I promised Aubrey I would meet with her and the wedding planner to go over the details of her wedding." She dries Maya on the spot and lifts her into her arms while she talks.

"I'm sorry, Ally. But you're on your own tonight. That is, of course, unless you would like to join us." Abigail's smile is sarcastic at best.

"Looking this good? That'd be a waste."

Abigail knows damn well that Aliah despises weddings more than anything else in this world. She despises love and all of that other girly crap that goes along with a lifetime of happiness too. She hasn't always been this single sighted. But ever since Hunter Wight crushed her heart into a blender and hit the pulse button repeatedly, she has vowed never to love again.

It was an easy task, really. She will never let a man get that close again. And if he dares try, she will cut off his balls and pin them to the wall as a reminder for any future takers. No man is willing to risk his balls to win that fight. It's a losing battle.

Saving her from another futile discussion about getting back out there, Aliah welcomes the company, as another woman rings the doorbell. Aliah opens the door and waves a dramatic hand.

"Come on in."

Aliah doesn't recognize her at first, but as soon as the girl opens her mouth, Aliah is quickly reminded that it's none other than that big-mouthed bitch, Ashley Clarke.

Ashley's eye bug out of her head the instant she notices her niece sitting in Abigail's living room. "Pheobe? What are you doing here?" she screeches.

That was my reaction exactly.

Abigail shifts from one foot to another and lowers Maya to the floor. "Pheobe, would you please take Maya to her room to get dressed? I've picked out her clothes. They're on top of her dresser."

Pheobe doesn't ask questions. She is old enough now to understand when adults need their privacy. Pheobe reaches for Maya's hand, then hikes her onto her hip. "Come on, Maya. I'll help you get dressed."

Ashley doesn't waste any time opening her big mouth. "I can't believe my brother even talks to you, after what you did to him. He's still a wreck. You've ruined him."

Abigail turns her head toward the floor and massages the top of her baby belly. You can see it in her features that she means what she says. "I didn't mean to hurt him, Ashley. I still care for Cameron, very much. But I'm truly happy now and I know in my heart that I made the right choice. Life couldn't be any better for me, really. Marrying Edwin was the smartest decision I've ever made."

As if waiting for the perfect moment, Edwin enters the door and piles into the overcrowded foyer. Maya hears her father arrive home and comes toddling back into the room at full speed, only partially dressed. She springs into her daddy's arms. Edwin kisses her all over her face, then blows on her belly, making her giggle even harder than she already was.

Pheobe renters the room and giggles too. Everyone admires the way Edwin is with his little girl. Even Aliah has to admit that he's a good dad.

Abigail makes eye contact with her husband. Those two are truly in love.

It's sickening.

"Can you bring the girls to Maya's room for a few minutes?" Abigail asks him.

Edwin kisses Abby on the cheek, as he caresses her belly, then he carries his little girl down the hall. "Ladies," he says, with a nod, as he walks away.

Pheobe follows after him, like a lost puppy. It is crazy, but the girl appears to have really taken a liking to him.

Ashley notices Pheobe's fixation too. "That isn't even right."

"What isn't right is you flapping your gums like that in Abby's house," Aliah vents.

It's bad enough Abigail has to put up with Ashley long enough to get through her sister's wedding. Aliah is happy to lend a hand, if only to get the girl to shut her big fat mouth.

Abby presses her hand to her forehead. "Do we have to do this now?"

Ashley seems to think so. "I just can't get over the fact that Cam's asked *you* for help with his daughter. Pheobe is *my* niece. She can come stay with me."

Abby clearly feels the need to explain. "Pheobe's not that happy at home. She likes coming here and she deserves the attention. The poor girl's had a rough life. You of all people should know that." Abby blows out a breath of exhaustion. "I like having her around, and so does Maya."

Aliah understands why Abby does it, but she's still curious about the entire arrangement. "How does Eddie feel about you playing mommy to your ex's kid?"

Abigail's expression shows how uncomfortable she is having this conversation, but they both wait patiently for her to answer. "Edwin knows I chose him. We have the family I've always dreamt of. I couldn't be happier to share that with Pheobe. I love the girl. So does Eddie."

Edwin returns to the room and slips his arms around Abby's waist, hearing her confession. He rests his chin on her shoulder and turns his head to kiss her neck. "Hey, baby. Everything okay out here?"

"I think so," Abby admits, flashing a pointed glance at Ashley.

Edwin catches the exchange and snatches Abby's gaze, so he can steal another kiss. This time he reaches her lips.

The two guests both stare, admiring the passionate embrace and the way Eddie takes away all of Abby's frustrations with his lips. Ashley has to shake her head to snap out of it, but not Aliah.

"Get a room. I don't need to see this!" Aliah grows very uncomfortable.

Edwin smiles, in between kisses, as Abby turns to face him. Everyone hears the kids sneaking back down the hall, but the couple doesn't stop gazing at each other, sharing chaste, intermittent kisses.

"Love you," Edwin whispers to Abby.

"Love you too, Eddie."

"You really think you should be doing that in front of Pheobe?" Ashley doesn't watch her mouth around the kids and everyone can see how angry that makes Abby.

Edwin winks at Abby, as he lifts Maya back into his arms, and it seems to bring back her calm. "Say bye bye to momma."

"Bye bye," Maya coos, reaching out for her mom.

Abby collects Maya in her arms and squeezes her tightly. "You be a good girl for daddy. Okay, sweetness?" Abby kisses a small, baby soft hand, and delivers Maya back to Edwin. She gives Pheobe a hug, and whispers not-so-quietly in her ear. "You keep an eye on Eddie for me. Okay, hun?"

Pheobe giggles. "I will." She runs off with Maya, and Edwin follows after them.

"You ladies have yourselves a nice night."

Abby's smiling, but after Edwin disappears from the room, the smile near-instantly disappears, as she turns back to Ashley. "I see no problem kissing in front of Pheobe and Maya.

"It's no big deal," Aliah agrees.

"We're married, Ashley. We're in love. I see no issue with sharing that in front of the girls. You would be pushing it to say that it is inappropriate."

Aliah nods in agreement. *She* can't even deny it. "It's sweet. The girls will see the way you two are together and know you're in love."

Abby smiles, catching Aliah's moment of softness. "Hopefully one day you'll find a love like that."

Aliah is very uncomfortable with that notion. She flags a hand in the air, to stop Abby and her crazy-ass comments. "Okay. I've had enough of this mushy shit. I'm going out."

"Ally, it's only seven. It's a bit early for you to hit up your usual stomping grounds, wouldn't you say?"

"It's Thursday night. The lights will already be low. I'll grab something to eat and bug Mitchell over at Riley's. I'm sure I can wrestle a few drinks from him, on the house." Aliah winks at her friend, but Abby doesn't look real impressed by the idea.

Neither does Ashley. "I'm surprised Mitchell even lets you in the place looking like that. Some of the patrons might get the wrong impression about what kind of establishment he's operating there."

"Stuff it, Ashley. You're just jealous because you have to pay for your drinks."

Abby explains it, so Aliah doesn't have to. "Mitchell's had a thing for Aliah as far back as I can remember."

Aliah scowls at Abby, even though she is doing her a service. "I can't believe you just told her that!"

"Oh, puh-lease. It's so obvious to anyone who sees you

two together. He still crushes on you hard."

"He has a girlfriend now, you know." Aliah tries to get Abby off her back, but it doesn't work.

"Yeah, I know. It hasn't changed the way he looks at you. I'm sure he's still hung up on you. He's just waiting for that one day when you'll come around."

Aliah stuffs her fisted hands under her armpits. "He'll be waiting a long time."

Abby smirks. "Why else do you think he would want to keep you that close, Ally? Come on. Think about it."

"Whatever," Aliah says, growing tired of always being under the microscope.

With her father being the City's fire chief, and she being his only daughter, all of the town folk think it's their business to know what and who she's doing at all times. She makes a good effort to keep out of the public eye. That way she can avoid the unwanted attention. Abby's not helping her situation any.

"Have fun?" Abby says, smiling.

Aliah answers with a smile. "You, have fun with the whole wedding thing. I'm out of here." Aliah tries to ignore the two of them, as she moves between them to reach the door.

"Be good," Abby teases.

Aliah smirks back at Abby, as she steps outside. "You know I won't."

CHAPTER THREE

Harley heads home from work early to get a head start on his investigation. He does his best work from home. His home office is like a shrine of all his achievements; the greatest of all being the research he'd done to find his daughter after the death of Hannah's mother.

He smiles. Researching Miss Aliah Brooklin will be a much easier task. He skips by his office and heads for his bedroom. He tosses his laptop on his bed and starts it up. Harley grasps onto the tail of his t-shirt and pulls it over his head, tossing it onto the floor next to his closet. He gets comfortable on his bed, slouching against his headboard, and loads the Google search engine.

Aliah Brooklin.

Ah, ha! This should get interesting. A large number of articles pop up about the only daughter of the City's fire chief. Why hasn't he heard of this girl before? He's been slacking.

He skips past all of the mundane articles, when he notices the images link.

Aliah Brooklin is a babe!

With each picture he scans over, she seems to look more and more beautiful. She isn't your typical beauty either, with blonde hair or blue eyes, but there's just something about the fiery look in her eyes that has him intrigued. She streaks her hair with dramatic colors, and that only seems to intensify the darkness in her large, almond-shaped eyes.

He can see why Mitchell Cavanagh is interested. *Allegedly.* Harley finds it hard to see how any man with a pair of eyes and a dick wouldn't be attracted to her. He scrolls down the first page of images, which are mostly of her, with Cavanagh creeping in the background of a few.

He clicks back to the search page and reads over her

social networking profiles, but there isn't anything there of much interest to him. Miss Aliah Brooklin doesn't seem too active on the social front. She seems surprisingly laidback, which is in stark contrast to the look in her eyes. Harley stares at a photo of her for a minute too long. She's looking right at the camera, and it feels like she can see right through him.

This one will be interesting indeed.

Harley figures it's best he follow his client's instructions and attend the bar Mitchell Cavanagh owns, that Miss Brooklin tends to frequent. It's shocking that this spicy looking gal is hanging out at a local pub with an oversized troll like him. Does she really think she's going to meet the right kind of guy at a place like that? Maybe she truly does have a thing for Cavanagh.

Nah.

As Harley climbs out of the shower, he hears his phone ringing off the hook. He wraps a black towel around his waist and pads to his bed to answer it. He's not surprised in the least that Ms. Hawkins is calling already.

"So, did you get any of the answers I was looking for?" the woman asks, without a friendly greeting.

Harley heads back to the bathroom to grab a hand towel to dry his upper body. "This sort of thing takes time, Ms. Hawkins. I have some preliminary findings, but I'd like to approach the accused before giving you anything definitive."

"Preliminary findings? Accused? She *is* guilty!"

He ignores her outburst. "I will do so tonight. I really don't think there is anything you need to worry about in the meantime."

"Tell me what you've found," she demands, with a clipped tone.

He knew she was going to be one of these. He'd better make this case a quick, clean cut. Like a rip off the bandage, take her money and run type of deal.

"What I've found online shows nothing but a long-term friendship. They knew each other as kids. They went to the same high school. Graduated the same year. I can see it in the pictures. Have you checked your own year book, Ms. Hawkins? I understand you went to the same school yourself. If you ask me, there's nothing going on there. At least, not from her perspective."

"I didn't pay you for your opinion," she shouts, overreacting once again. "I paid you to show me the proof. Did you know I walked in on them last weekend in his office? If I hadn't barged in, she would have fucked him."

Harley glances to the floor and sighs, digging his fingers into the corners of his eyes. He doesn't want to say it, but this Aliah girl is way out of Cavanagh's league. In every picture of the two of them, Mitchell looks like he has a case of puppy love. Little seems to have changed in the more recent photos. Harley can see why.

Miss Brooklin is a looker.

"Let me do the detective work here, Ms. Hawkins. Trust that I'll take care of it."

"You'd better."

"You should reconsider threatening me, Ms. Hawkins. I don't take lightly to that." Harley's voice does not fluctuate, but his point is taken.

"I apologize."

Against his better judgment, he goes on. "I have to admit, though, I really don't think you have this one pegged..."

"Fucked him, I tell you!" She hollers it into the phone. It has him looking over his shoulder to make sure his daughter hasn't heard her.

Suddenly Harley starts to see the depths of this woman's madness. It is like she's flipped a switch from plain Jane to crazy Connie in a matter of seconds.

"She's a whore. She feeds on friendly, nice guys like Mitchell all the time. I'm not going to let her have this one."

"Please, ma'am. With all due respect. Let me look into it and I'll tell you all that I find. That is my job. And from what I hear, I'm pretty damn good at it."

She huffs again and snaps at him. "Make it quick."

Again, he feels the need to reiterate the obvious facts. "Nothing seems to be out of the ordinary between these two. If there's something going on, then I will find out. I'll have to do a little searching, dig a little deeper, but I truly think that you're wasting your money here."

"It's my money. Let me decide whether it's a waste or not. Do it. I want the facts."

Even as she's barking the orders, Harley has a rotten feeling brewing in the pit of his stomach. When he first saw Aliah's photo, he admits he was intrigued, but he doesn't look at women as anything other than objects these days. That is one object he can't wait to get his hands on.

"I'll do it. Two for the price of one."

She's pleased when she hangs up the phone. His gut tells him that something is seriously wrong with this woman. His gut is rarely wrong. But the pay check has him pulling on his leather jacket and rolling out his Harley from storage.

What had started out as an easy investigation into a local bar owner, was quickly turning into a character assassination by Ms. Brandee Hawkins. Harley's agreed to follow Mitchell Cavanagh around, to make sure he's not cheating, but his client is clearly fixated on this Aliah girl. If Aliah is as close to Cavanagh as Ms. Hawkins suggests, then it's likely that he'll be running into her tonight too.

This should be fun.

When the sky turns dark, he kisses his daughter on her forehead and climbs onto his bike. After giving it a couple of revs, he lifts his feet and makes his way downtown, leaving a cloud of dust behind him.

CHAPTER FOUR

Aliah escapes that conversation by the nick of her teeth. It's no wonder she hates hanging around the ladies. They always have to pry at her personal life. She hates nothing more than discussing relationships, marriage and love. Those aren't things she ever intends on finding and so there is no point in acting like she cares to hear about it.

What she really needs is a fun man-friend who can meet all of her sexual needs. Then again her friend Abby had tried that with Edwin and look where that got her. Regardless, she isn't Abby and she has measures in place to ensure that history doesn't repeat itself for her.

She wonders when it became so difficult to find a man who can appreciate a casual, detached relationship. Her sex toys had helped her get through the first few months after Hunter Wight had dumped her, back when she knew that spreading her legs for another man would never mend her broken heart. But she needs a backup plan, for when she's looking for something more than a cold, trembling dildo.

After a long, lonely year, Aliah had finally drummed up the courage to give other men a try, but they were deficient in many areas. She has only hit up the best looking ones, even the ones she had a few years on, but they were substandard lovers. She supposes there were a couple of guys who might have lived up to her standards, with a little practice, but the bastards always break the rules.

Aliah doesn't want to meet the parents, or cuddle on the couch to watch a movie on Saturday night. She doesn't need dinner or shiny trinkets to fill the void in her heart. She doesn't need showered with gifts of flowers or chocolate. All she needs is an experienced sex god to tease and please her and hit the road when he's done lighting her bed on fire.

Is that too much to ask?

All those other things lead to one thing. The one thing she plans on avoiding at all costs.

Falling in love.

Aliah Brooklin will not be making that mistake again.

She can't believe a whole year has passed since she has gotten laid though. She has already burned out two vibrators, and has led a lot of men on, but she can't seem to go through the motions again. She's afraid, though, that if she doesn't find a friend soon, she'll die a lonely, old spinster, complete with crotchety cobwebs.

It isn't until her lifelong friend, Mitchell Cavanagh, finds himself a woman that she realizes how dire a situation it has become. Her and Mitchell go way back, that is true, but they're just friends. He does not fit the bill to be the man in her life, and she's just not attracted to him that way.

It's no secret that Mitchell has always had the hots for her, and it's true that she's always known it, but they've never let that get in the way of their friendship. They are buddies. And apart from Abby, he is her best.

Aliah pulls into the parking lot across from Riley's Pub. She glances across the main street at the warm brick building and the double wooden doors. The patio is surrounded in black rod-iron fencing and protects a number of tables with beer-branded umbrellas hanging above them. Despite the fact that it's a beautiful night, the patio is nearly empty. The heat from the afternoon has scorched the brick, and almost everyone seems to be hiding inside to take advantage of the air-conditioning.

By the time Aliah reaches the front door of the place, perspiration glistens off her exposed chest. She pushes the doors open and instantly sees that there is a lively crowd filling the seats at the bar. Her prospects are looking promising. She smiles at them all and acts like she owns the place, rounding the bar to grab herself a refreshment. All the bartenders are so busy filling orders that they don't even notice.

After bumping a willing young man out of a bar stool, Aliah takes her new found seat. Mitchell peeks out from the cold storage room and smiles at her.

"Hey, you," he hollers, stacking a few cases of beer in the refrigerator.

"Hey, yourself."

Mitchell wipes down the bar with a meaty hand and smiles at her. "Have you eaten?"

She pulls her stool closer, ignoring the fellow drooling over her shoulder, and reaches for her draft beer. She lifts it up and smiles at Mitchell.

"Aliah, you have to eat something."

"If you say so."

Ten minutes later, a plate is being slid in front of her. As Aliah finishes her meal, she drops her napkin on top of her plate and walks to the end of the bar with her dirty dishes. Mitchell hasn't reappeared from his office in the past 15 minutes, and the place is packed. He isn't one to spend much time in there, especially when he's clearly needed on the floor. She decides to check up on him.

Aliah carries her dishes to the dishwasher and smiles. "Is he in there?" she asks the girl in the kitchen, pointing at the closed office door.

"Yep. But I wouldn't go in there, if I were you. I think he's taking care of business."

Aliah barges into the room and catches Mitchell with his back to her, facing the wall. He's shouting into the phone. It sounds like an all-out screaming match. He must be truly mad too, because it takes a lot to get this brother to holler.

"Tanya. That's enough," he shouts into the phone. Then he peers over his shoulder and hints for Aliah to close the door. "This is not acceptable in my book. Three strikes you're out, honey." He hangs up the phone, as the door clicks shut.

Aliah can't stop smirking. She takes the seat from across his desk, lifts a heeled shoe and props it on the top of it. "Who the hell was that?"

"Tanya," he answers. Then he sighs and wipes a weary hand over his face.

"Tanya, the waitress, Tanya?"

"You got it. She was supposed to be here half an hour ago. But she was a no-show. That's the third time this month. So I called her. If she had told me she was on her way, then I was going to give her one last chance. But we're swamped here, we're understaffed tonight as it is, and she's out partying with her boyfriend."

Aliah nods, agreeing with how outlandish some people can be.

"I hate to let her go, Ally. But I can't let her act like that and get away with it. The last thing I need is the others thinking I'm a pushover."

Aliah gets up from her chair and walks around his desk. "You're not a pushover," she teases, as she shoves his shoulder backward.

Mitchell smiles, giving her the response she was hoping for. "Come here," he says.

She slips into his outstretched arms and gives him a great big bear hug. "If you need help, you know I'm here for you."

"Really? You would do that for me?"

"Yeah," Aliah answers. "I can help bus tables, or fill beer orders. But no dishes. Not looking like this." She waves a hand between them. She always dresses like a pop star, whenever she walks out of the house after dark.

Mitchell's smile grows even bigger. "You know I would never do anything to harm your beautiful reputation."

She slaps at him and breaks away from his arms. "You ass."

Mitchell chuckles, as his girlfriend knocks on the door. When Aliah glances over her shoulder, she sees Brandee peering through the window, like a nosy principal ready to scorn the teacher inside for canoodling with a student.

Aliah heads for the door and grabs the handle. "It wasn't locked."

Brandee's eyes are so narrow that they can barely be called open. "You looked like you might have been busy in here. Was *my boyfriend* keeping you busy?"

"*Your boyfriend* was giving someone the boot."

"And Aliah was so kind as to offer her help," Mitchell adds, merrily.

"How sweet of Aliah," Brandee moans, forcing an unattractive smile onto her face. "I have to run an errand. Do you think you'll be alright while I'm gone?"

The look Brandee gives Aliah is amusing. No one needs her for anything. She must know that.

All three of them make their way to the bar. Aliah's the last of them to pass through the kitchen. As Brandee tugs Mitchell to the door, Aliah glances up. A flash of light catches on the door and a man appears from out of the darkness.

Her eyes get hooked on this dude who's standing there, looking all bad-boy sexy. His look is complete with a tight pair of jeans and a soft leather jacket that fits perfectly over his sculpted muscles. When he peels off his jacket, it only gets better. Every inch of that body demands her attention. All six feet of it. His tattooed arms bulge from his shirt and she just wants to grab onto that ass and maybe take a bite out of him.

The guy nods at someone who's across the room and she tries not to gawk to see who it is. No one she knows. Then he finds himself a bar stool, at least four away from her, and casually glances over at her, snaring her eyes again.

"Hey," she shouts, finding it difficult not to talk to him now that he's caught her gawking shamelessly.

"Hey." His reply is short and curt.

Annoying.

He wears a sleeve of tattoos on one of his arms and a look of danger on that sexy face. He isn't wearing a ring on that finger, but he certainly isn't giving her the time of day. She doesn't know what it is particularly about this guy, but she just wants to lick him.

She moves closer, drawn in by his careless attitude. "Can I get you something to drink?" That seems to get his attention.

"Are you buying?" He's smirking and she just then realizes it's because she's standing on the wrong side of the bar.

"Sure. Why not?" She walks around the bar, pulls out two bottles of beer and slides them to the middle of the bar.

He watches her every move, but doesn't comment. She hands him one of the bottles and he takes it, but he doesn't thank her.

What an ass!

She is sure he can read her thoughts, because he is smiling again, and that's good for him. But she wonders why it's getting her blood pumping so hard. He lifts his beer, twists off the cap and slides it over to her, pressing it into her hand. Then he reaches over the bar and cracks open the second one.

"It won't kill you." He clinks their bottles together, and keeps his eyes on her as he draws a long, slow gulp from his own.

She sees the way tattooed-sexy wraps those lips around the bottle, and the way his eyes promise a whole night of dirty fun. It sends a shiver passing across her heated flesh.

"The name's Harley," he says, reaching out a rough masculine hand.

"Where's your motorcycle, Harley?" she answers, thinking she's *so* smart.

"What makes you think I have a bike?"

"Are you saying you don't?"

"No." He raises a brow and it is so damn sexy.

She can't stop her mouth from smiling really hard. "That's what I thought."

After a moment of silence passes, she decides to take a sip from her beer.

"You here often?" he asks her.

Aliah loves how he cuts to the chase. She can just imagine how much fun it would be to tumble around for a few hours with this sex stick. "Once or twice a week, if you must know." She answers like it's a bother for her to talk to him, but that doesn't seem to affect him one bit.

"I haven't seen you around here before."

She gives him a devilishly sexy look. "I guess today's

your lucky day then." The way he watches her makes her very conscious of her tongue when she speaks. His eyes continue to sear her parted lips.

"I'm surprised a beautiful girl like you is still single."

"Did I say that?"

"I just thought..."

"Well, aren't you smooth?" She pauses for dramatic effect and loves the way his name rolls slowly off her tongue. *"Harley."*

That seems to get his wheels turning. She loves the furrowed brow he gets when he thinks a little too hard. She serves a couple of customers and finds herself on his side of the bar again.

"So, you're not single?" He just keeps pressing.

"I didn't say that."

He lifts his hands in defeat. "I don't know who hurt you, but he's obviously ruined it for the rest of us." After he says the words, she can actually see a look of regret in his eyes. It's like he hates that he's letting her get to him. She loves it. Him? Not so much.

"The rest of who?" she asks, peering over her shoulder at the locals lining the bar behind her.

"Men in general. Your future husband, maybe."

Hah! Good One! "Who said I ever plan on getting married?"

"I just assumed..."

"You know what they say about that."

It'll make an ASS out of U and ME.

He chuckles and swipes a hand across his face, then looks at her again. "I just thought that most beautiful women your age will have found a man to have a kid or two with by now." He fumbles over his words and that makes Aliah smile.

"My age?" She loves how she's always one-upping him.

He doesn't know how to handle her. "I just meant... Forget it." His eyes touch her all over. "You don't really look like the marrying type."

Aliah narrows her eyes, even while a wave of excitement

floods her limbs from his slow perusal of her body. "You really need to learn when to shut your mouth." She slides the serving tray onto the bar so she can prop her hands on her hips. If she ever decides to have a kid someday, it'll be one kid. But it's not exactly a dream of hers. "Not everyone validates themselves by the number of babies they've popped out."

Now he's the one becoming defensive. "I never said that." His voice is firm and demands her attention.

Aliah ignores him. "I have no intention of wrecking this hot little body any time in the near future."

He smiles, even though he tries not to, while she struggles with the thought of ruining herself. "You said it," Harley answers, raking her *hot little body* with uninhibited eyes.

She smoothes her hands down the curve of her slim waist, appreciating the body God gave her. "That's right. I did. Because I have the balls to say it." Aliah notices how conflicted Harley seems. He obviously has something to hide. She doesn't know what it is, but it intrigues her to keep stoking the fire. She moves closer to him, sliding one of her legs between his thighs, so she can whisper provocatively in his ear. "Unlike some people."

Aliah leans back to catch his reaction, but he doesn't let her move far. His arm hooks around her waist, as Harley raises a brow. She loves the look he gets on his face every time she shocks him. Then he leans into her, until she can feel his breath on her ear.

"I may act like a gentleman in public," he growls. "But that doesn't mean I won't spank you behind closed doors."

Aliah smiles, loving the way his voice makes promises. "Is that a threat?"

He leans back and takes another good look at her. "What are you doing after work?"

She smiles, a genuine smile. "What do you care?"

"Do you always make it this difficult for a man to ask you out?"

"Yes. Most men don't last half this long."

He looks to the floor, smiling.

"Aliah! Are you waiting or dating?" Any other time and Aliah would have given Mitchell a high five for originality. But not tonight.

She groans. "He doesn't pay me nearly enough for this."

Harley's still smiling when she leaves him.

That smile is a weapon, I tell you.

He needs to put that thing away before she's *forced* to do something that will give him a good reason to smile that wickedly.

After escaping from Harley's attention long enough to serve a few tables and fix up a couple of drinks, she turns around and finds Harley standing there, like a brick wall. She slams right into him. He's even bigger than she thought. A shiver courses through her veins, the chill quickly spreading through her entire body, as she imagines what it would feel like to be pinned beneath all that man.

CHAPTER FIVE

Harley doesn't take his eyes off the prize. It's a simple task, watching over her, with that tiny waist and stunning child-bearing hips. This is turning out to be more fun than he anticipated. Aliah Brooklin is even hotter in person, if that is possible.

Thank the Lord for side boob.

She's just a petite little thing, with luscious hair and pale green eyes. Her attitude strikes you like a sword, or maybe like those skyscraper stiletto heels she manages to walk in. But Harley has come armed too. His charm will slowly wear her down, the way it always does with the ladies. Before long, she won't be able to resist him.

He loves every single minute of their bantering, and from the look in her eye, she loves it too. She has a mouth on her, that one. He'll have to be careful with her. She isn't exactly the kind of girl you'd want your teenaged daughter looking up to.

But even as he hears himself saying no, his dick is telling him otherwise. He'd love to teach her a lesson about that potty mouth too. He could have a lot of fun teaching Miss Brooklin a lesson or two in the bedroom.

When he watches Aliah finish up at the bar, he slides over to strike up another conversation with her. She slams right into him, pressing those beautiful breasts against his hard body. He struggles to find a respectful thing to say. Nothing thoughtful can come from a glance at those breasts.

Harley tears his eyes away and focuses on her face. Though her cleavage has burned the most beautiful image in his mind, he's suddenly having difficulty taking his eyes from those luscious lips. He gazes at them a little too long. He is sure that her mouth has a multitude of other uses that can be valuable to him.

"You're closing up soon."

Aliah glances up at him. "Yeah, so?"

"Do you need a hand with anything? Or is Cavanagh getting the job done for you?" He was careful not to push too hard, but she seems to catch right onto him.

"What business is it of yours, Hulk?"

She starts to hesitate, wondering what his deal is, so he drops her an angled smile; the one that slants a little to the left. It has always worked with the ladies and it looks like it works for her too.

"It's Harley, missy." He doesn't know what it is about this girl, but she makes him want to press her buttons. "Get it right or gets a stepping."

Aliah glances over each of her shoulders dramatically. "I was here first, *brother*. And *you* can screw off, it you're going to be such an asshole."

He looks at her incredulously. "Do you kiss your mother with that mouth?"

"That's not the only thing," she snaps back.

He nearly spews his beer all over her, excited by her insinuation even while she berates him. Unable to keep his distance, he draws closer, and glances down at her. She doesn't back away. Instead she thrusts her hands onto her hips and lifts her chin.

He leans down until they're nose to nose. Then he combs his fingers through her hair and wraps his hand around a good handful at the nape of her neck, pulling it back firmly until she has no option but to lift her chin to the sky. Her expression shows that she's straining to match his hardness but, because of the heat flickering in her eyes, she can't fool him.

"You like it when I'm rough with you?" He tugs a little harder.

Aliah lets out a strangled moan, but doesn't answer.

"Imagine all of the fun things we could do." His lips whisper over her neck and up to her ear. "Would you like to have some fun, missy?"

It's hard to keep his cool when this vixen is swooning at

his feet. "The name's Aliah. Get it right." She barely gets the words out, before closing her eyes.

She wants it. *Him.*

He knows it's a bad idea, but his lips brush across her throat before he can think to stop. His tongue licks across her warm flesh and he gets a taste of her skin. She's his flavor. When she whimpers again, he lightens his grip, ever so slightly, but not nearly enough to give her control over her head. He feels like he's in the power seat and smothering a powerful woman like that is a heady experience. He knows they're in public, but he can't stop.

Harley wants to taste her again. Hell, he wants to do a lot more than that. If this wasn't his hometown, she'd already be flattened against that bar and he'd be moving inside of her. With Aliah's small hands on his chest, he's unable to think clearly. She fogs his brain when she's this close. He needs to put some space between them. He needs to get back to business.

He smiles and lets go of her hair. When he releases the pressure, she looks a little lightheaded. "So, *Aliah.* Same place tomorrow?"

She seems to like that he gets her name right this time. And, though he's kind of joking, he has to fight off his smile when she reluctantly nods her head to agree with him.

"Does it look like I have a choice?" she snaps, trying to regain her attitude.

He shakes his head, not surprised by her snappy comeback, and heads for the door with strong legs and steady steps. To his surprise, she follows him out.

He turns back to her and raises an eyebrow, taking in every curve on that body. She shares an equally as suggestive glance, once she's stopped next to him. He can't waste the opportunity.

"I don't do this often."

She cuts him off, not much caring what he has to say. "Am I supposed to feel special?"

"Can I get your number?"

Aliah delivers him a slanted smile of her own. "No. I

don't give out my number."

"Can I give you mine?"

"Why? So I can do a background check on you?"

Harley laughs at that. "I'll take that as a sign that you like me."

She smirks at him, both of them finding it difficult not to respond to each other with upturned lips.

He pulls a business card from his wallet and pushes the leather fold back into his pocket. Before giving her the card, he rips his number off the bottom and stares at it. Then he stuffs the larger half in his pocket and hands the small piece over to her.

She reaches for it, but he won't let it go. Their eyes meet for a heated second.

"I *never* give out my number." His intensity appears to thrill her, but she can't help but sass back.

"That's why you have a business card. And I'm not even entitled to see the entire card. That's cool." She stuffs the scrap of paper into her purse.

"Allow me to rephrase." The depth of his tone captures her attention. His heart starts racing. "I never give my number out to a woman because I want to sleep with her."

His boldness seems to turn her on. He loves how her skin grows warm whenever he makes a lewd comment, but the color of her face remains a soft white. His words are meant to test her, to see if his sexual advance scares her off. If not the words, then maybe the oversized bulge in his pants. But it doesn't.

Now he's truly intrigued. He wonders what it'd be like to have her peel his jacket off him and skim her hands across his skin, looking up at him like he's a sexy slab of man, the way she is now.

His lips slant into a smile that is sure to melt her panties. "Are you going to call me? If you're not, then you might as well give that back." He points at her bag where the scrap of paper is tucked inside.

She turns her bag away from him, as if he might try to take it back if she made it too easy for him. "I'll get back to you on that, as soon as I have a chance to check you out."

"Ah, shit."

"What's wrong? Do you have something to hide?" Her voice sounds coy and it's very sexy on her.

"Nothing you'll find."

Aliah steps closer to him and lowers her voice. "Is there a shady history you don't want my *superior* investigative skills to uncover?"

Her confidence actually has him a little on edge.

Is she onto me?

Hiding that from his features, Harley brings his face right to hers, until their noses are nuzzled and his breath is rushing over her lips. "A little mystery never hurt anyone."

After a brief pause, with her full lips urging him to kiss her, he decides it might be fun to turn the tables on her. "What would I find if I looked you up, Ally?"

Her eyes look up into his, like a lost little girl, and yet he refuses to release her from his determined gaze. She looks terrified by the knowledge that he uses her nickname, and yet she doesn't stop him, as his hands swipe down either side of her head. He clutches over her hair and holds it firmly against her throat, toying with her air supply.

She should have been terrified, screaming for help. But instead he finds her swallowing another moan.

"Tell me to stop," he says, reading her eyes. If she doesn't, then he's not sure he'll ever find the control to. When she doesn't, his fingers magically loosen their grip, as he dusts a kiss over her lips. He doesn't want to hurt the girl, even if she could use a lesson in submission.

"Why did you call me that?" Her voice is hoarse, and even that is sexy.

"I heard a guy in there call you by name. The bartender who has the not-so-secret crush on you."

Her gaze turns cool. "He doesn't have a crush. We're friends. He's seeing someone else."

Harley brushes a rough thumb over her throat. When she holds her breath, it cuts off her air, just long enough for her to feel a slight bit dizzy, but no less excited.

"He wants more." His eyes flicker down between them, and he takes an eyeful of her exposed flesh. "I can't blame the guy. Look at you, all packaged up for my viewing pleasure."

"You like that?" she asks, urging him toward his more devious pleasures.

"I'd like it more if I could unwrap that." He flings her long hair over her shoulder. "I want to have a better taste." He licks at his lips, like he's warding off an uncontrollable hunger. "I want to see if you taste as sweet as you look."

She pants and he wants nothing more than to pry that bra off of her so he can bury himself in those swelling breasts and drag his tongue across her entire body. He'd like to discover her all over, just the way his deep voice promises. He edges closer to her mouth and descends on her lips.

Aliah expects him to play rough, and he does. He tugs her close and flattens her against his hard edges. His hands dig into her flesh, in stark contrast to the softness of her lips, as he teases her with a sensual assault that is sure to wet the girl's panties.

CHAPTER SIX

Aliah hasn't kissed a single man since Hunter Wight. Sex? Yes. Kiss? No. But with her blood boiling with lust for this man, she accepts his advance, knowing that she will live to regret it. He takes her in his strong arms the way she's only dreamt of a man taking her, and he kisses her.

She catches how her eyes have fluttered shut, and the way her rapid breaths are making both her head and heart scatter. Then he releases her, suddenly breaking all contact between their bodies.

"Think about it." His words echo through her mind.

Oh, she will.

It will be a miracle if she thinks about anything else, after that.

Harley turns away and her eyes flutter to that ass. She watches him wrap a powerful leg over his seat and start up his motorcycle. It's a shiny black Harley. And it's new. A real man's man kind of ride with all the fancy chrome details.

He sears her with a glance, as he takes off on his sexy machine. She stares after him, long after he's gone.

Holy shit. I think I'm in love.

Her panties feel like they have been incinerated and he has barely even touched her. She imagines what it would have felt like if he had.

That exchange rolls through her mind again and again, until Mitchell hands Aliah her purse and explains that it's time to go. She heads home, but when she enters her front door, she wonders how she's gotten there. The only other thing that runs through her mind, again a flashback of everything that is *Harley*.

After a night of erotic fantasies, all staring the mysterious *Harley*, Aliah tells herself that she has no choice but to return to the bar. She wants to get in those pants, but she doesn't want to look desperate. She manages to claw her way through the weekend, until Thursday night returns. She doesn't call him, but it's not because he's not on her mind. He's all she thinks about.

Instead of continuing to live in her fantasy world for another week, she calls up Mitchell the next morning and suggests that he needs her for another night. He can't say no, still being short-staffed. She pulls out her old uniform and dusts it off. She's always loved the cute plaid skirt that Mitchell makes all his waitresses wear, even if it is borderline skanky.

By day, she works for criminal defence lawyer, Joshua Bailey. Once the clock strikes five, Aliah rushes straight home and spends the next couple of hours spoiling her body after a rigorous workout. She gets all done up in a low cut black shirt with short angled sleeves and the fitted plaid skirt that is much too short to be considered appropriate. Luckily, she isn't going for appropriate tonight.

When she waltzes into Riley's, fashionably late, she realizes it's all for nothing. Harley's not even there. She wants to bitch slap herself for getting her hopes up. Aliah Brooklin does not get her hopes up for a man. She'll be more careful in the future to detach herself from such feminine stupidity.

Later in the evening, when Mitchell asks her if she can help out on Saturday night too, she declines. She needs a some time to recuperate from her disappointment. But when he calls her again Sunday morning, practically begging for her help, she can't leave her friend hanging.

Mitchell assures her that Sundays are slow, but the summer must be an unpredictable time. The bar fills up, until it becomes steamy and uncomfortable. The air conditioner is on full blast, but the steady traffic at the door ensures that it will never catch up. Aliah tries desperately to avoid the evil eye continually scanning over her from the blonde in the corner, but she loses the battle.

What is that girl's problem?

Brandee Hawkins is one jealous girl. Aliah doesn't know how her modest Mitchell has ended up with such an envious girlfriend, or what Brandee's deal is these days, but it's clear she has issues. For Mitchell's sake, Aliah's kept her mouth shut, but Brandee just begs to be told where to shove that look.

To top that off, nasty scum bags hit on her all night, until she starts to recall that most men are total pieces of shit. Harley being number one on her shit list. He was obviously just stringing her on. And she let him. She now realizes his implied intention to screw her brains out was but a false dream. She only wishes she can stop fantasizing about it.

Aliah's relieved when the drink orders are all filled and she has a second to herself. As the pace slows, Aliah clears the empty bottles from the bar, wipes it down, and sets out to prepare herself a thick milkshake. She hunches over the bar and sips from it, purely out of exhaustion. Her lips are puckered over the straw, but her eyes still remain latched onto the front entrance of the place.

She notices Harley the second he walks through the door. It's hard not to notice something so sexy. Has he come back for her? Did he look for her another night? Unwilling to wait for the answers, she instantly abandons her drink to pay him a visit. She walks right up to him, struggling to contain her giddiness and keep up her bad girl attitude.

"Back again?" She smiles, even though she warns herself not to.

"Back again."

"What can I do for you?"

Now he's the one smiling, teeth and all. "Now that depends…"

"To drink. What can I get you to drink?"

Harley chuckles and it gets to Aliah. She doesn't get flustered easily, but this guy just turns her crank in a really good way. She really wants to keep him smiling like that.

He glances over at the bar where she was hunched when he'd arrived. "What are you drinking?"

"Oh, you saw that did you? It's not on the menu."

He follows her to the bar and when she catches him raping her legs with his eyes, she needs a drink to cool off.

She brings the straw to her lips and, without thinking, speaks. "Look how thick and smoothie it is."

That makes him smile. Now he can't take his eyes off her mouth. A bit of her milkshake coats her upper lip. Her tongue darts out to get it, with parted lips. His eyes seem to warm at the sight. She chews on her bottom lip craving more of the attention he has to give. The temperature in the room suddenly feels like it's spiked another ten degrees.

"Hello!" a fat man hollers from across the bar. "Can I get a drink in this place, or what?"

Aliah crinkles her eyes and winces. "Excuse me." She knows exactly who is messing with her. She walks over to where Big Roy has landed and begins to fan her face.

Harley eventually finds a spot at the bar at the opposite end from the fat man. Aliah holds onto the beer and gives Roy a pointed glance. "I didn't hear a please on the back end of that question, Roy. You aren't getting anything until you use those manners."

"May I please have my drink, beautiful?" Roy answers.

Aliah slaps at him, and when she plunks his beer in front of him, it splashes over the rim of the glass. "Don't call me that." She stares at the bottom of her shirt, now soaked in beer.

"You used to love when I called you that. Is little Ally all grown up now?"

Aliah glances up, just in time to catch another slutty barmaid tending to Harley. "Yeah. Something like that," she mumbles. To say she was disappointed would be a mega understatement.

Seeing Harley chatting with the other girl only makes her remember that she's not about to bend over backwards for anyone. Hard to get is the way she rolls. It's always worked for her in the past and Harley, whatever his last name is, isn't getting any special treatment, starting now.

Rather than return to Harley's side and interrupt his

little conversation, Aliah keeps her post and tends to the other gentlemen waiting for assistance. When she gets caught up, she helps out the waitresses by taking a few plates out to diners, in order to keep herself busy.

With every glance in Harley's direction, her body heats two degrees. Within minutes, she's sweltering, even though she's wearing very little. Without any other option, she lifts her shirt over her tiny waist and ties it in a knot just below her breasts, exposing the black flames that lick across her hip. Then she moves to sweep all her hair up and off her neck.

When she takes another discreet glance at Harley, she sees that his eyes are zoned in on her midsection, his mouth slightly open, like it's watering for another taste of her. She lifts her chest and flaunts her rear end, accentuating the sharp curve of her waist.

She's unwilling to take her eyes from him first, but he doesn't look away. She wants to scream out.

Oh My God, he's sexy!

She swallows, relieved when the cook hollers out to her. Aliah turns for the kitchen, tearing her eyes away, and takes a much needed exit from the room. When she's in the privacy of the kitchen, she doubles over, and presses her hands against her bent knees.

She's *never* reacted like this to a man.

When the cook slides a couple of plates onto the counter, he gives her a funny look. "Everything okay?"

She doesn't answer, realizing she has to go back out there already.

"Aliah, could you please take this to table eight?" He speaks a little louder this time, as if she's not heard his last question.

She takes a deep breath and smiles, despite the butterflies taking flight just beyond her bare midriff. "I got this," she answers.

Aliah takes both of the plates and props them on flattened palms. Using her butt, she pushes open the kitchen door, to enter the main room.

"Coming through. Hot stuff," she hollers, with a plate lifted over each of her shoulders.

Harley instantly glances towards her, and she nearly tumbles onto the floor, just barely catching herself on a table and managing to not spill the dishes on the impatient customers.

How does he do that?

The way he looks at her is intoxicating. His eyes are insinuating that she is hot stuff. There is no need for words. Suddenly it feels like her skin is flaming, and it's not from embarrassment.

What is wrong with me?

She rocks shoes this tall on a daily basis. It's kind of her thing. But Harley has her stumbling over her own two feet. When she returns to the bar, Harley calls her over with a lifted hand and curled fingers. She can just imagine what else he can do with those fingers.

Trying to push that thought aside, she clears her throat and acts like he hasn't just caused her to make a scene. His eyes skim over her body. He's showing her that he wants it.

Welcome to the club, buddy.

He licks at his lower lip, nibbles on it and looks down at her with hooded eyes. "When are you working next?"

"Actually, I don't work here," she blurts, catching herself mid-sentence.

"Shit. You've been here waiting tables for the past two weekends. You actually expect me to believe that?"

"Believe it. Because it's true. I'm just helping out a friend." She points back to Mitchell, but Harley only seems to catch the evil eye the blonde bitch standing next to him shoots their way.

"She looks really friendly," he mocks.

"Brandee is Mitchell's new girlfriend. She's harmless. She only looks scary."

Harley chuckles and flashes another peculiar glare at Brandee. "I should get going."

What is that all about?

"Okay, then."

He walks away without another word, but he doesn't make it far. Some guy stops him to talk, and suddenly it looks like he has all night to chat.

"Rude much?" she mumbles to herself, a little disappointed that their nightly bantering had to end so soon.

Roy, the regular, who is nursing his fifth beer, lifts his head to talk to Aliah. "You don't want to get involved with that one, beautiful. He's trouble."

She nods her head in agreement, watching him. She knows Harley's trouble. But she likes it.

"Aliah!" Mitchell hollers, from the storage room door.

Aliah twirls around and hurries toward the kitchen. "Coming!"

She gives Mitchell a hand and finishes with the orders. By the time she finishes wiping down the bar, she notices Harley is gone.

Aliah watches the clock after that, for what seems like hours. It feels like time is ticking backwards. She knows that the bar is open until two, but it's practically abandoned by one o'clock. As the long hand creeps closer to the twelve, everyone leaves the place except for Roy; and he seems to be hanging around only to keep her company.

After cleaning the place up, Aliah throws the rag onto the sink. Mitchell walks up behind her.

"Looks good," he says, acknowledging the visible effort she has put into tidying up the dining room.

"Thanks. Do you mind if I get going?"

Mitchell tilts his head and smiles. "Sure. Of course. Thanks, Ally. You're a good friend." He reaches out to hug her, not noticing the murderous glare coming from his girlfriend behind him.

Aliah accepts the bear hug and waves goodbye as she walks toward the exit.

"Oh. Wait! Aliah. I found this on the floor behind the bar earlier. Is it yours?" Mitchell strolls toward her and holds out the ripped business card.

"Um. Yeah."

"I didn't want to throw it out in case it was important to you."

"Thanks, Mitch. You're a lifesaver." She flashes him a golden smile, and snatches the scrap of paper with Harley's number printed on it. "See you later."

Mitchell walks her to the door. "Do you want me to walk you out?"

"I'll be okay. I doubt Brandee would like that very much. Thanks, though."

Mitchell hangs his head, and sighs. "She'll come around, Ally. She just has to get to know you better."

"Doubt it. But it's all good. I'll catch you later."

"Okay, lady. Have a good one."

She walks outside, only wishing she'd find Harley out there so she wouldn't have to contemplate giving him a call. Now she is truly dreaming. Despite her sureness of Harley not being there, she hurries across the road and stops, scouring the parking lot for a motorcycle. At the very back of the lot, right near the river, she sees something in the shadows. She squints to see what could be a motorcycle parked in the distance.

"Looking for someone?" Harley's breath crashes over the back of her neck.

She freezes in place, relishing the warmth coming from his body, then spins around to face him, once she's regained her balance.

"You stalking me now?" She turns away and walks off, without slowing for an answer.

Harley smiles, but he doesn't follow after her. "Wouldn't you like that?"

She almost admits that she would, when he takes a step in her direction and reaches his hand out to her.

"I was waiting for you. If I was stalking, I would be a little less obvious about it."

Aliah twirls back around, and gawks at his outstretched hand, her long bouncy curls fanning out behind her. "Is that supposed to relieve me?"

Harley raises his eyebrows and holds them there. "Are

you always this confrontational?" His hand drops down to his side, but his posture is no less intimidating.

"Do you always answer a question with a question?"

"Wow. Nice chat." He makes to walk away from her.

She sighs and glances at the ground, before lifting her chin back up. "You waited all this time and you aren't even going to offer me a ride?" She knows she will live to regret this.

"You have your car."

"How do you know?"

He folds his unbelievably defined arms across his chest and smirks. "Do you have your car here?"

She rolls her eyes, effectively tearing them away from the tattoos wrapped deliciously around his arm. "Forget I asked."

"Wait," he grinds out.

She stands there silently for a minute, waiting for him to decide what he's going to say next. Her breath seems to be on hold, waiting for him to speak. It makes her a little light-headed.

His eyes lock on hers, and he looks more determined than ever. "Come with me."

She can't even explain it, when her body involuntarily responds. Her hand is gripped in his and she is being pulled away before she can even come up with a smart remark. As they get to his bike, the black of the gas tank sparkles in the moonlight. His motorcycle is almost as sexy as him.

This isn't anything she's ever done before. She likes to put up a good front, but she has a good heart underneath that push-up bra. She's always dated the knight in shining armor type. They seem to be drawn to her naughty-girl attitude. Quite frankly she has grown rather bored with that type of man and she is ready to live up to her sassy persona.

To see a bad ass biker like Harley dragging her to his ride has her body humming already. She likes it. Nothing has ever excited her more than the thought of him taking her to his bed and showing her everything she has been missing out on.

The only problem? She doesn't do one-night stands.

I guess we will just have to make it two.

CHAPTER SEVEN

Ten minutes earlier.

Harley gets on his motorcycle and rides. Sure, he is a man. He gets turned on. But this girl has his cock raging for hours. It makes it uncomfortable for him to walk, let alone ride his motorcycle home. He doesn't even mow his own lawn, but he plans to work to please her in every way possible, no matter what the challenge.

He had taken off from the bar before he did something stupid, like ask that beautiful bartender out. *What was he thinking?* He hasn't dated since... well, ever. He doesn't do dates. He had been forced to grow up and get out in his early teen years. He lived in an unhappy relationship for far too long after that and he has no desire to date another woman now or ever.

But damn, Aliah Brooklin is hot. And he would love to have another arguing match with her. He is sure it could end in some really hot sex, if he plays his cards right. He only wishes it was worth the trouble.

Harley doesn't have anywhere in mind when he gets on his bike, but before long he finds himself rounding the corner and approaching Riley's Pub again. He wonders if *she* is still there. A quick scan of the parking lot tells him she is. You can't miss her car. It's the flashiest thing a girl could buy, short of a pink Cadillac.

It wasn't all butterflies and sunshine for that girl though. Harley is good at watching people. He has watched Aliah. A lot. Though she looks like she could be a lot of fun, hidden just below the surface is a damaged little girl. He will have to be careful to keep that little one in hiding.

Harley parks his ride at the back of the lot and sits there for a few minutes in the shadows. He debates whether he should start his bike back up and get the hell out of there.

Though all signs point to *yes*, he kicks his leg over the bike and rests his helmet on the seat. He has no choice. He has to fuck this girl. Just the thought of sliding his hands under that short skirt and touching that soft, pale skin has his cock raging again.

He moseys toward the bar, second guessing himself with every step. He peers in the door before reaching for the handle and instantly notices Aliah near the exit with Cavanagh. He ducks swiftly to the side. The detective in him wants to eavesdrop, but it looks like she's just leaving. If he walks in now, he will be stuck for a beer. Does he want a beer?

Only if he can drink it from her unclothed body.

Knowing the likelihood of that to be close to nil, he steps back into the shadows and waits. He watches her eyes, even while they're smiling at another man. Those lips. Instead of reading them, like he should be, he thinks about how nice they'll be when they're wrapped around his cock. Aliah busies herself with her keys and before too long reaches for the door. He's in luck. Cavanagh accepts her rejection and lets her take off on her own.

Sucker.

Harley waits for her to step off the curb before following her across the road. She has absolutely no idea he's watching her. His long strides make hers seem like that of a child. When she stops and scours the lot, he wonders what she's looking for. Her car is straight ahead. It's not *that* she's looking for.

She focuses on his bike at the back of the lot, as if she were looking for it. Intrigued by that thought, he moves dangerously close to her; so close he can smell the sweet perfume melting from her neck.

"Looking for someone?" he rasps provocatively, the deep bass of his voice registering in his gut.

He tries to ignore the sparks flickering between them but, after some promising banter, Harley decides against it. He steals Aliah's hand and tugs her to his bike, ordering her to come with him. He doesn't actually think she will. She would have to be crazy to leave with him. But she slips her small hand into his and lets him pull her along. He has never felt so powerful. And he has been in some powerful situations.

She's done it now.

Her decision has been made. He refuses to take no for an answer. Not that she seems to be putting up much of a fight. But, knowing that this bargain can pass, he drags her to his bike as fast as her five inch heels can carry her. He feels so tempted to scoop her into his arms, so they can get there faster. He just barely resists the urge.

He believes it's officially in the bag, when they're mere steps away from his ride, until she pulls her hand away from him and stops. He turns around to see what the problem is, worry written across his brow. He really fucking needs this.

Aliah's eyes look so big and wide that he almost forgets his goal. *Almost.*

"You aren't a serial killer, who seduces his victims and then murders them, are you?"

She's trying to act scared. Like a little school girl. And he falls for it at first. But he quickly sees past the act. His entire body tightens. Her hesitation only makes him harder.

"If I was, I certainly wouldn't admit that to you now. Especially now that you're so close to giving in to me."

Aliah smiles and turns her eyes away. She loves his bluntness. He knows it. He decides now is as good a time as ever to give her a little truth.

"I may not be who I appear to be, darlin', but I assure you I'm no serial killer."

The look on her face suggests she doesn't even want to know, and that's just fine by him. She shrugs a shoulder, proving that he's back in the safe zone.

"Good enough for me." She gets closer to him and lowers her voice until it's soft and breathy. "If you like it rough, I'm good with that."

Just the thought of tumbling in the sheets with her

makes him tight in the pants.

"Just make sure you're gentle with my body afterward," she teases. "Nothing worse than crime scene photos of a woman propped up in the tackiest of poses."

Harley smirks at her. "Because you would know this."

"I do."

He ignores that, passing it off as a lie. She probably takes her pointers from the phoney late night crime shows. Regardless, she doesn't need to worry. He would never let another person touch her. That perfect little body will never be the subject of a brutal disfigurement put out on display for the cops to find. Not while Harley's on the clock.

He tries to forget about it. He wants to get her back onto the topic of sex. Yes. He likes that idea very much.

"I promise not to treat you like a trophy, although I can see why a man might want to look at you that way." His eyes touch her all over.

Aliah tilts her head to the left and presses her lips into a flat line. "Okay, quit with that creepy shit, before I change my mind."

She pulls the hair tie from her high pony and shakes it out, until long waves of silky hair are framing her face and dangling down to the curve of her lower back. Her hair whispers across the bareness of her skin, like chocolate silk.

"So, is that a yes?" He's not below begging at this point, if she is to say no.

"Yes to what? I recall that you asked what I was doing later. Was I supposed to *assume* that you meant you'd like to keep me busy?"

"I would like that. Very much."

"I'm sure you would. Unfortunately, I'm busy. Maybe next time. But not likely," she mumbles under her breath, as her voice trails off.

"Are you too good for me? Just say it, if that's it." His words stop her in her tracks.

She spins back around and props a hand on a flawless hip. "Do I look *good* to you?"

No. She looks bad. *Very, very bad.* Her sassy mouth and

bad attitude are really turning him on something fierce. He wants to spank her; to see his handprint marking her delicate flesh.

"*Good* isn't the word I would use." His eyes violate her entire body.

He reaches out and pulls a single strand of hair from between her lips, then dusts a kiss there, in stark contrast to the loaded machine gun he's packing in his pants.

He can see that she's flustered. He's getting to her. Little Miss Aliah isn't quite as hard as she lets on. He, on the other hand, is as hard as he can possibly get.

"You make me feel..." She huffs, not even knowing how to fill in her own sentence.

"Wow. So she does *feel*."

Aliah narrows her eyes, but quickly replaces that look with a smile. "Yes. I only *play* the heartless bitch."

He watches her fidget with her necklace, and then closes his hand over hers to stop her. "You're a good actress."

She shoves him backward, taking what he says the worst possible way. "Get away from me." Though she tries to put some distance between them, her attempt at moving him is wildly unsuccessful.

He catches her wrist, worried he's already pushed her too hard. With Aliah, there seems to be a fine line between *O-K* and *F-U*.

"I'm sorry..." he starts, but is cut off by Aliah's pleased cackle.

"I am pretty good, eh? I certainly had you."

He can't believe he has fallen for her act. "I feel like I have to tread carefully with you. Should I ask for permission before saying anything offensive?"

"Hah! Where would the fun be in that? It's all good. I'm sure I can handle you in real time."

"Is that right?"

Her hesitation is sweet, but the smug expression that swipes across her face makes him want to collect her hands behind her back to restrain her, while he moulds her soft curves to his hard edges.

Would she respond to him?

He moves his face very near hers and growls. "You only *think* you could handle me."

She doesn't back away. "No. I *can* handle you."

His body twitches at her bold statement, only leaving him to egg her on. He wants to taste her, when he inhales the sweet nectar inviting him to her skin.

His breath rushes over her ear. "Prove it."

He thinks she'll retreat, but then he feels her silky hands discovering the inside of his leather jacket.

"I plan to." She spins around, grabs for his helmet and pulls it onto her head. Then she straddles the bike and massages her hands over the length of the leather seat before looking back to him expectantly.

She looks stunning. He wants to take a picture.

"Are we going, or what?"

Harley takes a few steps closer and then pulls his helmet from her head.

"Hey," she shouts, as it snags her hair.

"That one is mine," he informs her.

Aliah shoves the helmet against his chest, startling him. "Aren't you Mr. Particular?"

With his left hand now free, he skims his fingertips across her cheek, sending a shiver sweeping down her body. His thumb brushes across her lower lip, and his own lips comes temptingly close.

"I am *very* particular." His kiss sends her thoughts swirling. "Is that a problem?" He kisses her again, hooking onto her lower lip and pulling.

Her strangled whimper is proof positive that she's into him. Aliah relinquishes the helmet, when his lips curl into the sexiest of smiles. She hooks her arms around his neck and leans back, until he's forced to toss his shiny black helmet into the grass.

He slides her back onto the cool leather, until she's laid out flat on his bike and he's hovering over her, their bodies mere inches from meshing. His voice growls before the words come out.

"You have no idea what seeing you like this does to me."

Aliah spreads her legs wider, the tightness of her skirt straining against her feminine curves. "Why don't you tell me?"

He presses himself against her. "I'd like to show you."

The touch of their lips starts out soft, becoming increasingly more necessary, until fireworks are exploding between them and he's drinking from her lips like it is a life or death situation. Yes, their kiss is heated, but the way their bodies are rubbing together is highly inappropriate for a public parking lot. Aliah curls a leg over his hip, flashing her wet panties to anyone who's watching.

He presses on her again, as if he's going to give it to her on the spot. If he weren't wearing any pants then he would be fucking her this very minute. When he flexes his hips against her, she moans. His cock swells even more, but he knows one too many respectful business owners who could be watching, and he isn't about to fuck up that arrangement... even if his cock is ready to bitch slap him.

Her voice turns breathy, as his fingers slip into her panties between them. "Yes."

His fingers slip over her. She's slick, but soft like silk. He sinks his middle finger inside of her, with his thumb making a circular motion between them. He watches her face as he eases his finger out of her and slides it back in. She's going to cum!

He rotates his finger and presses it deeper. He can feel her from the inside out. He grows tighter in the pants as she wraps tighter around his finger. It's a beautiful sight, her pale, perfect lips parted in pleasure, but it's not going to happen. He won't let it. When he retrieves his finger, she whimpers from the loss of warmth.

"Please!" she begs, watching him through half-lidded eyes.

"I will. Just not here."

"Where?" she gasps, ready for him to get back to it immediately.

He swallows hard, realizing he can't take her home with

him. "My sister's staying with me, so we can't go to my place." He says it much too casually. He's a good actor. "If you don't trust me at your place…"

"I trust you," she pants, making him harder yet.

He looks away to hide his wince. If she knew about his lies, she wouldn't be quite so trusting. Once she finds out the truth, she will never trust him again.

He makes a grab for the helmet and climbs onto his bike. He starts to adjust himself, but no adjustment can make him comfortable at this point. Until he's able to sink into that sweet pussy, he'll be in a whole lot of anguish.

Aliah pulls herself to a sitting position, as he settles onto the seat in front of her. She kicks a leg over his head, to wrap her legs around the bike and he nearly loses it.

"Here. Put this on." He hands her his prized helmet.

She keeps her big mouth shut, and his wild fantasy continues. She raises a brow and slides the helmet over her long, tangled hair. He rotates forward and turns on his bike. Her small hands curl under his arms and clutch onto his chest, as her inner thighs squeeze onto his legs.

She feels so good on him.

As the rumble of his motor soothes his nerves, he only wishes it could last. With a few small unnecessary directions to her house, he lifts his feet and they speed off. Neither of them say a word on the ride to her place.

Aliah's garage door opens as they pull up to her house. Harley turns his motorcycle off and, after taking his helmet from her hands, he rests it protectively on the seat.

"Nice place."

"Thanks. It's a little on the small side, but it meets all my needs. My dad bought me it," she admits, internally scolding herself for babbling to her two-night sex toy.

"Your family sounds very giving."

"My dad? Yes." She smiles, feeling it necessary to explain it to him. "My mom's a heartless bitch."

"Oh. So, that's where you get it from." He wears a pained look as he follows her into the house. He'd learned his lesson. He really had. But it is too easy to play the sarcastic asshole all the time, and he's been playing the part for so long that he's not even sure he can turn it off anymore.

She scowls at him over her shoulder. "She wouldn't give me a dime if my life depended on it. I may be a bitch, but I'm not that cruel."

Aliah reaches into the garage and presses a button, then waits for the garage door to seal shut.

"I was only teasing you."

She grabs Harley by the elbow and pulls him inside, closing the door behind them. "You're lucky I haven't been laid in a while, or that comment would have sent you packing." She makes to walk away.

He grabs her wrist and pulls her back to him. Then he whirls her around until she's pressed against the door to the garage and her arm is pinned just above her head. She closes her eyes to hide from his stare. He wants her to look at him.

"Hey. I didn't mean it." His breath washes over her.

He leans down to kiss her, and though his eyes are closed, he can feel the moment right before their lips meet, when she turns her head away to dodge his mouth.

"No kissing."

He presses his lips against her neck and retreats after a lingering caress of his tongue. He waits until their eyes connect and pauses for her to explain. He'd already kissed her, multiple times. Why the sudden change of heart? Was it something he'd said?

Aliah gives him a pointed glare. "Don't ask questions. That's the deal. You want the sex? Fuck me till your heart's content. But there will be no more kissing on the mouth."

It seems like a really odd request, but he doesn't have a problem with that. When he is done with her, she'll be kissing the ground he walks on, begging for him to touch his lips to that sassy mouth.

He tilts her head up to make her look him in the eye, regaining the intimate connection that had been broken. "That's it? Or do you have other exclusions I need to know about?"

His question heats her to the core. Just the thought of him doing things to her has her body vibrating.

"That's it."

He nods. "I'm glad." A flash of heat flickers in his light hazel eyes and the warmth seems to stay in the color. "We should probably get this out of the way now. I've been tested."

"I already told you. I haven't had sex in a while, okay? I'm not the whore bartender you might think I am."

"That's good to know, since I don't *make love* to whores." He wants so badly to kiss those feisty lips. Then he catches her eyes grow wide at his choice of words.

Most women swoon for a man who uses the word love, but not this woman. Nope, the second she hears the damn word, she looks like a deer in headlights. Then she pulls out that trucker mouth.

"But I'm sure you *fuck* them as you please." She tries to put up a stony front, but he can already read her weaknesses.

"You want me to fuck you? Is that it?" Just saying it out loud turns him on.

"Yes," she pleads, not even slightly afraid to ask for what she wants. Her voice is breathless and her chest heaves with every raspy breath.

She needs this too.

Harley presses his lower body against her, pinning her to the door, so she can't escape from him. He loses his jacket and drops it to the floor, not much caring for his expensive leather in comparison to the pleasure he's about to receive from tasting this woman.

When he removes his shirt, he looks into her eyes and growls. "Your turn."

Aliah's expression is incredulous. "You expect me to undress myself? Most men would have had me naked by now."

"You say you're not a whore..."

"I mean, most men would strip a willing woman with his teeth if that's what he had to do to get her naked."

Harley squeezes his eyes shut, forcing away the delightful image that slams into his head. "I like to take my time."

He sees Aliah swallow. She's intrigued. Has a man never taken his time with her? He leans in to kiss her, then immediately catches himself before she can turn away and throw him out. He's straining against his pants, and her softness only compliments him. He wants to sink right into her, but he wants to do it his way.

Harley can see the way her chest rises and falls, as she waits to see what he's going to do next. Aliah acts like she's a take-charge kind of girl, but he knows better. She wants to be taken.

"Why won't you just fuck me already?"

Oh, he plans to. But not until he is good and ready.

He skims his hands over her heated flesh, tickling her sides with the gentleness of his touch. He flexes against her, demonstrating how much the anticipation intrigues him too. Then he finally lifts her shirt over her body, but leaves it covering her head.

While he kisses her neck, she doesn't even complain. He lets his tongue have a taste of her skin, as his hands warm to her slim core. When he cups a covered breast, she gasps for a breath and suddenly notices the misplaced shirt.

"What the fuck!" She is not impressed.

Why does he need her face, if she isn't going to let him kiss it?

He helps her fumble with her shirt, until it lands on the floor next to his jacket. His smiling lips find her neck, but she shoves him backward. Not giving up, not even a little bit, he kisses her neck again. He feels when she softens beneath him, but he's not going to let her forget.

He grasps onto her chin and turns her head away, as he sucks her skin into his mouth, giving her pleasure bites from her jaw to her ear. She's clearly pleased with his tongue, now that he's shut his mouth. But she still struggles to fight him off, knowing exactly what he's doing with his tight grip on her chin.

She pries his fingers off her face. "What's your problem?" Even while sassing at him she arches her back and presses into him, to get the full effect of his hard on.

Harley's only response is a smile. He kisses his way across her chest and presses a warm tongue into the hollow of her neck. His lips skim up to the sensitive spot behind her ear, and trace her jaw downward, coming much too close to her mouth.

He knows she wants to stop him. He can feel the tension coming off her in waves. But he revels in the fact that it feels too good for her to actually spit out the words to make him stop. His lips close around her chin and she opens her mouth, to get more air into her starved lungs. Then he kisses the corner of her mouth, and she almost gives in.

But not quite.

She takes his face in her hand and squeezes, searing him with a glare. Then she reaches between them and grabs him by the balls. He grunts; but not unpleasantly.

"You have some big balls, doing that after I told you not to."

He smiles, loving the way she chews at her lips as she stares at his.

She tightens her grip, finding her resolve. "Do it again, and this thing we have going on right here - it's over. Understand?"

He ignores her and licks at the crotch of her hand; the one that is trying really hard to chastise him.

She grabs onto his long, extended tongue with two fingers. "You have no idea how badly I want this tongue inside of me. But you've disobeyed my one and only rule. Now nod your head like a good boy and tell me that you won't do it again."

Her actions stump him. Has he read her all wrong? He thought she liked it when he controlled her. But then she pulls out a sexy-ass move like that. Maybe it could be fun if he let her call the shots. Just maybe.

She lets go of his tongue. His silence isn't a sign of any disagreement on his part, but the look on her face in response to his unsmiling expression is priceless.

"Well?" she urges him.

She still wants it. And he wants to give it to her. But he refuses to nod *like a good boy*.

"I won't kiss you," he agrees. "But know that it's not because I don't want to."

Her tongue darts out to moisten her ruby lips, and they're just begging for him to kiss them. He can't even tear his eyes away. Why won't she just admit it? Their chemistry is mystical; dangerously so. It has him acting out of character. He's acting like a total pussy.

That's about to change.

"You want me to fuck you?" Though he means for it to be hypothetical, she responds to him with parted, passionate lips.

"Yes," she moans, as she strokes him through his pants.

He pulls away to keep the power out of her hands, and it takes all that he has to do it. Energy flows from his fingertips, as they whisper over the dainty lace trimming the top of her black bra. "How much do you love this bra?"

"What?" she whimpers, too caught up in the moment to realize what he's asking.

He tightens his grip on the cups and shreds her bra in half, with one swift rip. She moans loudly, as her breasts bounce free, as if it has turned her on so greatly that she nearly climaxes on the spot. He instantly replaces the lingerie with his hands, lifting and squeezing her like a stress ball.

With her breasts pressed together, he can't help but bury his face in them, to kiss and lick the hollow between those two delicious mounds. Aliah wraps one of her short, little legs around his hip and digs her heel into the small of his back to move herself against him.

After paying sufficient attention to each milky breast, giving careful consideration to her fully aroused nipples, he grabs onto her foot, unwinds it from his hip and lowers it to the floor. Then he unbuttons her skirt, pries it open and slowly eases it over her hips, one at a time, licking his lips as he anticipates how pleasant this is going to be for him. He sees her tattoo, up close and personal.

His fingers disappear beneath the fabric and smooth over her thighs as he lowers her skirt and panties to her ankles at once, exposing more black flames. He's careful not to snag what's left of her lacy lingerie, as he pulls it past her heels, until he's left her standing there before him wearing nothing but those fuck-me-now shoes and a sassy smile.

He picks up one of her heels and presses a kiss to the swell of her foot. Harley was never one to obsess over a woman's shoe, but seeing Aliah like this puts a whole new spin on things. He looks up at her, but finds it difficult to look past her perfectly trimmed pussy.

Forgetting to restrain her arms while he divested her of her clothes was his first mistake. She reaches down to hurry him along and help him with his shirt. Not taking any of her cues, he continues with his slow provocation. His rough hands whisper over every inch of her exposed flesh, focusing on those healthy thighs. He just wants to dig right into her, as he squeezes a supple ass cheek and presses a kiss just below her belly button.

When she shivers, Harley decides it's time to make good on one of her expectations. Their eyes connect briefly.

"Are you ready for this?" he growls, so excited himself he can barely wait to have a taste.

She swallows and nods, intrigue flaring in her eyes as he swiftly lifts each of her legs over his shirtless shoulders and regains his stance. He presses her into the door and seals his mouth onto her precious pink pussy. Her body shudders the second his tongue brushes across her.

He smiles, satisfied that she's enjoying herself. With a lick of his tongue, up and down, he splits her in two and has a taste, growing more and more hungry to please her with every pleasant whimper she voices.

Harley's mouth moves against her soft lips, as his tongue languidly swipes and stabs inside her to get a better taste. She arches her back, but again he presses against her to flatten her to the door. Aliah's fingers claw into his hair and dig in, to hold herself onto something stable, as he continues to lick and tease her.

With his arms flattened against the door on either side of her, he curls his tongue a little lower, using the come hither motion, eliciting the most appealing moan from her lips. He does it again and again, learning quickly how she likes it most, until she's wound so tight around his neck he knows she's about ready to explode.

So is he.

His cock throbs against his pants, begging for him to stop and sink himself into that sweet, sweet pussy. He needs her to cum as badly as she wants to. Harley glances up at her and finds her eyes squeezed closed, her chest heaving and her middle firm and flat. When he wiggles his tongue, her ruby lips part and a gasp escapes from her mouth.

He knows she's close and he's ready to take her there, knowing just what to do to get the job done. He slips his hands between her and the door and grips onto her luscious ass cheeks, holding her firmly against his soft, wet mouth.

She pants and gasps for air, but he wants more of a vocal reaction from her. He starts to move her lower body in sync with his mouth, so she can feel the slow rhythm of his tongue entering and exiting her body, as her pussy fucks his tongue. He loves the way her insides tighten around him, her thighs squeezing against his ears. Then, when he knows she is only seconds from orgasm, he slips a long finger in there and licks her with a firm tongue.

Aliah is not afraid to express herself. She screams, as she comes apart, and it's the most erotic thing Harley's ever witnessed. He nearly loses it himself, the only thing saving him being the sound of a knock at the unlocked door. He isn't even done with her, as she remains tightly coiled around his face.

He greedily drinks up his prize and she ignores the visitor. She can't seem to descend to reality, while propped up on his shoulders, sitting on his mouth. Shit. Neither can he. But the visitor is relentless, and starts pounding on the door.

When Harley breaks his mouth away from her, Aliah shouts, "No," not wanting him to stop. She doesn't want it to be over and neither does he. He continues to suck on her, until her body stops shuddering. He kisses across her stomach, before licking his moist lips and lowering her trembling legs to the floor.

She stands on wobbly limbs and quickly collects her scattered clothes from the floor. After pulling on those see-through panties, she crouches to hide in the corner. He grabs her around the waist and hugs her mostly naked body so it's pressed up against him. She gasps for air, a big smile on her face.

"They'll see you!" Her voice is but a harsh whisper.

The pounding ensues, after a barrage of rings from the doorbell. "I know you're in there. I can hear you breathing!" a man hollers.

They're both smiling like school children and she's on the brink of a giggle attack. They're flattened against the wall, just barely out of sight of the partially glazed side-light next to her door.

They can hear the beginnings of a conversation right through the door, which suggests that Aliah's earlier ramblings were vividly clear to their visitors.

"I'm worried," the man says, knowing Aliah's on the other side of that door.

Harley glances down at her for some indication of who it might be. He doesn't even have to ask.

"It's Mitchell," Aliah mouths, clearing up any guess work.

Harley nods and smiles, a sardonic smile. He wants nothing more than to chew on those kissable lips. He could care less who is on the other side of that door. He has a relentless lover, who's happy to accept what he has to offer her. Everything except for kisses, that is. On the mouth. He's plenty happy to kiss the rest of that body, knowing before long she'll be longing for the touch of his lips on hers.

Right now though, with her naked little body wrapped up against him, her lips have slipped to the back of his primitive mind. His fingers drift up the curve of her hip and smooth over the soft flesh next to a pair of perfect tits. He's so very tempted to lay her out on that ceramic floor and pummel into her with fast flicks of his pelvis until they're both swept up in a mindless release.

Then a woman adds her two cents to the conversation happening on the other side of the door, and it tears him from his daydreams in an instant.

"She obviously doesn't want to talk to you. She would come to the door if she did. Get the hint, Mitchell." Her voice is snappy. She isn't happy to be there.

Mitchell puts his fist to the door one last time. "Come on, Ally. I know you're in there. Open up."

"Enough!" Brandee shouts. "Leave *them* alone."

Them? Shit. Brandee knows Aliah has company. How could she know that? He doesn't know Brandee Hawkins very well, but anyone with such an unhealthy paranoia is guaranteed to lead into a bad situation. Does she know it's him there with Aliah?

That woman is nuts. Harley hopes Mitchell takes the nut bag's advice and gets her out of there. He's worried that Brandee's fixation on Cavanagh's sex life has already become more of a fixation on Aliah.

"Let's go!" Brandee shouts, and it sounds like they're finally leaving.

Forgetting about that, and living in the moment, Harley lifts Aliah's mostly-naked body into his arms and carries her up the stairs, plunging them deeper into the darkness of her unlit house.

"Where am I going?" he asks her.

She slaps at him. "Put me down."

"I'm not putting you down. So why don't you point the way?"

Aliah kicks and squirms, but soon realizes that she isn't going to break free from his grip of death. She points a finger and he takes a direct route to her room, lit only by the sliver of moon beaming through her windows. He brings her to the bedroom and lowers her body, until she's slumped at the foot of her bed. Aliah just stares up at him, not quite sure what's going to happen between them.

"I'm not about to make you do anything you don't want to do."

She grabs onto his waistband, her fingers dipping inside his pants. "Do you hear me complaining?"

"Every step of the way."

Aliah scowls at him. "Fine, then. What do you want to do?"

His chuckle is dark and seductive. "I'll give you two options. One: You tell me to get the hell out of here and I will leave right this minute. Or two: Get up on that bed and spread your pretty little legs for me."

CHAPTER EIGHT

When Harley asks for a silent invitation, her legs involuntarily part for him. That voice is a weapon. Her body aches for him before it even knows what it's missing. She hopes he'll just strip from his t-shirt and jeans and show her exactly what she's working with. He doesn't.

He loses his shirt in a matter of seconds. For that she is grateful. She can't take her eyes off those large sculpted arms, loving the way wings of a predatory bird stretch across the expanse of his strong upper back. He turns toward her and puts his hands on his hips. Now it seems to be his turn to peruse over her body.

Harley stands there, stationary, but his muscles are doing magnificent things under her warm scrutiny. She hasn't realized how a simple glance can have her twitching with exhilaration. She licks at her lips and his own mouth parts, as he sucks in a breath. The anticipation has the room in flames, together with her panties.

When Harley climbs onto the bed, it dips under his weight. She wonders why he hasn't stripped yet. Then his mouth is on her over-sensitized flesh, and suddenly she's not so concerned about his pants. His palm slides up and down her body, leaving a trail of goose-bumps in its wake, as his tongue works his magic on her.

When his hand slips between her legs, she makes to squeeze her thighs together, but is stopped when his large thigh captures her leg. She feels so exposed and yet completely and utterly content to let him have his way with her. And he did just that.

Harley gives her a night of the most unbelievable pleasure she's ever experienced, the attentions rolling over well into the early morning hours. Aliah doesn't know how she is supposed to explain this one to herself. Harley had delivered, all night long, and he hadn't even given her what she wanted most - him inside of her.

Sure, his tongue went there and he let her wet his dick in her mouth, more than once, but she needed that sizable thing between her legs. It was bad enough that she was stuck in this hazy purgatory between sleep and sate. It was worse when she's suddenly stuck thinking about nothing but the flexibility of his pelvis and how ram-rod straight he becomes every time she touches him.

Aliah's eyes open sleepily, expecting to find a vacant bed next to her. She was certain he'd have bolted before the sun was up, but that naked slab of sex was still sprawled out in her bed, just snoring away. Her teeth dig into her smiling lower lip. Why does that make her smile?

Terrified by her reaction, she slips out from under his arm and hides out in the bathroom for close to an hour. She hopes that is enough time for him to wake the fuck up and skedaddle. But this dude isn't like other guys she's dated. Not that *they* were dating, but Harley was so attentive to her needs.

Harley had restrained himself from orgasm completely, even when she'd sucked him hard and slid him between her breasts, begging him to cum all over her. The look in his eyes told her he wanted to, but he'd denied himself the release. He'd exerted sheer willpower like she'd never seen before. What man does that? He's like superman or something.

That thought alone has her wound so tight, she can feel herself contracting between her thighs, the rest of her body quivering with excitement. She presses her ear to the door, but she can't hear anything. She figures he's finally taken the hint and left quickly and quietly. With a smile, she opens her door. On the other side of it is a sleepy Harley, and he's naked, with a hard-on from hell.

Aliah's mouth falls to the floor and stays that way when his massive arm stretches up and over his head to scratch the back of it.

"Good morning." His voice is low and husky; very sexy.

But not half as sexy as that fit body.

He leans forward and plants a kiss on her lips, before passing by her to enter the bathroom. If she hadn't closed the bathroom door behind him, she was sure he would have taken a leak right in front of her. *Is he on drugs?*

What the hell had just happened? That wasn't half as awkward as she thought it might be, and maybe a little too comfortable really. Aliah hurries to her room, collects up her things and carries them to the kitchen, trying to avoid that man's amazing body, with him wearing it all naked and erect like that.

When he steps out of the bathroom, she half expects him to ignore her, but he acts like he's completely comfortable standing buck naked in her living space. He seems to think that she would find no offence to that. She doesn't. Especially when she notices how he's still semi-erect. It draws her eyes to the place where two powerful legs meet.

Her eyes zero in on one large piece of meat. He can hardly expect her to ignore that thing, when he's flagging it out there like that. She smiles for a second and quickly hides it behind a mask of responsibility. She hooks her last earring into her ear and reconnects with those dreamy eyes.

"Um, maybe you should get dressed. I'm sorry, but I have to work and I'm already running a little late."

"I thought you were a bartender." He looks only slightly confused.

Oh shit. "I wear many hats. This one is a little less agreeable with me being late, so…"

"I understand, but Aliah…"

"Yeah?"

"Do you think you could spare one minute for me?"

Oh. Shit! What could he possibly want?

Maybe he wants a quickie. That doesn't sound like such a bad idea. In fact, that sounds like a fabulous idea. She smiles. "Are you getting fresh with me?"

Harley chuckles, and even though he says that he isn't, he starts to stand at attention again as he begins to speak.

"I just thought we would sort out what happened here."

"We had a good time last night, and you crashed here. It's no biggie." She waves a careless hand at him.

"Okay." He continues to smile and it starts to make her a little uncomfortable.

She can feel the heat rising to her cheeks. "Why? What did you think happened?"

She wonders if she has missed something important. When she flashes a glance at his waistline, he raises his eyebrows incredulously. It is hardly a crime. He can't actually expect her to stop looking at his flag pole, when he's waving it around in her kitchen.

"How about I pull some clothes on and I'll walk you out?" He doesn't wait for her to answer. He's gone in a heartbeat and back in the room fastening his belt within that same minute.

She watches him pull his shirt over his head, then he reaches for his jacket, scrunching the leather in one hand. She stares at him, like an idiot.

"You were just leaving?" he offers, and he says it like she's only said it in an attempt to get rid of him, when in fact that's exactly what she's doing.

He follows her to the garage, and it's not until he holds the door open that reality begins to sink in for her.

"Shit!"

He smiles, knowing damn well that she has no wheels, except for the unused bicycle hanging from her ceiling.

"Need a ride?"

"Obviously." She sighs and slaps her hands down, staring at the beautiful motorcycle sitting perfectly centered in her garage.

His eyes never leave her. "You're going to have to ask nicely."

"Really? You'd leave me stranded like that?"

"If you insist on being a bitch, then yeah."

She groans and exaggerates her curse. "*Fuck* me."

He smiles at that. "While that idea is very intriguing, you've already said that you're running late. I really don't think we can fit that in." He's teasing her now.

Where does this guy get off?

"I just finished doing my hair. I'm going to have funky helmet-head if I wear that thing."

She throws a hand out to point at his helmet, but she reaches for it anyways. He pulls it back, before she can get a good handle on it.

"I'm sure you'll look good, no matter what hairstyle you go with today. But I'm still waiting for you to ask me nicely. Can you do that, Aliah? Can you be a *nice girl*?"

"Most men look for something a little different than that. Tell me you're any different."

"Oh, I'm different, sweetheart. You can bet your pretty panties on that. And I've already seen that you don't mind getting a little dirty, and that's good. I like a little variety. Is that something you can give me?" He chews on his lip, trying his darnedest to wet her panties.

It's working too, but their conversation has turned way too intense for this hour in the morning; especially with the knowledge that she had only just closed her eyes mere hours ago after a night of unrestrained ecstasy. She feels herself squeezing her thighs together, but it hardly helps to douse her attraction to him.

"Harley."

"Yes?" he answers immediately, smiling.

"Can you *please* take me to my car?"

"No."

"No?" she squeals.

"That wasn't nice enough. I guess you don't do nice. Sorry. Maybe you'll have better luck next time." He rests the helmet on his seat and hits the button to open the garage door.

Aliah follows him back to his bike and waits for him to turn around. She cannot believe that he is pulling her own stunts on her. When he doesn't turn to face her, she grabs onto the helmet, pulls it on, and swings a leg over the seat until she's straddling his machine with both hands resting in front of her. She strokes the length of the conditioned leather seat, relying solely on sex appeal to get what she wants.

"Please, Harley? Take me with you?"

He quirks a brow and flattens a hand over his bristly face. "Shit."

She smiles when she sees the twinkle in his eyes. *It's working!* She thinks she's won, but he's not prepared to give in quite that easily.

"On one condition."

"Whoa, whoa," she says, shaking her head and waving both hands in a criss-crossed fashion. "Wait right there. No one said anything about conditions."

"I just did."

She huffs, realizing how much time they were burning over such a minor thing. "I asked nicely." Maybe she should have just called a cab and saved her hair from the disastrous mess it was quickly becoming.

Harley doesn't take his eyes off of her. *This man is serious.*

"Fine. A condition. What is it?"

"Dinner. Tonight. I'll meet you at Orlando's."

She glares at him, wondering if she's heard him right. "You do realize Orlando's is fine dining. I really doubt you want to take me there."

"You can't appreciate the finer things in life? Would you rather I meet you at a flea bag motel and fuck you against a filthy wall?"

Her insides twitch at the thought. Even that nasty remark turns her on. She has to think about it for a minute. It did sound a bit intriguing, but was he not trying to be a jerk about it? "That was rude! Maybe I don't want to meet you at all, after that asshole comment."

"I'm sorry," he blurts, but it hardly sounds thoughtful. "I just thought I could take you somewhere nicer than Riley's."

"You're a motorcycle dude. Any random restaurant would be fine. You really don't have to try that hard."

A smile slants across his face when he catches her admitting that she is already smitten.

"Oh, I didn't mean *that!*" she blurts, but he's already convinced himself that she really likes him.

Harley catches her chin in his hand and sears her with his molten gaze. "I know exactly what you meant."

A nosy neighbor walks down the sidewalk in front of her house and stops when his small dog starts barking erratically at them. The man catches Harley's overbearing stance, and the way he forcefully cups Aliah's chin, mistaking it as an unwanted gesture.

"Everything okay in there, Miss Brooklin?" the neighbor shouts, looking a little concerned.

Harley instantly releases her chin, when he realizes that his affections are being broadcast to the entire neighborhood.

Aliah glances around Harley's imposing frame. "Everything is just fine, Joe."

After satisfying Joe with words, she seals the deal by hooking her arm around Harley's waist and delivering a soft smooch on his cheek. Her softness seems to melt against him, making her knees weak and her mind all wishy washy, as Harley holds her there with closed eyes. He stays silent, hovering close to her face, long after he should have retreated. Then his eyes open and catch onto hers.

"You kissed me."

"Yeah, on the cheek," she snaps, as though it meant nothing to her. Her legs still feel like jelly. "I had to. Unless you prefer that my friend Joe there call the cops on you."

"Oh."

"So, are you going to give me a ride, or will I have better luck hitchhiking?"

"Tell me you're only joking."

"Yes. I only hitchhike on evenings and weekends. It's too unpredictable for a work day; especially Monday mornings. So can we go already?"

"I'll drive you. Soon. But first, there's another ride I want you to take."

Harley steals her hand and pulls her into the next room where he seats himself on the stairs, pries her button open and all but tears her clothes off of her. He unzips his fly and pulls himself out for her to pounce on him. After rolling on a condom, Aliah straddles his lap and slowly eases onto him. Harley hisses as he fills her insides with his rigid length.

It's so tight and it feels so good, but Aliah's surprised by the intimacy of their contact, face to face. As she settles down on his lap, he grasps onto her hips and jerks himself deeper, a snarl passing across his face. When their eyes lock, she feels like kissing him, but she quickly brushes that thought away as sensations below the belt demand her undivided attention.

Before long, she's bouncing on top of him, her climax spiraling out of control, like the waves in her hair. She continues to move on him, but she's so sensitive, quivering from the delicious contact. Harley grows impatient from her slowed pace and stands to his feet, without breaking their connection. He presses her into the wall and fills her with a furious erection. She's never felt so complete.

His nose brushes across hers. "Okay?" he asks, as he thrusts into her again.

When she nods, he pushes into her once more.

"Yeah?" he asks softly, demanding that she be more vocal, as he quickens his pace.

"Yes!" she shouts, sounding exhausted and breathless. "God, yes!"

Her back is flat against the wall, but she's clinging to his rippled muscles. Every touch has her body aroused beyond comparison. He drives into her again and again, until she's crying out and he's finding his first release inside of her.

A sated pride blooms in her belly as she retracts her nails from out of his back and he returns her to her feet. She quickly redresses and joins him in the garage.

When Aliah slips outside, Harley's straddling his motorcycle. But now she's wearing a helmet of her own, looking a lot like the girl of his dreams, her cheeks flushed with a healthy glow. His bike rumbles to life, as he pulls on his helmet and she mounts the bike behind him.

Harley eases his bike down her driveway. He lets them roll to the curb, and he watches in his mirror until the door presses shut behind them, before pulling away from the house in a flurry of speed. The wind is chilled, but it feels good in her hair. He feels good in her arms. Believe it or not, she feels like she could get used to this.

When they reach Riley's parking lot, he stops a few spaces away from her yellow BMW. It's the only car in the lot.

"Before you go, don't you think we should settle the terms of this date?"

"Date?" She can't believe he's actually asking her out after last night. "I don't date. Been there. Tried that. A monstrous waste of time, if you ask me."

"Alright then, I won't call it a date. Dinner sound okay? You have to eat. I can pick you up..."

"No. If you pick me up, then that would make it a date."

"Then I'll meet you there."

"Fine," she snaps, like she really doesn't want to. Unfortunately, the look on her face tells another story.

"Orlando's at six." He winks at her, and he's smiling when she slips inside her car.

She settles into the driver's seat to hide behind the dark tint of her windows. Harley doesn't know it, but her eyes follow his exit like a moth to a flame. When he disappears around the corner, she sits there for a moment and tries to collect herself. A glance in her rear-view mirror has her inspecting the rosy quality affecting her cheeks.

This is new. And she's not even sure that she likes it.

CHAPTER NINE

Harley leaves the lot before Aliah even has her key in the ignition. But he doesn't get far before he turns down an alleyway and rolls to a stop. He turns his bike around, remaining seated, and walks it back up to the edge of the tall building to wait for some indication of where she is heading.

He already hates where this is going. He'd tugged her back in her house and had gone against the one rule he had set for himself... no topping out. After relenting so shamelessly he should have felt guilty. All he felt was satisfaction. He'd claimed her. It was written all over her face. She is as good as his, if he wants her. *Does he want her?*

His employability relies on strict confidentiality. He has a job to do. His latest client, the one with the overactive jealousy and violent temper, is the last person he needs to be pissing off right now. He has to finish this job. It's not like he believes that Aliah is guilty. And even if she is, he refuses to let one little hussy take him down.

He's met chicks like her before. Well, maybe not anyone *quite* like her. She's not exactly an endangered species though.

Harley wishes he could just throw her back to the wolves, but he can't stop thinking about how perfect Aliah looked straddled on the bike and how good she felt behind him. He'd asked her out. On a date. And she's outright denied him. He's never asked a woman out before. Never. But something has him forcing the issue with Aliah. He wants to woo those sassy shoes right off her.

Aliah's car passes in a flash. She drives so quickly that he almost misses her flying by. He turns into traffic and maintains a safe distance behind her, having to travel a lot faster than he usually would in rush hour traffic. He watches her turn into a parking lot and examines her every move.

She rushes the front door of a lawyer's office, Bailey & Miller LLP. It's only the top law firm in the City. Joshua Bailey happens to be the most renowned criminal defence lawyer north of Toronto. Harley wonders what kind of trouble she has gotten herself into. He can only imagine. It's no wonder she's lied about where she was going.

Harley drives right past the lawyers' office and heads straight to work, skipping home for a fresh change of clothes. He loves the scent of her on him. He'll have a pleasant day. After collecting himself, which is rather difficult when he can still taste her on his lips, he decides to spend the better part of his morning finding all the dirt he can on Miss Aliah Brooklin.

That is, after all, what he is hired to do.

Jillian takes a step into Harley's office before she realizes he has crashed behind his computer monitors. "Eh hem!" Jillian makes a dramatic sound, artificially clearing her throat to get his attention.

Harley jolts awake, looking like hell. "Oh. Hey, Jillian. I must have nodded off."

"I'd say. She must be keeping you busy."

"Who? Oh. Her. Right." He tries to act ignorant, but he can sense that Jillian's reaction to his sleeplessness is rather peculiar.

That's too bad for her. It's not against the law to have sex with a beautiful willing woman, even if he might have a *minor* conflict of interest in the matter.

Jillian tries to hide her impatience, but fails. "Any luck?"

She must be referring to the investigation. He doubts she cares to hear how exactly he got lucky.

"Not exactly." Harley clears his throat, squirming in his seat, as his body rises at the mere thought of Aliah's silky soft skin. He wonders how he can work around the truth without lying to his trusted assistant. "She's a handful, that one."

"I bet." Jillian's clearly annoyed with him. "What's the plan now? Do you need me to scoop her cell phone? Because I will."

"No, no. Nothing like that. I don't actually believe the girl is guilty. Ms. Hawkins might just be one with an overactive imagination."

"What?" Jillian's face is painted with scepticism. Her voice turns snappy. "You've never given the suspect benefit of the doubt before. Why start now?"

Aliah Brooklin.

He clears his throat again, as if Jillian might have heard his thoughts. "I just have a feeling about this one."

Jillian takes a step closer and stares at his crotch, but there's no way she knows his dick is still twitching just talking about her. "A feeling, hmm?" She props her hands on her hips, slouches to one side and stares at the crotch of his jeans. "I think you should quit thinking with your other head and concentrate on getting the deal closed. I mean it, David. Get it together."

He waves her off, as her eyes meet his. Since when did Jillian give him a pep talk? He wonders how invested she is in the outcome of this investigation. He kicks his boots up onto the desk to remind her who's the boss here.

"You're way off base. I haven't found even a smidgen of evidence against her. It's not the girl's fault that Cavanagh looks at her a certain way. Last I checked, it's no crime to wear sexy shoes and flash a little cleavage every now and then."

Jillian seems to soften to his easygoing attitude. "I'll have to remember that." She smiles, a little too intrigued by the idea. "Maybe I'll give it a try tonight. Some friends invited me to join them at Riley's. Want to join us?"

Every time she asks, Harley gives her the same answer. But she keeps on asking anyway.

"I would. But I actually have a thing."

"David H. Gates. Don't tell me no lies. Do you have a date?"

His expression remains deadpan. "Something like that."

"Why don't you bring her too? I'd love to meet the girl."

"I appreciate the offer, Jillian. I really do. But I don't think I'll be dressed for the part tonight."

Jillian is not giving up. "What do you mean? Riley's hardly has a dress code."

"I know. But I'd feel a little out of place wearing a suit past five."

"A suit? Oh, you're pulling out all the stops for this one. I'm jealous."

He raises his brow, wondering why she continues to flirt with him after all these years. "Don't be. It's nothing special."

Jillian lifts both of her brows in a dramatic display to the contrary. "You in a suit? That's pretty special in its own right."

She pauses, and seems to think better than to carry on with the swooning. "If you change your mind, stop on over for a drink."

Harley nods his head, but he has no intention of bringing Aliah there. He has a date. A date. That's what he's calling it because that's what it is. No one spends a plate at Orlando's on someone other than a date. Aliah has to know that. Since she's agreed to dinner with him, but not *a date*, then what is she looking for? A good fuck? He certainly hopes so.

His dick suggests he's doing the right thing, and he seems to agree at this time. In reality, he's on business. He shouldn't be fucking around with the suspect, even if she is one smoking hot chick. But he wants her, from those high heels to her potty mouth. And he isn't against flashing a wad of cash, if that's what he has to do to impress her.

Jillian is right. He's ready to pull out the big guns for this one. And, for the first time in his life, he's looking forward to it.

CHAPTER TEN

When the clock strikes five, most of the staff rush out of the office. Everyone bolts early on a Monday night. But not Aliah. Not tonight.

Bailey had just dropped a stack of files on her desk ten minutes earlier, and every last one of them had been called to the docket for Tuesday. Bailey needs the files ready for tomorrow at nine. She really doesn't have much of a choice in the matter. There is no one else. Just her and Bailey and a stack of files for four.

Bailey peeks his head back inside her cubicle. "You're sure you don't mind working late tonight? You know I hate doing this to you, but it really is an emergency."

She knows how important it is to Bailey that these matters be heard tomorrow. She bites her tongue and smiles. "I can do it. It shouldn't take too long."

That was an understatement. She had quit looking at the clock at six. She knows there is no way she can make dinner with Harley now. Maybe it's best this way.

Bailey offers to order takeout at seven. "It's the least I can do."

She can't even imagine eating a bite, while dreaming about the meal she has missed. "No thanks. I'm not hungry."

She ignores the food when it arrives and finishes her work.

"I think that's it." She drops the files on Bailey's desk. "Why don't you take a quick look and make sure there isn't something I've missed?"

"No, no. You go on. I can take it from here."

"You're sure? Because I don't mind staying a little longer."

"It's after 8:30, Aliah." Bailey swallows a mouthful of

food before continuing. "I've already ruined your night."

You have no idea.

"You get on out of here," he insists. "And don't bother to come in until after lunch tomorrow."

Her smile is genuine. "Thanks. But you don't have to do that."

"I insist. You'll be paid for your time. No more fussing. Now get lost." He waves a hand to shoo her away.

She smiles and walks off. "Good night."

The cool evening air rushes her when she steps outside. The sky has already turned dark and shadows are lurking around the private parking lot. She hurries to unlock her door, and instantly relocks it after she drops into her seat. She rubs her eyes with both hands, smearing the black mascara under her eyes.

Aliah holds one of her hands over her face and starts to laugh, but it's not out of humor. She has totally blown off a sexy bad boy, who also seems to have the desire to wine and dine her. Oh well. He probably would have paid for her dinner with drug money anyway. She drops the pouty face and snickers to herself, as she starts her car.

What is this guy's deal anyway? He plans all this while still believing that she's a trashy bartender. It is likely for the best that she didn't call him. He'd get the hint in a hurry when she didn't show.

Can you even say you stood up a man when it isn't a date?

Yes. Because that's exactly what she did. And it *was* a date. Her realization only makes her feel like the piece of shit that she is.

As she turns toward her home, she contemplates why she had even agreed to go out with him in the first place. She could have dropped the act and caught a cab the other night. But a part of her, the one hiding deep down inside of her, secretly wanted to see where things could go with him. She wanted it to be a date. Why did she want it to be a date?

Instead of calling Harley to apologize, or calling a friend to confess, Aliah drives straight to Riley's to drown herself in a few shots. She convinces herself it was a good thing that she never made it to dinner with Harley, since then they would have went back to her house for more sex. A bitch could get addicted to a man like that. It's best this way. She keeps telling herself that repeatedly, hoping that it will make it feel more true.

After whirling her car around, she speeds to Mitchell's bar and wheels into the parking lot. She climbs out of her car, shrugs out of her stifling suit jacket, and then tosses it into the backseat. Still feeling overdressed, Aliah pulls her blouse over her head and readjusts her tank top to make sure she is showing the most attractive amount of cleavage.

With her tight shirt tucked into her high-waisted pants, she reaches for her purse and pulls out a wad of cash, leaving her baggage in the car. She checks her reflection in her mirror and once she is satisfied that she looks fuckable, she makes her way across the road to Riley's.

She hates that the place is packed. Monday night wings never fails to fill the place. She knows though, that it is only a matter of time before the happy hour crowd clears out and returns to their families, to settle snugly into their beds for the night.

Usually Aliah is content to go to bed at ten, snuggle in with a good book, and save the drinking for the weekend. But usually Aliah isn't asked on a date by a man who she is very attracted to. Then for her to stand him up without an explanation even when she has a perfectly good one.

She has issues.

As the bar quickly clears out, Aliah makes herself more comfortable, kicking a heeled foot up onto the barstool next to her.

"Bartender!" she shouts, though he's only a few feet away. "Another tequila shot, please."

"Sorry, Aliah. But I won't do it. Mitchell would have my neck."

Aliah looks at the row of empty shot glasses in front of her. It was only three drinks. But she did just drink one – two – three in a row. She could easily handle a couple more.

"What the hell?" she shouts, frustrated more with herself than the poor bartender. "I'm barely even buzzing and you're cutting me off?"

She becomes more pissed when she realizes that she'll have to face her troubles soberly. "Maybe I'll just have to take my business elsewhere. Why don't you go tell Mitchell that?" She shouts it loud enough for everyone else in the place to hear.

Not only does the owner hear, but she manages to drum up the attention of a certain individual who had been collapsed in a booth, drowning himself in liquor.

Mitchell comes out of the back room and steps right in front of Aliah, as Harley pulls himself out of the booth and onto unsteady feet.

"Ally. It's a work night. You really shouldn't be drinking like that. What's with you tonight?"

"Who are you to decide how and when I should be drinking? I'm my own woman, Mitchy boy. If I want to drink, then I'm going to drink."

Harley steps out from the crowd, unbeknownst to her, but Mitchell notices immediately. He points his next words at him. "I just want you to be safe."

Aliah catches the evil eye and knows she has company. Company who Mitchell apparently doesn't like very much. She spins around on her stool. There's someone standing there, looking tall and dark and sexy, but it can't be her Harley because he is wearing a suit! Her eyes bug out of her head as she takes in such a sight. Now she feels like an even bigger douche.

Harley gives Aliah a pointed glance, but his voice is casual. "You have some nerve showing up here."

Aliah sighs. "Let me explain."

"No need. I get it. I'll keep my distance." He turns away and stumbles down a step and back toward his booth.

"Wait! Harley!"

Shit. He's really drunk. And that's because of her. With a few insignificant glances, he disappears back inside the confines of his booth. He manages to make her feel like a horrible person. *She is one.*

He had gotten all dressed up, wearing a tie and everything. A god-damned tie! By the look of the quality, he had visited a tailor too. And she'd stood the guy up. He is clearly trying, and she has to admit that seeing him dressed like that had her heart swelling with an unguarded desire. Oh, she loves the bad-boy, biker look on him, but the fact that he could pull that shit off too just does something to her insides.

What is wrong with her? Why does she even care? She isn't supposed to care like that.

"Ally. Don't do it." Mitchell's voice comes out of nowhere. All of his statements lately have had her on the defensive.

She hadn't noticed until now, but Mitchell has been watching her. She rests her back against the bar, giving him the cold shoulder, her voice turning snappy. "Don't do what?"

He points toward Harley's booth with his eyes, as Harley waves a finger at a waitress to get him another drink. Harley's eyes catch onto hers for not more than a second, but she feels it in her bones. He acts like she is a nobody; a piece of garbage beneath his polished shoes. She feels like trash.

"Don't do it, Ally," Mitchell repeats. "He's not the type of guy you should be hanging around. Especially alone."

"Is that right?" Aliah twirls around and stands there surfing momentarily, waiting for her balance to catch up with her. "Who exactly do you think is the type for me? I'd really like to know."

Aliah raises her voice, catching Brandee's attention and every other nobody sitting between them at the bar. It was no secret that Mitchell has always tried to protect her. He has ever since high school. He has always been a great friend. But he also has a thing for her. And by the way Brandee watches her, Aliah knows that she knows.

Mitchell grabs onto her arm, to keep her from falling, and apologizes. Mitchell is a lot of things. But a cheater is not one of them. Aliah knows he is a safe bet as a friend, since she will never settle like that and he will never grow the balls to make a move beyond friendship. She just isn't attracted to the big, beefy type. Unless of course that beef is solid, grade-A, Harley.

"Thank you for looking out, Mitch. But I don't need a babysitter. I can manage fine without you."

Aliah slips to the floor, suddenly feeling very sober. She stills for an extended moment of truth, before taking a step in the right direction. What is she doing? If she doesn't want to date Harley, then she has already gotten that point across. Her intentions were voiced loud and clear by her silence. But now it is something else drawing her to his table.

As she grows closer, something in the back of her head nags her to stop. But she can't stop. And she doesn't stop, until she is standing across from him.

What a mistake!

Her heart rams up into her throat and cuts off her air supply.

Poor, little Harley... my ass!

He's sitting there with a sexy little slut smiling up at him. Her dress has a deep v neckline and her youthful bust is exposed for every man in the place. But it is Harley's eyes that she is concerned most about and they seem to be concentrated on the girl's chest.

Before Harley even notices that she's standing there, the girl slides across the bench and rests her hand on his, leaning into him.

Slut.

Aliah overhears the girl's confession. "You know I'm here for you, David. For whatever."

He'd lied to her about his name. Smooth move, *Harley*.

The girl senses that Aliah's standing behind her and glances over her shoulder. It isn't long before they're scowling at each other. Aliah watches the girl slide out of the booth and walk away, giving a pointed glare at her, as she passes. Once she rejoins a guy across the room, Aliah clears her throat.

Harley only just then notices that he has company, as Aliah slips onto the seat across from him. His sigh is exaggerated, like it's a bother for him to deal with her. Then he lowers his voice.

"It's you," he mumbles.

"Don't sound so excited about it."

"Because you give me good reason to be." The rude tone he uses with her hits like a shock to her system. All warmth has left the building, along with their unforgiving chemistry.

"Can I say that I'm sorry about that?" She reaches out for his hand to show him some sort of affection, but he pulls his hand away before she can even touch him. She pulls her hand back and clutches onto her belt loop, feeling scorned.

"You look sorry." Even when he tries to scorn her, his eyes take a suggestive inspection of her body.

It doesn't stop her from reacting to his attitude. "What the hell is that supposed to mean?"

"You didn't even bother to pick up a phone. I waited for you, you know. For close to an hour." He lifts a pitcher of beer to his lips and guzzles it down, like he has an overwhelming need to quench his thirst.

"When you didn't show, I'd figured I might as well enjoy a peaceful dinner. *Alone.* And I did. Without your big mouth there to ruin it." The slur in his voice is the only indication that he is the one who'd polished off the many pitchers of beer cluttering his table.

"Nice." She doesn't know how else to respond to him.

"What? You think you're the only one allowed to act like a jerk? It works both ways, darlin'."

"You know what?" She pauses, carefully considering her words. "Fuck you."

"Fuck you, too."

She scowls at him and leans over the table. "I came over here to apologize for being such a bitch. But now I almost want to take it back."

"That was hardly a worthy apology anyways. You *should* take it back, and do it right this time."

Aliah flips him the bird. There's no sense in arguing with him when he's in this state.

"What?" he shouts.

She narrows her eyes, preparing to rip him a new one. "You can't just shut your mouth long enough for me to tell you how fucking sorry I am for ruining your night. I would have even added how nice you look, but you reek like a case of beer, which is not incredibly attractive."

"Fortunate for me, that isn't the look I'm going for tonight."

He could have fooled her. He had loosened his tie and unfastened the top three buttons on his shirt, showing just enough flesh to toy with her imagination. His tie is flapped over a broad shoulder and it looks like his facial hair is making an early appearance. Everything about him screams sexy and she can't even deny it.

When Aliah notices that the girl from earlier is returning to the table with a fresh pitcher of beer, she shuffles to the edge of the bench seat. Aliah supposes she's the reason why Harley's bombarding her with ignorance.

"Again, I apologize," Aliah snaps, as the girl slides up next to Harley. But no one would believe her, with the anger in her tone. "You and your girlfriend can have fun. I'll get out of your hair."

She hurries away from the table, before she shares an emotion that she prefers to bottle up and save for the privacy of her own lonely bedroom.

Why is she reacting so strongly to this dude?

She doesn't want to care. But to see him with that other girl has her feeling royally rotten. She can't stop the hesitation in her breath, and that just barely allows her to maintain her cool. Aliah stops at the bar and grabs onto it for support. She leans over and whispers in the ear of the college-aged guy next to her. He gladly orders a pair of shots for her. She tucks a bill in his pocket and he smiles, crushing the bill back into her hand.

"It's on me." He licks a smiling bottom lip, as if that generosity might have earned him another sort of reward.

He looks sweet, with his ball cap pulled low over his glimmering eyes. She smiles sideways, taking in the way his shoulders are broad like Harley's.

"Thanks."

When the bartender turns away, and Mitchell disappears into the back room, she takes the first small glass from the guy's extended hand. As she edges it closer to her parted lips, a large, strong hand cups around hers.

"Drop it."

The deep, dangerous voice that rushes over her ears can't be mistaken for anyone else. *Harley.*

She releases the glass and tucks her hands into her lap. Unexpectedly, Harley downs the first shot and chases it with the other one. She glances over her shoulder at him.

His eyes are soft and bloodshot. "I needed those more than you. They cut me off an hour ago."

He is suddenly the only man in the room. She is shocked by his slurred admission and makes it her responsibility that he make it home safely. The last thing she needs is for him to crash and drown in a ditch along the way.

What Aliah doesn't realize is that the young man who had just purchased those drinks for her is not very pleased with Harley's selfish swallow. This guy is on his feet and takes a swing in a matter of milliseconds, connecting with Harley's face, only inches from her own.

Harley's slowed senses kick into gear and he lays the guy out with one upper cut. The guy crashes onto a table behind him, knocking a girl to the floor, splashing a full pitcher of beer on the guy next to her. Within seconds, the place breaks out into a full on beer soaked brawl.

After knocking two more jocks on their asses, Harley tosses Aliah over his shoulder like a damsel in distress and dashes toward the door. He exits the bar and crosses the road with her that way, even as she slaps at his back. He doesn't put her down until he reaches his motorcycle and begins to pulls his keys from his pocket.

Aliah snatches them out of his hand. "I don't fucking think so. You're hammered. Why don't we catch a cab?"

"The cops are guaranteed to be here any minute."

"Then come with me."

"I can't leave my bike. You go ahead. I'll be fine." Harley stumbles over his own two feet and laughs sardonically.

"Harley, please don't do this. I already feel like shit for everything I've done to you. It's bad enough you're going to have a black eye in the morning. But I couldn't live with myself if you died because of me."

"I'm not leaving my bike," he repeats, swiping a hand across his bloody lip. "I'd rather die a slow and painful death."

"Then let me drive it."

"No one drives my bike but me."

They both turn their heads to see the flashing lights approaching. Aliah spins back around to face him, as he snaps up his helmet and climbs onto his motorcycle.

"You'd rather drive it into the ground, than let me take you home?" She's so very frustrated with him right now.

"I don't sit backseat to anyone."

Ignoring his comment, she plugs the key in and hops on in front of him, practically sitting on his lap. "Get over yourself. I promise to take good care of her."

He can't believe his eyes when Aliah has the bike off its kickstand and they're speeding toward the stop sign before the cops even make their appearance. She makes it two blocks away before he can even lift his chin off her shoulder. Then she takes a sudden left.

"My house is the other way," he shouts over her dainty shoulder.

The motorcycle veers down a long, dark alley and she clutches the brake, until they're stopped at the bottom of the incline. It's a dead end, ending right at the water's edge. She parks the bike and tugs off his helmet.

"What are you doing?" he asks, angered by the change of venue.

She turns off the bike and tucks the keys into his pants pocket, gazing up into his eyes.

He catches her chin and doesn't let go. "Can I ask what

the hell we're doing?" He says it like he's forgotten that he had only just asked that a second earlier.

She pries his hand off her face and walks away. She spins back playfully, to smirk at him. "It's called a park, Harley. What do you do at a park?"

He looks stumped.

"You play," she informs him.

He still doesn't get it.

"I left my wallet in my car, so I don't have my license. It felt like you were going to roll us. If you want to kill yourself, fine. But I'd like to get home in one piece."

Harley can't even deny that he's three sheets to the wind. "It's not like you're licensed to drive a motorcycle. There's a test for that, you know."

When she turns back to goad him, he's right there. "No shit. I've passed the test." Her voice turns breathless in response to his proximity.

Now he can't stop smiling, licking at the fresh blood on his lip.

She slides her hand under the collar of his shirt and back down his chest. "You're too drunk to drive and I thought you were going to pass out on me back there. I doubt you'd like me very much if I crashed your bike. You need to sober up a bit before we go any farther." She pats his cheek twice and then saunters toward the play equipment. She can feel his eyes following her.

"Are you still referring to riding, or is this more about *us* now?" His voice is but a low growl.

She freezes in place, intrigued by that reference. "I'd really like you to accept my apology, if that's what you mean. But I'm not going to throw myself at you to do it." She takes a few steps and spins around, slouching into a black slat swing. Her hands hang from the chain above her head. "So, if that's what you're waiting for, you'll be sorely disappointed."

"You want the truth?" His voice sounds painfully honest, as he grasps onto the chains on either side of her hips and pushes her backward, leaving her suspended a few feet in mid-air above his shoulders. "I don't know if I can do that so soon – accept your apology. The wound is still gaping."

The dangerous flicker in his eyes shows that he's only kidding. Aliah reaches out to slap him, but he grabs onto her hand and tugs her close. She crashes against him and their gazes collide. His eyes are sparkling midnight, like a dark, dreamy nightmare. She wants to kiss him, as she slides down his body. Gravity has her standing on tip-toes but something else has Harley held rigid against her.

She hasn't wanted to kiss a man in years. But as he eases closer, her parted lips quiver and she considers it. With eyes pressed closed, she turns her cheek. He kisses her there and pauses, absorbing the silence.

"I'm sorry," he finally says.

"*I'm* sorry," she interrupts. She doesn't know what her problem is either. "I'm messed up, alright? I'm just not ready for that kind of commitment."

"A little harmless kiss is commitment to you?" His smile has butterflies battling in her lungs and tumbling in her stomach.

Aliah inhales sharply. "It's not the commitment I'm afraid of."

She instantly wishes she hadn't shared that with him. He gets her talking too much. Besides, it is only partly true. She has no issue with commitment herself. It's him she's worried about.

"Then what are you so afraid of?" Harley's eyes are squinted, as if he's trying to sneak a peek at her soul. His moist, warm lips are so close she can almost taste them. She steps away and discreetly gasps for air, as though he has been starving her of it.

"I have my reasons, okay? Can we just leave it at that?"

When he steps up behind her, she doesn't step away. He reaches for her right hand and grabs onto it. "It's okay to feel scared. This shit can get scary. But do you see me running?"

The warmth of his body against hers is superficial but soothing. She squeezes his hand involuntarily. "You don't understand."

"Don't I? *You* stood *me* up tonight, woman."

She glances up at Harley over her shoulder. "Look... I've been hurt, okay?" Her pale eyes share her hesitation. "I've battled for love and lost. I'm not looking to have my heart trampled on like that again any time in the near future."

He squeezes onto her hand. "I didn't realize how fresh it was."

Aliah turns away and glances at the ground. "It's not fresh. It was two years and three months ago."

"You're counting."

"Wouldn't you?"

"No," he answers frankly.

Aliah's voice is soft and careful. "You act like you know. But how could you?"

"You're right. I couldn't."

Aliah really wants nothing more than to run away from this conversation right now, but she senses his sarcasm and knows it has to happen if they are ever going to get past this night. "Why..." She sighs, not even knowing what she's trying to say. "How do you know?"

"Are you sure you want to hear that answer?"

She really does, but she catches herself backpedalling. "You know? You're right. You're drunk and you'll probably regret this whole conversation tomorrow. Maybe we should lighten up and save it for another day. Maybe after our first date."

Harley's laugh echoes through the dark night. "Are you calling this our first date?"

She tries to tug her hand away, but he won't let it go. "No!" she screeches, like she's horrified.

"You just did."

"I did no such thing!" The higher her voice rings, the more he laughs.

After the echoes of laughter drift into the night, Harley nuzzles his nose next to her ear. "You need to let him go, if you're ever going to move on." He releases Aliah's hand and she walks away from him, to look out over the calm water.

Aliah has always found it easier to get her thinking done at night time. She likes it when she's alone. She has spent many a nights at that very same park, expressing herself to the wind. The only thing missing tonight is her can of mace. She had forgotten that in her car, in a rush to drown her troubles.

She stands there wondering why so much time has passed and yet she's still clinging to the short-lived love affair that happened between her and Hunter Wight. He was sweet, gentle, kind. But then he'd cheated on her. Harley was right. She'd never gotten past the sting of that deed. It had nothing to do with love. They'd kissed and made up, but it was never quite the same.

Aliah had fallen out of love with him over time. She'd been more married to the idea of love, then to its relation to Hunter. She'd only refused to admit it to herself then. Apparently it only takes a surprisingly sweet, hulking drunkard to teach her that.

She seethes near the water, wondering what this means for her. She certainly isn't ready to throw another two years away on a man who doesn't want her. It is then when she realizes that Harley is standing behind her again, and she wonders how long he's been waiting, listening to her thoughts.

She glances at him over her shoulder and smiles. He tucks a lock of hair behind her ear and traces the length of her jaw with his index finger. She closes her eyes, shivering from the intimacy of his touch.

Harley reaches his arms around her tiny waist and inhales the sweet scent emanating from her neck, then he presses his lips there. "Do you want to talk about it?" His lips move softly over her sensitive flesh.

"I don't know if I'm ready."

Harley laces his fingers with hers. "I've got all night."

Aliah smiles softly and tugs on his hand to put them in motion. They slowly traverse the gravel path that winds next to the water's edge. Neither of them speak. They just listen to the summer night. The crickets. The rustling leaves. The soft water flowing next to them.

The moon makes the swelling water sparkle, and the serene feeling envelopes her, as she walks hand in hand with this ethereal beast, dressed in a suit.

Aliah smiles up at him, as they grow closer to his bike, having walked the entire park circulation, her eyes glittering with acceptance.

"You should smile more often. It looks good on you."

She bites down on her lower lip. She tries to stop herself from smiling like a fool, but loses the battle.

Aliah's eyes flutter to the ground. "It wasn't all good."

He squints at her, having not read her thoughts. "What wasn't?"

"Love. It hurt more often than not. I'm not really sure what the excitement is all about."

Harley tilts his head to capture her gaze. "I wouldn't know."

Aliah drops her chin and looks up at him, incredulously. "You've never been in love?" Her voice echoes down the long driveway, as she props her rear-end on a chipped, old picnic table.

He releases her hand and grips onto her waist to help her up. "Not that I know of," he admits, sounding completely serious.

Aliah smiles softly. "If you have to think about it, then you definitely haven't. It's not a feeling you forget too quickly." Her voice floats over them like a whimsical cloud of dreams.

Harley nods slowly. "You're still in love with him." He states it like a fact and doesn't even disguise his disappointment.

"No," she answers matter-of-factly. "It's hard to love someone when they don't reciprocate the feeling."

Harley clears his throat. "So I've heard."

"It sounds like you've had love before. Is it that girl from Riley's?"

That slut certainly wishes it is.

"Jillian?" He looks shocked and appalled by her

suggestion and tries to cover his response with a chuckle.

Aliah shrugs her shoulders indifferently. "You two looked pretty cozy tonight. She kept touching you like you were intimately acquainted."

Harley raises a brow and smiles. "I'm afraid Jillian is taken."

"Are you disappointed about that?"

He outright laughs this time. "I *do* wish I had more say in her selection of men."

Aliah's confusion shows on her face. "What do you care, if it's not you?"

Their eyes connect, his smile transmitting a secret message to her. "I need my assistant to be happy. There's nothing worse than working next to a miserable woman all day."

Aliah nods her head, but she's not completely satisfied with his answer. What kind of job can he possibly work that requires an assistant? She only wishes that was her main concern.

"Any other questions?" he asks, almost goading her.

"Yeah. One," Aliah admits, unafraid to stir the pot. "Did you fuck her?"

His head snaps up to look at her again. His words remain on his lips for a few seconds before he shares them with her. "We have a very good *working* relationship."

"You fucked her." Aliah turns away, with an unfriendly snarl on her face. Why is she suddenly so angry?

"I didn't fuck her."

"You want to."

Harley sighs, not liking where this conversation is going. "No. But there was a time when she wanted me to. That was quite a few years ago now. We've had a good laugh about it since then, and everyone's moved on."

"You think so."

Harley's voice turns harsh and convincing. "I know so."

"You're saying you've never thought about sleeping with her?"

He tilts his head, bringing his face closer to hers. "She's

cute. If you like the leggy, blonde type."

"And you don't?" Aliah can't help but smirk, as she hunches over and rests her elbows on her lap, happy to take any disruption from that gorgeous gaze.

"She came to work for me when she was eighteen. She was a misguided youth. I'm not attracted to her that way. She's more like a daughter to me."

"Skanky daughter you have there."

"Says the girl downing shots with a random college kid at the bar."

Aliah can't stop smiling. "For the record, you downed those shots. I only wanted to."

"Why?"

"Why?" She looks like she's stunned that he doesn't know.

He nods.

"I don't know."

"You know," he presses. "You're just too embarrassed to admit it out loud."

Aliah lays flat out across the picnic table and closes her eyes, stretching her arms above her head. "Maybe I am."

Harley leans backward and props himself above her. "You don't seem like the type who embarrasses too easily."

"You think you know me."

"Am I right?" he persists, maintaining eye contact.

"Yes," she admits, smiling.

"Thank you... for saying that. It's the first step toward admitting that you've already fallen madly in love with me."

"What?" Her voice screeches once, but it seems to echo infinitely into the endless night.

"It's okay. You're not ready to say it yet. I can be patient."

She turns her head to smirk at him, and he flashes her a mouthful of pearly white teeth. "Smart ass."

"You love it."

She puckers her lips to feign a pout, but he can see her aversion to love unravelling between them. Harley pulls himself away, to lay down on the tabletop next to her. He curls his arm around her and pulls her close to his side.

He's so warm. She only wishes that she can enjoy it. But he doesn't give her another second to settle down, getting right back to the nit picking.

"You sounded pretty upset when you thought I was fucking the blonde. Why is that?"

Aliah snuggles back against him and she can feel him stirring beneath her thigh, now hooked over top of him. "Is it really that hard for you to figure it out?" Aliah rolls her eyes, but she won't say it.

"Why won't you just tell me?"

After a thoughtful pause, Aliah blurts it. "Because I want to be the only one fucking with you, okay?"

He rests his head back against the table and his smile disappears. "Not really the answer I was looking for, but it'll have to do."

"You don't like me?" Aliah hates that she is turning into *that* girl.

She reaches for the end of the table to pull herself away from him, but he catches onto her hand.

"Oh, I like you alright."

Aliah scowls at him. "Then why won't you have sex with me?"

Harley returns her hand to the table next to her and retrieves his own. "Let's see. You stand me up. You want to be the only one *fucking with* me. You won't let me kiss you... on the lips. Should I go on?"

Even with him verbally prodding at her, she can't stop her insides from quivering at the memory of just how good of a kisser he is, both on her mouth and between her thighs.

"Please," she breathes, as if his words might be enough to send her sailing into an abyss of pleasure.

He turns his head to share his disbelief with her eye to eye, then he brushes a strand of hair away from her face. "I'd be good to you."

His statement strikes her from her high horse. They lay there quietly for a long while, gazing into each other's eyes, too afraid to face the emotions stirring between them. She hides behind their rainbow of physical chemistry and slides a hand up his muscular middle.

"Tell me again why you won't sex me up." She refuses to admit there's more to it than raw, unguarded desire.

It sounds like he thinks about it before speaking. "I don't want to hurt your feelings."

Aliah steals her hand away. "You can't hurt my feelings. I've little left."

He leans into her, with his nose very near hers. His eyes are swimming, but he's gazing right into her. Harley licks his lips and his eyes turn down to hers, looking like he wants to taste her mouth. But when his eyes slide closed and his lips descend on hers, she rolls out from under him like a ninja, acting like she hasn't just dodged his kiss.

She retreats to his bike before he does something to make her regret ever getting involved with him. *Shit.* She is already involved, which is exactly what she was trying to avoid.

"Come on." Her voice rings sharp, as a stab of guilt claws at her insides.

He remains facing the picnic table, with his eyes squeezed shut. Then he slams a closed fist on the tabletop, and it looks like he very nearly pummels a hole into it. He growls angrily, and it actually makes her feel bad. She's frustrated too, but she can't let her heart all in. She knows what happens when she opens herself to a man, and one broken heart in this lifetime is all this girl can handle.

CHAPTER ELEVEN

Harley doesn't understand what's going through his mind. He wants to be the man to fit her life, whatever life she may lead. This idea would not please her. Hell, he's not particularly pleased with himself at the moment. This was not the plan. No woman has ever wiggled her way into his empty chest cavity, the way Aliah has, but suddenly he's feeling a little less vacant.

He chases after Aliah and tugs onto her shoulder until they're standing nose to nose. He gazes into her eyes and considers telling her everything. The truth about him. The truth about how they came to meet. But as he moves to kiss her, she bolts again from his arms. Any progress he thought they'd made seems tarnished and she's just as guilty as he is, if not more so. Telling himself this gives him a second wind.

"You lied to me," he growls. "Why did you have to lie? A two second phone call."

Aliah flips her hair over her shoulder. "I told you. I had to work late. That wasn't a lie."

"You told me you were going to work. Then you turned around and went to see your lawyer. If you're in some kind of trouble, maybe I can help."

Aliah's eyes blink wide, as she stifles a laugh. "You truly are stalking me! That is so not cool. If we're going to try this dating thing, then that's got to be one of the boundaries."

Even as she says it, he can see she's cringing on the inside. But damn, he cares about her.

"I think you should just tell me what you're charged with. The receptionist told me you were with Joshua Bailey. He's the top defence lawyer in the City, Aliah. Admit it. You must be in deep."

"Not exactly." She smiles. And he can tell from the look in her eyes that he's not done very good detective work.

"Why else would you go see a lawyer then?"

She raises her eyebrows. "You really don't know?" She still can't seem to get over the fact that he'd followed her.

"Tell me you aren't dating the man, Aliah. He has to be double your age."

She breaks out in laughter. "Some detective you are."

He freezes in place. She's got him now. His cover is blown. The world starts spinning around him, as he tries to catch his balance. No one finds out David H. Gates. No one.

Aliah stomps toward him as he crumbles to one knee. She pushes him, until he falls backward landing on his ass. She mounts his waist and presses him into the grass, dirtying the knees of her expensive pants.

"Easy, boy. I'm not dating Bailey. He's my boss."

He squints up at her, through lazy, drunken eyes. "I'm confused." He stares at her for a long few seconds. "Bailey owns Riley's? I thought Mitchell Cavanagh was the owner."

Aliah sighs out of frustration. "Yes, Mitchell owns Riley's. I don't actually work there. I was only helping a friend out. He was in a bind, okay?"

He closes his eyes and scratches his head, as a gentle finger skims over his lips. His eyes pop open to find Aliah with her tongue wetting her thumb. He swallows, as she smears the dry blood from the corner of his mouth. That touch right there shows him that there's more to her than the desirous sex fiend she tries to act like.

"I'm not a bartender. I'm sorry if that disappoints you." The way she says it has him thinking that it should.

"Then, what are you?" he asks.

As she sighs, she rolls off of him. Then she curls up in the crook of his arm and rests her head on his chest. "A girl," she whispers.

The night is quiet and so are they. He's surprised to learn that she isn't the slutty bartender that disrupts his sweet dreams with wild fantasies. Was he so blinded by her beauty that he'd overlooked the basics of this investigation?

Harley never drops the ball on research.

Jillian had suggested that Aliah is an educated woman with a real job and a large bank account, but he told himself that it couldn't possibly be true. He was so sure she was a daddy's girl, soaking him for money and working a petty part-time job for kicks. He hates to learn that she works in criminal law. He knows the kind of clients Bailey rides with. Just one more thing for him to worry about.

After a spell of silence, while he tries to process the new information she's shared, they both find sleep. Aliah sleeps much lighter than Harley.

She awakes to a spot light being shone in her eyes. "Shit! Harley. You have to wake up. Harley!"

He doesn't move a muscle. She thinks he's out cold. In truth, he's just not in the mood to deal with it right now.

Aliah scurries to her knees, wipes the dead grass from her pant legs and struts toward the unmarked police car. The cop's window eases down and a handsome officer stares back at her.

"Is it even possible for you to stay out of trouble?" His accent is the only thing that indicates he is from England. Everything else about the man screams American athlete.

"Hey, Spence. Long time no see."

She knows Spencer Caldwell personally? Maybe she is in deeper than he knows. Harley listens in on their conversation to figure them out.

"I seem to recall seeing you a couple days ago, speeding through a stop sign."

"Oh!" Aliah snickers. "I thought that was you."

Who snickers at a cop detailing their crime?

"You're lucky that was me, or you'd be stuck with a sizeable ticket and a court date."

"Do you want me to thank you?"

Oh, so she is smart like that with everyone. Harley can't believe this girl.

"No. I want you to stay out of trouble. Speaking of... Who's that guy you're with?"

Harley resists clenching his fists, as he's flooded again by the white hot spot light.

"He looks real lively tonight."

Knowing Spencer all too well, Harley figures his motorcycle plate is good as run. Not that he needs a computer to tell him that it's Harley's bike. Spencer has been popping up a lot lately. Harley suddenly feels like *he's* the one under investigation.

"Are you telling me you don't know him?" Aliah asks, noticing the way Spencer smirks at her.

With Spencer's attention surely focused on Aliah, Harley dares a glance in their direction. Spencer is smiling at her. Harley doesn't like the way he smiles at her.

"I just wondered if you got his name before getting on his bike. That's dangerous for a girl like you."

"A girl like me?" Now she's playing coy.

"Or any other girl, for that matter. Downright stupid."

"His name is Harley – er, David, maybe," she blurts, then pauses.

Harley realizes then that he's never told her his last name. And with good reason.

"What else do you know about him?"

"Not much. Only that his sister is staying with him. He owns a house in town, has a tongue that rocks my world, and that's his Harley right there."

Harley tries not to smile, but that has him beaming with pride.

"It's a nice bike."

He'd better not touch my bike.

Spencer glances at his phone and Harley fears the worst. *Information.*

"Did you know that Harley is his middle name? I didn't even know that one."

Aliah doesn't seem to pick up on the connection. She acts like she doesn't care, but on the inside it bothers her how little she knows about him. "I didn't know that. Why? Do you know him? Is he a criminal or something?"

Oh, no.

"Don't you recognize him? Take a closer look, love. His

face is plastered across every other sign downtown."

She draws a blank, while Harley holds his breath. She shrugs her shoulders. "His name is Harley. That's all I know."

"Maybe his full name will ring a bell. David H. Gates."

"No." She shakes her head erratically. "That's not him."

"It is."

She glares at the sky, trying to place him. "But he's so bad ass."

Spencer snuffs unattractively. "You only think he is."

"No. He is," she mumbles, unwilling to accept the truth.

Spencer chuckles. "I'll give him ruthless. Cunning. Conceited even. But bad ass?"

"Okay. I get it. You can shut up now."

"Maybe next time you'll do a little digging before spreading your legs for a guy."

"Fuck you, Spencer."

"Easy, love. Or I'll have to arrest you. Don't think I wouldn't enjoy every second of getting you into the cuffs."

She wants to provoke him; to say something that would wash that smirk right off his pretty boy face. But she bites her tongue. "If you're done making fun of me..."

He gives her a curt nod. "You might want to consider getting the hell out of here. The park closed at midnight."

"Sorry. I didn't know."

"Well, now you do. So get a move on."

"Yes, sir." Aliah gives him a mocking salute.

"I mean it, Aliah. Collect up your boyfriend and move on for the night."

"Okay. Okay."

"I mean it. Get out of here," he urges.

Spencer scans her with his icy eyes, as he puts his car in reverse and pulls away from the grass. Aliah lifts a hand to wave at him, but he ignores her. She promptly returns back to Harley and crouches by his side. She proceeds to gently shake his arm.

"Harley. We have to go."

He springs to his feet and pulls a gun from his pants, but

he doesn't aim it at anyone. He keeps it hidden beneath his suit jacket. Aliah jumps backward, with both her hands raised, like she's a criminal.

Harley scans the perimeter with eyes of a hawk. "Get on the bike."

She takes a second to scowl at him and then stomps back to his parked motorcycle. "Fine. But you can put the gun away. Are you trying to kill someone?"

"Aliah. I swear to God. I'm not going to say it again. Get on the bike. Now."

She yanks the keys from his hand and starts it up. "What an ass," she grumbles.

When she looks back at him, he can see she's not very happy that he still has his gun drawn. He keeps it hidden inside his jacket. But he's not putting it away. It's for her own protection. And his. They're surrounded. If they don't get out of there fast, they're both going to be laid out on the pavement, bathing in blood.

He climbs onto the bike and wraps his body around her. "Someone is watching us," he whispers in her ear. "Don't act funny. Just go. And don't stop until I tell you to. Can you do that?"

Aliah gulps and whimpers softly when she nods. It is obvious she has never found herself in a similar situation before, which begs the question: Why are these people following her?

She takes off a little too fast, nearly losing him off the back. But it's good enough to get them away from the park before the trackers can respond.

"Now you can give it a little gas," he purrs, trying to keep her calm.

They were already speeding, but he needs her to go faster if they are going to avoid an untimely accident. In a matter of seconds, headlights appear behind them, down an otherwise blackened street.

"Now, Aliah!"

She gives it more gas and winds back into town."

"What are you doing?" he shouts.

"Losing them." She looks so determined that he can't argue with her.

The way she maneuvers through the downtown roads, he knows she's done this before. She seems to have mapped the fastest route to her house, and she manages to skip any other vehicle interaction on the way. It is impressive, and has dick aching to claim her again.

Aliah wheels into her driveway and Harley holds up the motorcycle as she pounds the code into the keypad for her garage door. He rides the bike inside, as she runs into the house and presses the button near the door to close up the garage. They both stand there, frozen, waiting for the door to seal shut, as if the bad guys might appear out of nowhere and attack them.

The idea isn't completely far-fetched, and so when the door clicks shut, they both take a deep breath before entering her house. Harley slides the gun into the back of his slacks and smiles while he double checks the deadbolt on her front door. "Where did you learn to ride like that?"

Aliah climbs her stairs, two at a time, and flicks the light switch on. "I know these streets like the back of my hand. My dad's the City fire chief. He knows the fastest ways to get across town, and so do I."

Harley nods, still smiling about it.

"My turn to ask a question." She stands at the top of the stairs looking down at him, surrounded by a mist of light.

He holds his breath again and the smile falls off his face.

"Why do you wear a gun, *Harley*?"

He doesn't like the way she pronounces his name, but that's an easy one. "Protection." He doesn't elaborate and she doesn't ask for him to.

Aliah tries to take a deep breath, but the adrenaline has her limbs shaking and she can't seem to slow her nerves.

Harley scales the stairs and stops at the top. He flicks the light out, but not before seeing her standing there, looking all small and helpless. "We don't want anyone to know you're home," he explains, while the image of her trembling frame haunts his present.

He opens his arms to her. "Come here."

She recklessly obeys and crashes into his arms. Even though he still has to be well over the legal limit for alcohol consumption, with her in his arms, he feels strong and protective. When he cups her cheek, he feels a tear trickle down her face. She lets it fall.

Harley's finger traces its path and lands under her chin. He tilts her head up with a finger and stings her with his midnight gaze. "I will *never* let anyone hurt you."

She holds his stare and it is as if they are sealing a promise. "Never?"

He steals a chaste kiss, and it happens so fast that she can't even stop him. She presses her lips together and narrows her eyes.

"What are doing?" She sounds so exasperated.

"I kissed you," he states, as if he's proud of his misdoing.

"I told you not to," she whispers, as if someone might be listening in on them.

Harley's smile slants across his face. "I never was very good at listening to reason."

Without warning, Aliah's mouth crashes into his. Harley instantly lifts her into his arms. She wraps her legs around his torso, and he doesn't stop kissing her as he kicks off his shoes and maneuvers his way blindly to the kitchen table.

He can sense that she's wondering what the hell he's doing as he unfastens his belt. Then it seems to dawn on her when his pants slide down to his ankles. He puts her down to remove her clothes and he doesn't stop until she's completely naked. Then he makes a grab for his shirt and watches the way her eyes widen in the shadows when she gets a good look at his tattooed abs.

She pounces on him, feverishly kissing every rigid muscle, as he tugs off his tie and tosses it aside. He takes a seat on the chair, with his massive thighs exposed, and his overpriced slacks pooled at his ankles. Aliah climbs on top of him, knowing exactly what he wants. She reaches for his unyielding cock and lowers herself on top of him.

He groans with every roll of her hips and enjoys every

inch of her pussy perfection as her breasts rub up against his chest. Her strangled moan has him harder than a surf board, and he has to grip onto the chair to hang on for the ride. He loves that she's going slow, but he's about near ready to drill a hole through her. He needs things to go fast.

Taking control, he clasps onto her wrists and locks them behind her back like he's arresting her. Then he latches his mouth onto a straining pink nipple and sucks from it like he's a starving infant. Aliah's head rolls back and she cries out in pleasure, as he grips onto her hip with his free hand, demanding that she bounce faster and drop harder.

She squirms on top of him, until he's the one thrusting upwards, lifting her feet from the floor. Aliah wraps her suspended legs around the back of the chair, and closes her pussy around him. That single act represents the sweetest of surrenders, leaving him in control everything. Needing more friction between them, he releases her wrists.

"Hang on," he grunts, as he pumps into her repeatedly.

Knowing exactly what he means, she grips the chair behind him, until she's white in the fists. It looks like she's hanging onto the chair for dear life, as he thrusts into her again and again, their skin slapping in a magical medley of sounds. She's bouncing up and down from the sheer force of his thrusts and it all feels celestial as he seems to leave his body in a moment of complete bliss.

"Holy shit!" Aliah screams out, as he drives into her harder. The chair breaks into pieces beneath them, as her pussy squeezes around his dick in the most amazing of finales. They're both panting, with eyes closed, not quite realizing what has happened. Then Aliah releases her clenched fists, dropping the back of the chair onto the floor.

A masterful smile curls onto Harley's lips, as he starts to chuckle, realizing it was the force of their joint orgasm that totalled the dining chair. Aliah joins him in a fit of laughter. With every giggle, her insides tighten around him and he winces from the sensitivity still affecting him.

After climbing off of him, Aliah points at the floor behind him. "Look what you did to my chair!"

He thinks to plead the fifth, but decides against it. "It was me."

Her jaw drops, but her smile is still gorgeous. She loves his honesty. Now only if he could be more honest with her. She escapes to the washroom with her clothes, and he gives her a few minutes to wash herself, as he tries to put the hopeless chair back together.

Not going to happen.

After pulling on his underwear and an unbuttoned shirt, he peers out the front blinds. No one is visible, so he barges into the bathroom to see what is taking her. Though she can't believe the intrusion, she doesn't make him leave. Their smiles eventually soften, but when he leans down to kiss her, she doesn't stop him. He reaches for the warm washcloth, snatches it from her hand and gently caresses between her thighs, as his lips descend on hers. His excitement bubbles back to the surface, as he strokes her tenderly and she accepts his tongue through parted lips.

Washing up only instigates their next engagement. He drops the cloth to the floor, his fingers continuing with the sensual assault on her clitoris. When Aliah's legs get wobbly, he lifts her into his arms and carries her to the bedroom. His weight bears down on her as they crash onto the bed. He knows she wants him to conquer her body again, but she looks so scared. Scared for her life.

Scared for her heart?

It's written all over her face in a painful mix of color, as Harley continues to kiss her. He can't stop, afraid that she might take back the silent offering if he does. But eventually his lips slow, until time freezes between each emotional peck. The sound of his lips connecting with hers and the draw back to him every time he pries his lips away seems to trip her up.

Aliah starts to slide his shirt open, but he catches her hand.

"It's been a long night."

Her face looks so sad that he considers giving her a pity fuck. She's using all her wiles to her advantage. He relies on sheer willpower to push through the temptation. It *has* been a long night, and he doesn't want her turning to sex as her only comfort. He wants her to need him in other ways too.

What the fuck?

He did not just think that. Since when did he care about that kind of shit?

Aliah gulps and he thinks she's going to demand they do it again. If she does, he will have to screw her to the headboard. But then she rolls over and curls up into a ball, without a mess of words. There wouldn't be any more sex after that move.

Harley skims his fingers down the length of her leg and unlatches the surprisingly dainty shoes from her feet. He presses a kiss to each foot, just then realizing that she has been wearing them all along. When he drops the heels onto the floor beside the bed, they land with a thump, much like the steady beat of his heart.

He pulls the sheets out from under her, so he can wrap her up in the them. He doesn't try to hide from her, as he stands next to the bed. He watches over her for a minute, but she doesn't look up at him. She's so delicate when she wants to be; a small, colorful flower in full bloom.

Harley leans over top of her and plants a kiss on her forehead. Then he climbs onto the bed and huddles against her back. The moment feels so intimate, the room so quiet. Everything about this moment feels *just right*. He hasn't felt this way before. He's putting Aliah's needs before his own. He can hear what her body's asking for.

Sex.

And *he* wants it too. But more importantly he can see what she needs even more.

Love.

Aliah is doing right by herself. She is a smart girl to protect her heart from the Big Bad Harley. He'll surely huff and puff and blow her life in. But she has failed herself. She *has* let him in.

Why did she let me in?

Aliah reaches for his hand and wraps his arm all the way around her. He has a sudden urge to tell her the truth. Right all his wrongs. Lay it all out on the table.

"Aliah?" he whispers. He starts to think she's fallen asleep already.

"Yeah?" Her voice is as soft as her curves.

"There's something I have to tell you." He sighs and he feels her cheek lift into a soft, contented smile.

Why is she smiling?

"Not tonight. Okay?" she insists softly.

He doesn't answer, and neither of them speak again, as they fall asleep in each other's arms.

Harley wakes and glances immediately at the alarm clock. It's three in the morning, but Aliah is nowhere to be seen. He pads barefoot out of her bedroom and instantly finds her in the kitchen. She's sitting in the dark chewing on her fingernails, the light of the moon illuminating her beautiful features through the kitchen window.

She glances over her shoulder. "I'm sorry. Did I wake you?"

"I can't sleep," he admits gruffly.

"Me either."

He takes a few hesitant steps toward her and toys with a piece of her hair that is dangling in her eyes. She's been crying, but he won't bring attention to the unattractive smears across her cheeks. Instead, he takes her hand and leads her back to the bedroom.

He slides into the bed first and tucks a few of her decorative pillows against the headboard. He opens up the covers and drags her underneath them with him. He props himself against the headboard, and pulls Aliah toward him, until she's flattened against his chest.

When she sighs softly, he knows he's exactly what she needs. Whether she knows that herself yet or not is another thing.

Her eyes close, as he kisses her forehead, but there are no more tears. He isn't sure he'd know what to do if there were.   He strokes her hair and closes his own eyes, comforting himself with his continuous caress.   He isn't used to being this gentle. It is a different feeling, that is for sure. But it feels good.

He'd never tell her this, but he can see himself wanting to make her feel this good for many more nights to come.

CHAPTER TWELVE

Aliah awakes to an unfamiliar ringing sound and a sexy as sin man standing in the corner of her room with his back to her. She gawks at the winged bird spread across his expansive upper back. She's never seen anything more sexy.

After ending his call, he picks up his pants off the floor and pulls them over each long leg. His agile fingers have his shirt done up in seconds flat. She fears if she doesn't say something quick, he'll be blasting out her door without saying goodbye.

"Harley?" She rolls up to a sitting position and rubs a tired eye.

"I have to go." Harley doesn't say another word as he pulls on his jacket.

Angered by his avoidance, she yanks off the covers and retrieves her silky robe from the floor. She heads to the kitchen before wrapping her naked self up. After getting her coffee going, she struts to the bathroom, wearing nothing but the crumpled silk from the previous night.

When she returns, she finds her bed not only empty, but made. She takes off sprinting to find out where the hell Harley thinks he's going now. She isn't done with him yet. He can't just up and leave when he pleases. Not until she says so.

She stands in the door of the garage, with her arms folded across her chest, watching the way he paces the driveway. She wonders what has him so muddled. Then his eyes connect with hers. It's broad daylight but still he looks dark and menacing. It's then when she realizes she's not wearing any panties. A scalding heat pools at the juncture between her thighs and her lips part for a breath.

"Why don't you come back inside for a cup of coffee?"

Her voice sounds soft, because she's trying to act like it's no big deal either way.

The way he stares at her, she knows he's heard her. His glance continues to sear her as he considers what he's going to do next. She's not about to make that decision for him. In the blink of an eye, Aliah flips her attitude upside down.

"I'll be inside, in case you decide *not* to be a prick." She goes for the dramatic bitch voice, hoping to make a point. Then she turns away and slams the door between them.

She can't believe he was just going to take off. Was she the only one who thought they'd shared a special moment last night? He was probably too drunk to notice.

Why do I even care?

When the door opens behind her, she starts up the steps. She was not expecting that! She hurries upstairs, but not nearly fast enough. Harley's hand flattens against her ass, making a loud smacking noise.

"Harley!" she screeches, feeling the sting across her naked flesh. The tingles sprinkle across her senses, only amplifying the delightful ache she's been suffering from since she'd opened her eyes.

"I'm sorry, but you can't be flaunting that sexy thing around my face and not expect me to touch it."

She finds it hard to argue with the man, when he makes such a good point. She continues to her kitchen and immediately pulls two mugs from an upper cabinet. She reaches for the carafe and pours them each a cup of coffee. The only reason she knows he's still seated behind her now, is the scent that is undeniably Harley clouding her judgment.

Her eyes give a provocative look over her shoulder, but she's not quite smiling.

"Which one of those is for the prick?" he asks, trying to get a rise out of her.

She smiles. He always manages to get her body curling, whether it's her lips or her toes. She hands him a mug. But it's not just any mug. She's pulled out the special hot pink one with zebra stripes, just for him. She smiles, as she adds sugar to hers. He drinks his black.

Neither of them speak, but he's looking down at her, waiting for her to give him the time of day. She can't stop smirking, as her nose hovers over her cup, hiding her smiling lips behind her plain black mug.

"You're seriously going to make me drink from this one?"

Aliah glances up into those beautiful eyes and grins. "If you're thirsty, you'll drink it." She takes a sip from her simple black mug. "Mmm. This is so good."

Harley reaches out to take her mug and she has to turn away to avoid him. "Why can't I drink from yours?"

She walks around the table and takes a seat at the opposite end, while clinging to her coffee. "I've already had my lips all over it." She sticks out her chin, to teach him a lesson. "That makes it mine."

He sips the coffee from his girly mug, and takes a seat on the wobbly stool next to her. He sears her with a glance that has her desperate for air. The memory of what had happened on that chair the other night has them both fidgeting in their seats. He tears off his jacket, acknowledging the rising heat in the room, and it pulls at his shirt, exposing a set of washboard abs.

He clears his throat. "Following your theory then, wouldn't that make you *mine*?" Another layer of clothes comes off, until he's beautifully bare chested.

She's sure the deer-in-headlights look wasn't the most brilliant response. But he freaks her out and she doesn't know how else to respond. She anxiously licks at her lips.

"You really shouldn't do that around me." The promise in his growl terrifies her even more.

What the hell is he up to this morning?

Not quite sure how to handle Harley at the moment, Aliah takes her leave to the washroom. She blames it on the coffee she's only sipped on, but she knows *he knows* she's only trying to hide from him. It is no wonder he's started stripping. The temperature in that room seems to have spiked beyond one hundred degrees in a matter of seconds.

Aliah stares at herself in the mirror, trying to look for

something, but not finding it. Not having anything else to do, she turns on the water and splashes her face. The coolness helps a little, but she still doesn't know what to say to get Harley to stop with the sexy mushy shit.

Everything was going just fine until he'd said that!

She blows out a breath. She knows she can't hide in the bathroom forever. In fact, it was only a few minutes earlier that she was practically begging him to come back inside. Maybe she could tempt him for another round in the bedroom before he takes off. That would be enough to take her mind off of other things.

With renewed confidence, Aliah opens the door. Harley's not in the kitchen, and after peering in her bedroom, she realizes he's not there either. She hasn't heard the front door open or close, so she assumes he's roaming her house.

As she rounds the corner, she catches him casually slipping into her spare bedroom. She peers in the door and decides to keep quiet and see how long it takes for him to realize that she's there with him. He takes a good look at her desk, like he's looking for something, then he flips through her mail with a fleeting glance. There's nothing out of the ordinary he's going to find there. Junk mail. Bills. More bills.

She finds it difficult to concentrate on what he's doing, when he's shirtless, with the sexiest of tattoos painted across his back. Then he seems to redirect his attention to the diploma framed on the wall.

Shit!

As he reads it over, she watches his mug drop to the ceramic floor. It crashes with a horrific clash of sounds, as chunks and shards scatter and black coffee splatters across the floor, staining her desk and wall.

"Looking for something?" Aliah stands in the doorway with her arms clutched across her chest, trying really hard not to overreact. She still appears on edge, as if he is nosing around where he doesn't belong.

That's because he is.

"I see you have a university degree, and you've graduated from a prestigious law school." He points it out like it's an utterly shocking find.

"Yeah. So?" Her posture doesn't budge.

Harley raises his eyebrows. "I'm impressed." Then those sexy eyes scour her body. "That's a mighty accomplishment for a lowly bartender."

That is a low blow!

"Lowly? Get out of my face." She spins away, scoots to her bedroom and slams the door shut. "Asshole," she adds, under her breath. She is truly pissed.

He has really done it now. He invades her privacy, mocks an honorable profession and calls her names, all in a matter of minutes. He really has no clue what he's doing when it comes to women. Especially this one.

She doesn't claim to be special. But Harley really is clueless. Master in her bedroom, he is. A danger to her heart, for sure. But it is clear he hasn't had the life experience to know how to deal with women. Even Aliah's four brothers have more concern for her feelings than he, and you would think they had been born in a barn.

As she contemplates staying locked up in her bedroom forever, Harley's on the other side of the door, without any ideas up his sleeve. He grabs his jacket and pulls it on over his shirtless chest. If she needs some time to settle, then he will give it to her. He stands outside her door, with his forehead almost pressed against it. He can't hear anything. That makes him worry.

He couldn't have known that she was on the other side of that door, doing the very same thing, near tears.

"Aliah. I'm sorry. I didn't mean to offend you." His voice sounds believable, but she doesn't buy it.

"I find that awfully hard to believe. Get out of my house."

He presses his eyes shut. "Please forgive me."

"I said!" she shouts, clearly growing more impatient with him, as the door swings open and he nearly falls backward from being startled by her vagrant attack. "Get. Out. Of. My. House!" She pokes him with each word, and she truly means it.

"But last night..."

"Forget it ever happened. Goodbye, Harley. It's been fun." She shoves him, until he's standing at the top of her stairs. "Now get the fuck out."

He doesn't say another word. He's fucked up and he knows it. What's new? He'll have to suffer from his own stupidity. *But last night...* She'd said it right. Forget about it.

She follows him out to the garage and clicks the garage door opener to help him get on his way faster. He pulls on his helmet and delivers her a pointed glare, to show her that this isn't over. He revs his engine and pulls away. The garage door comes down so fast that he just barely makes it out in time, having to crouch to avoid being knocked from his bike.

Son of a bitch.

Aliah lifts her phone with a trembling hand. "Abby. Please come. I need you."

She hangs up the phone before Abby can ask any questions. She can't cry. The emotions won't come, even as she scrubs her soiled office, begging for them to. She wants to scream. She wants to cry. She just hopes by the time Abby comes over she'll have it together.

Wishful thinking.

Within thirty minutes, Abby's knocking on her door with a baby in tote. Nothing has changed. Her head is still spinning. She still doesn't know what to feel. She must be out of her mind.

Aliah opens her door to Abby and they stare at each other in silence. The only sound that breaks her from this nightmare is that coming from the lips of a happy little girl reaching for her mouth.

Baby Maya's little fingers hook onto Aliah's bottom lip. Aliah responds by nibbling at the adorable little hand, saving herself from sharing her condition in other, less productive, ways.

Concern is written all over Abby's face. "I got your message. I came as soon as I could."

Aliah opens the door wider and lets the two of them come in. But she still can't find any words. Abby will figure her out for sure. This is kind of her thing.

"What is it, Aliah? Is everything okay?" Abby slowly eases her pregnant butt onto the leather recliner and looks up at her expectantly. "Well?"

"It's happening again." Tears start forming in Aliah's eyes, but they won't fall with another person in the room. That's her own rule. There will be no waterworks here. She isn't the emotional girl who needs her friend's shoulder to cry on. But she's having difficulty keeping it together this time.

Aliah turns to run off, but a little girl latches onto her leg and giggles.

"Ally," Maya mumbles, in the sweetest little voice.

Aliah starts to laugh, scaring away the tears. "Come here." She scoops Maya into her arms and gives her a great big hug. "Hey, little one. I'd bet a hug from you is just what I need. What do you think?"

Maya giggles again, loving the attention.

Aliah takes the seat across from Abby and swallows a deep breath. "I'm seeing someone. Well... I was. Now... I don't know. It's complicated."

"Okay," Abby starts, then smiles. "Let's start with his name."

"Harley."

"Ooh. Sounds sexy. But I don't know any Harleys. Is he not from around here?"

Aliah chews on her bottom lip. "To be right honest with you, I don't know much about him."

"How long have you been *seeing* this Harley? You didn't say anything about a new man last week."

"Let's just say you're right when you say new. We only just met last Thursday. But our chemistry..." Aliah looks lost in her dreams.

"I get it. So what went wrong?"

Aliah throws a sideways glance at Abby. "Where do I start?"

Abby smiles again, and it eases her worry just a bit. "Why don't you start at the beginning and we'll go from there?"

So she does. And wouldn't you know it, Abby convinces her to give Harley another chance. How she does it is anyone's guess, but the second Abby and Maya are out the door, Aliah finds herself at her desk, feverishly searching her phone for his home address. She is sure it must be plastered online somewhere, if he is who Spencer says he is.

After doing a little digging, Aliah makes a stop at Harley's office. Jillian, his assistant, advises her that Harley's already gone home for the day and that she can't give her his home address. But when Jillian excuses herself to answer the bell at the back door, Aliah helps herself to the woman's contacts. That's what she gets for not password protecting her cell phone.

Aliah photographs his information with her cell phone and shouts out to Jillian. "Thanks anyways."

She wants to pay him a visit but loses her nerve. She has stolen his information after all. But by noon the next day, she has a plan in place. Abigail agrees that making him wait another day won't kill him. Aliah wants to make him sweat. At least she sure hopes he's sweating. If he isn't already, then this visit will certainly get the job done.

Aliah makes the trip across town and double checks the address. Now she's the one who's stunned. If this is the right place, then Harley Gates is living pretty damn high on the hog. There's a mint black Camaro in the driveway, with the windows tinted to black. Aliah's willing to bet on her life that it's his wife's ride.

The house is practically a mansion. All brick and grand, with a country style porch and three car garage. If the stamped concrete driveway doesn't give away his family's wealth, then the rod iron fence, bound by brick pedestals every ten feet, certainly does. The front lawn is so perfectly manicured that she wishes she had a dog just so it could take a shit on it.

Aliah casually approaches the house, steps onto the massive front porch, and knocks on the front door, eyeing up the two-seater swing.

Why would an unmarried man have one of those?

She fends off her pouty lip, but just barely, replacing it with an angry snarl.

Harley opens the door to her. He's shocked to find her on the other side. In fact, he's completely and utterly surprised. "Aliah." He glances over his shoulder, like there's someone in there that she's not supposed to see.

Like his wife, maybe.

Aliah barges inside, ready to be over with the lies. She sees a beautiful young girl there. It's even worse than she thought. Not only is he married, but to a girl who looks ten years her junior. Aliah starts to put the pieces together herself.

"Do you even have a sister? Or was that just a cover for your sugar baby?" she snaps, glaring at the girl.

"Dad?" the girl says, looking incredibly confused by Aliah's intrusion.

Aliah makes a grab for the end table to stop herself from crumbling to the pristine marble floor. "Back that up a second. What did you just call him?"

Harley throws his hand down from his forehead and confesses. "She's my daughter."

The poor girl looks so uncomfortable, and that's because Aliah is so indelicate. She's convinced herself that Harley is a cheating bastard, when in reality he's just a father. Aliah instantly feels like a cruel toad, but if that is the case, then Harley must be the *lowly* toadstool. She still wants to walk all over him, with her tallest heels on, and is sure his baby momma is about to make her appearance any minute.

Aliah glances at his daughter. She's clearly not used to seeing her father around other women. She watches Aliah with eyes of a predator. Aliah turns her eyes back to Harley.

"You have some explaining to do." Her first impression of Harley's daughter is that she is an innocent, so Aliah's completely shocked when the girl gets right up in her dad's face, interrupting their private conversation.

"Aren't you going to introduce me, dad? Or are you not planning on keeping this one around long enough to bother?"

This seems to anger Harley. "Your mother did not raise you to have a mouth like that. Apologize to Aliah. Right now."

The jab about her mother seems to hurt her, but it doesn't permanently remove the sass from her voice. "I'm sorry," she says, but it's about as believable as the idea of a witch bursting into the house and flying around on a broomstick.

"Hannah," he warns.

"I'm sorry," she says, magically making the sarcasm leave her voice. "My dad doesn't bring prostitutes home every day. You're his first."

Aliah has to laugh at that. "A prostitute? That's what you think I am? Trust me, honey, I'm no prostitute. If you ask me, marriage is prostitution. I don't see your dad buying me any jewellery and I certainly haven't seen any money out of this relationship."

"Oh, so you're a gold digger. Big surprise there," Hannah mumbles.

Aliah's mouth drops open. "Oh, hell no. No amount of money can buy this, sweetheart. You can't just give them all the goods up front. You have to make them work for it."

She tries to act like their relationship has been based on something more than desire, which is the exact opposite of the truth.

"Hmm, good talk," Hannah mocks, then shares a roll of her eyes.

And just for a second, Aliah sees a glimmer of herself when she was a teen. She smiles over at Harley. He has never looked more uncomfortable than he does this minute.

"I'm Hannah, by the way. Not that you care."

Aliah turns back to the girl, stunned by the offering, and smiles. "Aliah." She reaches her hand out, but Hannah steps backward and scowls at her like her hand might have cooties.

Harley sighs out of frustration. "Hannah, could you please give us a few minutes?" Harley flashes a glance at the girl, who bears a striking resemblance to him. "Please?"

Hannah leaves the room, but stares back at Aliah again, this time flashing a smile. But not just any smile. A devious smile, that looks so painstakingly similar to Harley's that it stabs at Aliah's heart and makes her wince once she's relieved of the teenager's glare.

Hannah stomps off and heads for the front door.

"Where do you think you're going, Missy?" Harley's tone doesn't manage to scare her in the slightest.

"Anywhere to get away from you." After snapping at him, she slams the door shut.

Aliah snickers. "She listens well."

Harley flashes her his angriest glare. "She reminds me of someone else I know."

"Don't look at me."

"Oh, I am looking at you."

After an awkward silence, Harley reaches for Aliah's hand. "Is that why you really came here? For an explanation?"

She refuses to allow him the pleasure of her touch, after he's just drilled a hole through her heart. He's had his chance. Now it's her turn. She throws his shirt at him and it swats him right in the face.

"*Actually*, I came to return your stinking shirt... and to hear your apology. Maybe I should have burned it instead."

"You're still mad," he mumbles, more to himself than to her.

"If you would have just told me you had a daughter, I wouldn't have been faced with murderous thoughts when I walked in that door. And maybe, just maybe, things would have gone down at little differently."

"I doubt it." Hannah's outburst has clearly made Harley

irritable. "She's been getting more and more sassy these past few weeks. Tonight, it's hit an all-time high. I thought it was because I've been spending less time at home. Because of you."

"Blame it on me. She's clearly having boy troubles. But leave it up to a dad to get it all wrong."

Harley waves a hand at her, but the words don't make it out at first. "No. No. No. No boy troubles here."

Leaving their own argument alone for a second, Aliah delves into another doozy. "Face the facts, Harley. You're daughter's getting to that age. She's a beautiful girl. How old is she now? She doesn't look a year over twenty."

He grabs at his heart in a dramatic display of pride. "I may be old, but I'm not that old. She'll be celebrating her eighteenth birthday in a couple of months."

"You're in trouble."

He's glaring at her, just waiting for her to take another jab at him. "Why am I in trouble?"

"I can see that she's already having boy troubles. You can only hope that it's not too late. The ones without a good mother figure in their life are usually the worst ones."

"You?"

"Not me. But most. My father would have killed me if I went sleeping around. But by age seventeen, there weren't many of my friends who could still call themselves virgins. I hate to be the bearer of bad news, but..."

"Then there's still hope," Harley blurts, unwilling to believe what Aliah's implying. Besides, Hannah knows better. She's a smart girl."

"You can hope." Aliah turns to leave, but he stops her with a firm grip on her shoulder.

"Oh... uh. Thanks for the lesson in marriage, by the way." After giving her a sarcastic squeeze, he releases her.

She shoots him a narrowed glance. "I only speak the truth. Sorry if it isn't the perfect picture you try to sell your little toddling princess."

Harley makes a fast approach around her, and it has her back stepping. "You've really thrown the idea of marriage under the bus?" he asks. He's standing over her now, his eyes a sight of dark seduction. "Tell me you haven't given up all hope."

He's so big and tall that she should be scared. But intrigue is all she feels screaming from every orifice in her body.

"For me?" She pauses. "Yeah. There's not a hope in hell." Aliah shrugs her shoulders and slides away. She's already given it a lot of thought. Her chances at a truly happy life are non-existent.

"You're so young yet."

Aliah rolls her eyes at that. "Oh, and you're such an old man. If you wanted a wife, you could have one. Look at this house. It looks like you've ripped a page straight out a home magazine. You clearly have money. And you aren't a bad looking guy. For all I know, you have a hoard of girlfriends you pick from to take out each night of the week."

"Gee. You paint me in such a pretty picture."

"The truth," she states, as he reaches out to her and skims a finger down her cheek. It has her shivering, as he leans in closer.

"I have a good housekeeper," he growls. "And my gardener is pretty damn good too." His words are by no means intimate, but the way he says it has a delicious chill skipping up her spine. "There are no girlfriends. There's only you."

That confession has Aliah swooning, but she refuses to let it show. "So clearly you've given up too."

Harley *boops* her on the nose like she's an adorable child. "I gave up a long time ago. But just because *I* didn't find love, doesn't mean I don't want that for Hannah. There's no reason why she can't secure a marriage based on love, trust and companionship. I'm trying really hard to teach her that there is such a thing as true love. Can you respect that?"

"I think so. Just because *I'm* doomed, doesn't mean your beautiful daughter is."

Harley smiles. "She is beautiful, isn't she?"

Aliah nods, glancing up at him adoringly. "She has your eyes." She wonders how she manages to let that one slip.

Harley steps toward her and she steps backward again. He glances over his shoulder at the closed door and then turns his gaze back on her. He reaches out to her, waiting for her to give in, then lets his hand fall.

"Why are you being like this?" He's begging for her forgiveness, but he hasn't confessed anything.

"You must think I'm stupid. You haven't given me an inch."

"I don't think you're stupid at all. I don't invite stupid women into my home. Hannah doesn't need that kind of shit in her life. She's an impressionable young girl, and she has enough issues of her own. I'm not about to add daddy's ditsy girlfriend to that list."

Did he just call her his girlfriend? Maybe, in some fucked up sort of way. It confuses her. "Why were you looking through my things?" You can hear the hurt in her voice.

He pauses for a minute, and she takes that opportunity to order him to be real.

"The truth."

He sighs, and she knows she's not going to like what he's about to say. "Let me explain."

Hannah re-enters the room at the most inopportune time, interrupting his confession yet again.

"Really, Hannah?" he shouts, in the heat of the moment.

It clearly upsets her. "Screw you!" she shouts back, with a horrifying screech. Then she narrows her eyes at Aliah, forgetting why she's returned, and leaves the room in a huff.

Harley presses his eyes shut, a wince of pain wrinkling the corners of his eyes. "Shit."

"She'll get over it." Aliah tries to make it better, but Harley obviously feels like a piece of crap.

"She doesn't have anyone else, Aliah. I can't push her away like that. She needs me. There's no mother here to caress her hair, shower her with kindness and nurture her love for her dad. It's all me."

It's a drastic change of topic yet again, but Aliah senses

his guilt and decides to leave it alone for now. "I know all about it. My mother's around, but she's pretty useless."

A glimmer of hope flickers in his somber eyes. "Maybe you can talk to her for me. Hannah definitely does not want to talk to me right now."

Aliah squints her eyes, trying to figure this man out. "Why do I feel like this has suddenly turned into a counselling session?" She wishes he would realize that this is supposed to be about *us*, not about *them*.

A smile slants across Harley's face. "It'll be good for you both."

"Really? Because I doubt me telling her what an A-hole her father is will help your situation."

His smile slides off his face. "At least you're guaranteed to have one thing in common." He's completely serious when he says it, which makes it that much more funny.

Aliah can't help but smile. She doesn't want to smile! But she can't even force it away. "I'll do it."

"You'll do it?" He seems shocked.

"I said I'll do it, so I will. Don't make me change my mind. And don't for one second think that this will make me brush all that other shit you've done under the rug. You've got some major ass-kissing to do if you think you're going to get another piece of *this* ass, I tell you."

It's too late when Aliah realizes that Hannah has snuck back inside unnoticed.

"I'll pretend I didn't hear that." Hannah makes a grab for her purse and slams the door again with a definitive snap.

Aliah palms her forehead. Harley smirks, but inside he's horrified. This is new to him too.

"That's my Hannah," he says, shaking his head. "I'm sure the last thing she wants to hear is that her father is having sex." He winces at the reminder of her untimely interruption.

"Oh, please. I bet the boys are knocking down your door to get to her. Is she seeing anyone?"

"Whoa. What do you mean?" he snaps.

It makes Aliah smile again. "Dating, Harley. Like a

boyfriend, maybe?" She says it like a tease.

"No. Not my baby." He really is that clueless.

"Oh, boy. You need my help worse than you thought."

"I need help?"

Aliah scrunches her nose up and nods. "Desperately."

"Help me then," he growls. "Give me the help I need."

The way he pleads leaves her wondering if there is more to it than that. He leans in close to her, until his breath washes over her lips. It looks like he's going to kiss her. A breath catches in her throat, as she quickly turns away.

"Where do you think she's gone? I'll go talk to her now."

"Now?" It is clear he believes he's done enough talking to get her back to sharing that ass with him.

"Yes, now," Aliah answers.

Harley smirks, as he tugs her back against him. He's grown in his pants and his abs are equally as hard against her back. "I was hoping to ask you what you thought of *our* relationship first." He flexes his love muscle against her.

"I'd hardly call it that." She spews it out before she even realizes that he means the sex they're having.

"Then what would you call it?" he asks, smirking. He leans into her and presses his cheek to hers. Then he reaches around her hip and strokes between her legs.

"A hit of good clean fun?" she starts, with a feminine gasp.

His fingers are circling on her and he knows just the right spot. She tries to act unaffected by him, but he really knows what he's doing. His lips brush across the nape of her neck. The hair on his face is rough against her skin. It has her other body parts humming.

When he doesn't agree with her, she feels the need to give another explanation, now that her skin is covered in tiny bumps of arousal. She rests her head against his shoulder and comes up with her best excuse.

"Something to kill the time while my massage therapist is on holidays?" She poses it like a question, and while it is mostly true, the heat in Harley's eyes gives away his disbelief.

He slants his head while he thinks about it, but doesn't lighten the pressure on her clit. "I can handle that."

"Good. So, you won't be asking me on anymore dates then?"

"It wasn't a date. Remember?" He presses into her back with his erection, then he lightens the pressure.

"Whatever you say," Aliah says, smiling. She pries herself from his tempting arms, trying to ignore the cry of her body from the loss. "I'm going to go now. Is there somewhere I should look for Hannah first?"

He gives up, realizing that she isn't going to stay for a quickie. Though seeing him hard up like that really has her reeling.

"Head up the road westerly. I doubt she's made it very far."

"Why's that?" Aliah's blood still hums sweetly through her veins.

He dangles the car keys from his finger. He's right. Without those, she likely hasn't made it very far at all.

Aliah heads out to her own car and opens all the windows. She never expects to find herself in the position of a role model, but she feels some responsibility to help the poor girl. Her father is clueless, and Hannah is so close to the girl she once was that it scares her.

Aliah slides her car into gear and eases out of the driveway. Sure enough, maybe five houses up the road, she finds Hannah walking next to the curb. When Aliah pulls up next to her and stops, she doesn't say anything, but Hannah does.

"Great. You again." Hannah doesn't look real impressed to see her.

Aliah knows the feeling. "Just get in the damn car."

"My dad's taught me not to accept rides from strangers."

This girl truly is a sassy bitch. As sassy as Aliah, even. Maybe even more so. Aliah can't deny she recognizes it. Hannah really needs someone to talk to.

"Look. I know where you're coming from. I only want to talk. I'll buy you a coffee. You don't even have to say anything, if you don't want to."

Hannah looks like she thinking about it.   Then she glances over her shoulder, like she's considering making a run for her house. "Fine." Her voice sounds exasperated, but Aliah knows she's made some progress.

One step at a time.

CHAPTER THIRTEEN

Harley never thought that Aliah would volunteer to have *the talk* with his daughter, after only having just met her. Aliah continues to surprise him every day.

He can't believe she's going to be the one to talk to Hannah about sex, when *they've* only had sex together a handful of times themselves. That has to change. He wants to sex her five ways to Sunday. Anything to make it so that he is the only one sexing her up from now on.

He's thinking this, while Aliah is chatting over coffee with his daughter. Had he really believed that he'd be fine with sitting here, not having a clue about what they are discussing? He paces his living room, trying to steer his thoughts away, but how does he even know that Aliah's telling her the right things? Harley had met Aliah at a bar, after all. He'd screwed her not much more than a week after that.

That's certainly not the kind of behavior he'd condone from his teenaged daughter. *I would hope she knows this.* Harley slaps his hand against his forehead. *What has he done?* He isn't one to sulk, but this girl has really gotten to him. He hardly even knows her, and now she's out with his daughter.

What the hell was I thinking?

He must have officially lost his mind. That would be the only explanation for his actions around this girl. Truth: Aliah is crazy. But no one is as crazy as he, right now.

Crazy in love?

He did not just think that. He does not *love* anyone, except for his daughter and himself. He is not capable of loving another person. But if there is a love for him to have, then this is it.

This is it.

Aliah's last name should be spelled trouble with a capital T, and yet it feels like she is the missing link in his life. He's now fed her so many lies he can't even keep them straight. Maybe he should tell her his name isn't actually Harley.

Shit!

To take his mind from his own issues, he focuses on hers. Why are people following her, and why the hell do they have guns? He thinks about it for a long time, rolling all of the possibilities through his brain. He still can't get over how sexy Aliah looked maneuvering his bike through those city streets. She was hunched down like she was on a mission and he'd crowded over her like her protector.

She is so hot.

Aliah would make one dangerously sexy sidekick. He doubts Jillian would share the same enthusiasm, but they could make a good team together. Not that Aliah would ever do such mediocre work. She has a friggin' law degree.

What the hell was he thinking, calling her lowly?

Sometimes he wonders if he has any access to the other half of his brain. Harley shakes his head, trying to refocus on the facts. The people following her were male. There were at least two of them. They appeared rather mediocre, being far from stealthy. He'd noticed them rather easily the other night, and he was drunk. Clearly they weren't trained very well. Either that or they were just plain stupid.

Most likely, they were hired muscle, so to speak. It was difficult to call them *muscle*, when one of them looked like a lazy slab of flab and the other long and lean and gangly. The two of them reminded him of the Jack Sprat rhyme. They make the perfect pair. But who would hire such a clan of morons?

Every question he poses has him running back to the same name. The very person he's been avoiding these past few days. He's actually quite surprised that she hasn't been harassing him for more information. He circles the name on the pad of paper sitting on his desk and pulls out his phone.

His call goes straight to voicemail. "Ms. Hawkins. David H. Gates here. I have some information for you." He hangs up abruptly.

That ought to get a response.

In a matter of minutes his phone is dinging. He swipes his finger across the screen of his cell phone and checks the text message.

Meet me at the river, across from Riley's. I'll be there in ten. — Brandee Hawkins

He slips his phone back into his pocket. He could be walking into a trap. But the river is a rather public location, and it's not far from the business district. In all likelihood, she's going to come unarmed. She's only looking for information. He'll give her some.

Harley rolls up to the river on his motorcycle, passing Aliah's car in the parking lot. He sees that Brandee Hawkins is already fidgeting by the water, and he wonders if she's even noticed Aliah's car parked nearby. Brandee looks awfully anxious, and scowls toward him when he stops his bike at the curb. He kicks out the stand and leans the heavy bike against it.

When he approaches his client, his boots sink into the soft grass with each step. "Ms. Hawkins," he greets her.

"Let's skip the pleasantries and get down to business, shall we?"

Her ignorance doesn't surprise him. "Right."

"The information. Do you have it, or what?"

"About that." He sighs, preparing himself for a battle. "I've done the digging. I've talked to the suspect. I've seen the inside of her office."

Brandee gives him a pointed glare and makes a sexual inference. "I've never heard it called that before."

He smiles, but it turns into a disgusted snarl against his best efforts to keep his lips curled upwards. "I mean literally, Ms. Hawkins. Please try to keep your mind out of the gutter for the next five seconds."

"I didn't think I was paying you to fuck the girl."

"About that." Harley hands her an envelope full of cash.

She peeks inside the flap at the money and smiles. "At least you got her off of Mitchell's back for a change."

He clears his throat to regain her attention. "As I was saying. I've done the research. I have the facts. I'm ready to give you the results of my investigation."

"Please do," she insists, waving a hand at him.

"She's innocent."

"Unbelievable! She's clearly worked her wiles on you too."

"I've found nothing to support your theory that she wants Cavanagh romantically. Their relationship appears to be purely platonic."

"Appears to be?" she screeches, like a maniac. "I could have told you what *appears to be*. What actually is, is another thing. You just don't want to admit that your girlfriend is fucking my man. You are one messed up fellow."

"I'm sorry you feel that way." Their conversation is going nowhere fast.

"You're a sucker, is what you are."

"That's enough," Harley snaps, and it has Brandee blinking erratically, as if he has struck her with his hand. "I'm done with this. You have your money. The investigation is closed."

"Oh, I don't think so. You haven't delivered a shred of evidence." She hands him the wad of cash, but he doesn't take it. "Take it back," she screeches, like it's an order.

Harley lifts a hand. "Keep your money. And just leave the girl alone. She hasn't done anything wrong here."

Brandee spins away and stomps toward her car. "This investigation is not over," she shouts, kicking his bike as she passes. "If you won't help me get some answers, then I'll have to find someone else who will."

Harley sees red, at the sight of her foot touching his chrome muffler. As she squeals away, he stomps toward his machine with adrenaline coursing through his veins. After a quick glance at his bike, he turns and watches her peel into traffic. When she's out of sight, he instantly notices his daughter emerging from the café next to Riley's. She's alone.

Ms. Hawkins is lucky. Harley's temper is not his most attractive quality, and she manages to bring it on full force. He takes two deep breaths and steps closer to his motorcycle, fully preparing himself to chase down that chick to break her neck.

After checking for damage, he buffs the exhaust pipe with his shirt until there's not a mark to be seen. Satisfied that he doesn't have to murder Brandee Hawkins anymore, he swiftly moves across the parking lot to cut off his daughter. It's not until he's two cars away that Hannah notices him. She freezes in place, but she looks surprisingly happy. He hasn't seen that smile in quite a while.

He's kind of missed it and it doesn't last long. As he walks closer, the smile falls off her face.

"What are you doing?" he asks. But his voice sounds more concerned than overbearing.

The smile returns to his daughter's face when she dangles out a single key in front of his eyes.

He doesn't get it at first until he recognizes the BMW key fob. "No," he says.

"But, dad!"

"How did you get her key? Haven't I taught you that you shouldn't steal?"

"I didn't steal it." She sounds angered by his insinuation. "I was heading over to Karen's house and Aliah offered me her car. As if I could say no to that."

"She offered you her mint new car to visit a friend?"

"Yes. I'm not kidding you, dad. Isn't she great?"

"Yeah. Great."

"So I can take it?" She pulls out her trademark pouty lip.

"What are you going to do with her car when you're done there? Do you even know where Aliah lives?"

"No. But she said I could just drive it to our house, as

long as I'm home by ten. It's a work night," she informs him, and it sounds like it's come straight out of Aliah's mouth.

He gazes at her, considering his options.

"Please, dad?" she begs. Hannah appears to be really happy about this.

"Fine." He sighs, giving in to his only daughter. "I'll see you at ten."

"Yes!" She wraps her arms around her father's neck and dangles from him like an air freshener. "Love you, dad. I promise to get your girlfriend's car home in one piece."

He gives his daughter a squeeze. "Go on. Be safe," he insists, as she lets herself in the flashy yellow car.

As he heads for the main street, he hears his daughter's squeal. He shakes his head as he crosses the road to pay a visit to his *girlfriend*.

CHAPTER FOURTEEN

Thirty minutes earlier.

The Thorncliffe Café is packed with people and Aliah and Hannah don't look the slightest bit out of place. They could have passed for a couple of girlfriends. Aliah grabs them each a coffee and takes a seat across from her.

"I'm glad you decided to join me."

"Don't get too excited," Hannah blurts, rolling her eyes.

"Can you quit with the attitude? I get it. You don't like me."

"I really doubt that you get it, but whatever."

Aliah manages to keep her cool. "Trust me when I say that I get it. I grew up without a mother too."

"What did yours die from?"

"Oh, she's alive and well. Sometimes I wish she were dead. At least then I'd have an good excuse for why she's not around. She never wanted a daughter. She treats my four brothers like gold. I'm an outcast in her eyes."

"That blows."

"It really does." Aliah feels like her mini-confession has actually brought them a little bit closer. "I know what it's like to be a teen without a woman in the house. I just want you to know that I'm here to answer any questions you might have. I know you don't know me. I'm sure this feels super weird. But I want to help you. I know there's things you can't tell your dad. I refused to talk about sex with mine."

"It's just too weird," Hannah admits.

"Right?"

Hannah nods and takes a sip from her mug.

"So, you're having sex I take it."

Hannah instantly shies away.

That's a big fat no.

"Hannah," she says. "If you haven't, that's not something to be ashamed of. If you can believe it, I saved myself for the longest time."

"What happened?"

"You first."

Hannah huffs, but she can't deny that it's a fair trade. "I've been seeing this guy for the past couple of months. He's cool, I guess. He's a really good athlete and totally hot."

"So, what's the problem?" Aliah can see that her whole heart isn't in it.

"He's been bugging for sex lately, trying to coax me to do it with him."

"But you don't want to?"

"I don't know. Kind of. I'm really nervous. I guess I'm mostly scared of getting pregnant. I'm not ready to be a mother. And I don't really have anyone to talk to about it. My friends have big mouths and I refuse to talk to my dad about it."

Aliah holds her hands up in surrender. "I'm with you there, girlfriend. I get it."

Hannah laughs anxiously. "I don't know if he's the one, you know? He's a lot more experienced than me, and I've always pictured losing my virginity to a virgin. It's corny, I know. You probably think I'm a total loser."

"Do you love him?" Aliah asks bluntly.

"No."

"Then don't it. I can guarantee you'll regret it if you do. Can I give you my honest advice?"

"Yeah," Hannah says, with a smile. She leans over the table, like Aliah has some magical wand that will give her all the answers she's been waiting to hear.

"You can only lose your virginity once. You've saved yourself this long. I'm sure you can hang on a little longer. You're young. I'd bet love is out there for you, just around the corner."

Hannah smiles. "You really think so?"

"I do. And anything that needs rushed isn't right. You should get yourself on birth control first anyways."

"But I'm not even having sex."

"It doesn't hurt to be prepared. You shouldn't wait until you're having sex to start birth control. Then it's too late, wouldn't you agree? If you're not comfortable asking your father to go with you, I could take you." Aliah rushes to insist that she doesn't have to agree. "I mean, I understand if you don't want me to."

"No. I would really appreciate it. Would you?"

"I'm getting off early on Thursday. I can take you then, if you want."

After exchanging phone numbers, a silence envelopes them. Aliah feels surprisingly content.

"My mom and dad were never in love, you know," Hannah admits, out of nowhere. "My mom told me so before she died."

Aliah nods, slightly gleeful to hear the news. "Does your dad know you know this?"

"No. And please don't tell him."

Aliah draws a cross over her heart. "I swear."

Hannah seems to trust her. "Thanks. What do you think I should do about Jared?"

"Is that the jock's name?"

She nods her head, as her eyes grow wide.

"What's wrong?" Aliah peers over her shoulder and instantly glances back at Hannah. "Jared?"

"Yeah."

Jared walks directly up to Hannah. "Hey, baby."

Hannah stands to her feet and he drops a kiss on her cheek, as he hooks an arm around her waist. "Who's your hot friend?" He smirks seductively at Aliah, making eye contact. "Maybe she can teach you a few tricks for the bedroom."

Aliah bites her bottom lip and has to grip onto her seat to stop herself from punching the jerk. To her surprise, Hannah pushes him off of her and her hand makes an amazing connection with his face.

I couldn't have done better myself! Go, Hannah!

Jared's friends walk up, after witnessing her assault. At

first they appear shocked. Then they start to snicker at him.

"I'm not your baby. And you won't be on the receiving end of any of those little tricks I've learned. Now get out of my face. You're dimming my light."

She turns back to Aliah and takes a seat, acting like Jared's a worthless piece of junk that doesn't deserve her attention.

"*You're* dumping *me*?" he belts out hysterically. He's clearly never been dumped before.

Hannah glances over her shoulder, like she can't be bothered to turn around and face him. "Are you deaf? I'm not interested. Do I really need to repeat it in front of all of your friends?"

Another guy grabs onto his elbow and tugs him toward the counter. "Come on. She's not worth it."

Jared yanks his arm away and scowls at Aliah. Aliah flashes him her best *take that, asshole,* smile.

Hannah takes another drink from her coffee. Aliah can see that she's shaking, so she takes her hand and pulls it under the table.

"Can I just say that you're amazing? Good for you."

"You said it. I've saved myself this long. Thank God I didn't have sex with him. I would have regretted that for the rest of my life."

"I'm so proud of you. I wanted to knock his block off, but you did a pretty damn good job yourself."

"Thanks." She smiles. "It felt pretty good, if I'm being completely honest. Oh, my God. I can't believe I did that." She starts to giggle. "Are they gone yet?"

"Nope. They're all staring over here, as we speak."

Hannah looks like she wants to curl up and die.

"Here. Take my car. Why don't you pick up a girlfriend and cruise around for a bit or something?"

Hannah's mouth drops open. "You're going to let me drive your car?"

"Go nuts. Actually, no. Take it easy on my baby."

Aliah smiles and she knows that she is scoring major points with Hannah right now. She doesn't know why that's so important to her, but suddenly it is. And it feels good.

"Oh my gosh. You are so cool. Thank you!" Hannah cheers.

Aliah unhooks the key from her keychain and hands it over to her. "Promise you'll take good care of him?"

"Your car's a him?"

"Is that a problem?"

"Absolutely not. I love it!"

"You're in business then. Just please have my car back to your house by ten. Does that sound fair?"

"Fair enough. Thank you again, Aliah. I really appreciate it."

"You're welcome," she answers.

Hannah looks so giddy when she spins around that she almost skips to the front door of the café. Hannah really is a sweet girl. A virgin too. Her father will be happy to hear that, when she gets around to sharing it with him.

Aliah finishes her drink, wondering how she's going to get home. As her quiet time starts to turn into loneliness, the bell on the front door clanks across the glass. She instantly looks up and locks her gaze on the hunk of muscle entering the place.

Harley Gates is easy on the eyes. Looking at him never gets old. He doesn't seem to notice her at first. She quickly tears off her glasses, before he can catch her wearing them and buries them in the bottom of her handbag. She glances back up at him, looking a lot like a giddy fool. When his eyes meet hers, an electricity strikes her core, and the longer his eyes rest on her the hotter the fire grows.

"Can I sit?" he asks, holding the back of the chair as if she might say no.

With a great deal of effort, she manages to remove the smile from her face and waves a hand at the vacant chair. He takes a seat and gazes at her some more.

"You won't believe who I just met with," he starts.

"Jillian?" she guesses.

He seems shocked by her sureness. "My Jillian?"

"Please don't call her that."

He smiles. "If I was meeting with my assistant that would hardly be remarkable. Why don't you like her?"

"I don't know. There's just something not right with that girl. I can't put my finger on it. It's just a feeling. Intuition maybe." Aliah circles the rim of her mug with an index finger. "I don't like the way she looks at you. There are unresolved feelings there, I think."

"You're seeing things."

"Whatever you say. But don't say I never told you."

"Okay," he growls. "It was Brandee Hawkins." He freezes in place when he realizes that he's never shared the connection with her.

"Ugh. You did not just say that name."

"I did." He clears his throat. "And you're not going to be very happy with me when I tell you why."

"Then don't tell me."

"You're going to have to face the truth at some point, Aliah. I've been trying to tell you this *little* secret I've been keeping from you, but you're not making it very easy for me to come clean."

"Out with it then, if it's that important to you." She doesn't even think before she speaks. *Is she ready to hear his secrets?*

"Brandee Hawkins *was* my client. I'm a private investigator who goes by the name of David H. Gates. She hired me to look into Mitchell Cavanagh's personal life. The case is now closed." He blurts it out, hiding the fact that he's been hired to nose around her life too.

Is that the only reason they'd ever met? Did he get the evidence he was looking for? Is he still using her to get the goods on Mitchell?

Aliah has so many questions, but she refuses to react to it, unsure how this new information is supposed to make her feel.

"Harley?" she asks, her tone begging him to tell her why he'd lied about his name.

"My middle name."

She nods unhappily, but nothing can clear the horrid

feeling from her gut. "It's about time you tell me. I was starting to wonder if you would ever come clean."

"I know we didn't meet under the most honest circumstances, but it's my job. It's what I do. And what I feel for you is real." He pauses, but not nearly long enough for her to sort out her jumbled thoughts. "I am truly sorry to do this, but we have to stay focused here. Brandee Hawkins," he repeats.

"What is that girl's problem? What she needs is to take a chill pill." Aliah's not impressed with Harley's evil ways, but she's smart enough to know that now is not the time to dwell on it. "She's constantly gawking at me," she points out.

Harley smirks and rakes her body with hooded eyes. "That could have something to do with how provocative you dress."

"I'm wearing a flowered shirt and a pair of shorts. You can hardly call what I'm wearing right now provocative." She pauses, then gives him a pointed look. "Quit looking at me like that."

Harley's gaze warms her to a boiling point in an instant. Even after feeding her a handful of lies, she can't evade the desire coursing through her body.

"That outfit fits you like a glove. You look incredibly sexy in it. Your breasts look perky and perfect; your skin soft and flawless. Those legs... Should I go on?"

Aliah is now trying to fight off a smile. "I certainly won't stop you, if you insist."

Neither of them can remember the importance of the secrets being unveiled only seconds earlier. Harley reaches out and runs a finger over her naked shoulder. When he growls, it sends her nerves firing off like firecrackers.

"You're a beautiful girl, Aliah. People are going to stare at you no matter what you wear. Like those boys over there," he says, nodding toward the fixated teenagers.

She acts unaware of the attention, skipping the part where one of them just got bitch slapped by his daughter. "I'm used to a little attention. But it's felt different lately.

Catching people looking at you is one thing. It's another thing entirely when they're hiding in the bushes waiting to jump you for God knows what reason."

"I can protect you."

"Can you? Are you going to walk me to my lobby at work every morning and tuck me into bed every night?"

"If you'll let me," he answers.

He looks completely serious. The thought has her head spinning. She can see herself enjoying that for some reason. She hates the idea of relying on anyone at all. Why now, all of a sudden, is she okay with depending on this man? Especially after he's lied to her on more than one occasion.

"I was only teasing. I can handle myself," she says, even if she wants him to handle her.

"If you change your mind, I'm always a phone call away."

His proposition has her changing her mind already. She nods her head, smiling.

"There is one request I have to make though," he adds.

"What's that?" Aliah polishes off her second cup of coffee. It's no wonder she's so jittery tonight.

"Don't go anywhere without your own transportation."

"Oh." She feels like he's got her pinned under his thumb. "I can explain." Even she can see how dumb a move it was abandoning herself at the café in the circumstances.

"You offered my daughter your car?"

She turns her head down and smirks. "You noticed."

"You do realize she's only been licensed to drive on her own for a few months now."

"I trust she'll be extra careful. If I were her, I know I wouldn't choose now as a good time to fuck up."

"Shit happens, Aliah, and Hannah is not you. Remember that."

"Shit certainly does happen, but let's just say that the benefits outweighed the potential loss at the time. You might not see it now, but you'll thank me later."

A look of disbelief covers his face like a mask. "I know how much you love that car. That must have been some discussion the two of you had."

"We understand each other."

"I hope for your sake you're right."

"I am. And I can see how much she respects you. Even if she acts out from time to time, she's only a girl and she loves you."

He nods his head, suddenly very curious to hear about their discussion. "Are you going to tell me what's going on, or do I have to threaten it out of you?"

"That depends on the question, and the punishment."

"You tell me what she told you and I promise not to be gentle."

His words have her pussy twitching, but she won't admit that to him. "Ooh. So tempting." Her words are dripping with sarcasm, but she really is intrigued. "Unfortunately, I made a promise to your daughter, and I'm going to have to keep it."

"You aren't going to tell me anything, are you?"

"Oh, I'll tell you something. I'll give you everything you need to know. The rest isn't really for a father's ears anyway."

"Why don't you get talking and let me be the judge of that?"

"Okay. You asked for it. But don't shoot the messenger."

"If you don't spit it out right now, I might be tempted." He bends his elbow and settles his hand over his hip where she knows he parks a gun.

She looks over her shoulders as if someone might be listening in on them, her face turning more serious. "You're sure you don't want to go to a more private place to discuss this?"

His voice turns low and seductive, ignoring her concern. "That doesn't sound like such a bad idea. What time did you say Hannah is due home?"

"I didn't tell you that."

"Oh, right. I had a little chat with her out in the parking lot just before I arrived. She said a time."

"Ten o'clock," Aliah tells him, certain of it. "Why?"

He checks his phone and glances toward the front door

of the café. "That gives us two hours all to ourselves. My house is guaranteed to be empty. I guarantee you, Hannah won't be home more than a minute early. That is unless you'd rather stay and talk about my shortcomings."

She does not want to talk anymore. "You're sure you want to take me there?"

"I'm sure." He stands from his seat and clasps onto her hand. "You can tell me the important points from your conversation with my daughter on our way to my bike."

Aliah delivers him a sly smile, as she slinks past him and pulls her hand free from his. The look exchanged between them doesn't go unnoticed by their teenaged spectators.

Harley is surprised by the gawking. "Who is that?"

"Jared," Aliah says, without turning to look at him.

He has no choice but to follow after her. "Again, I ask, who is that?"

She waits until they cross the road, making sure there's some distance between him and the boy before sharing the truth with him. "That, my dear, was your daughter's ex-boyfriend."

CHAPTER FIFTEEN

Still lying naked in his bed, covered by a thin sheet of silk, Aliah turns her eyes on him. He wants to have her again. He knows there has to be more than sex between them, but he can't get enough of it. He needs more – wants more.

"You should get dressed. Hannah's going to be home any minute now. We shouldn't be locked up in here when she shows up."

Aliah slides out from under his sheets. "Impressionable youth. I get it."

Once they're both fully dressed, they head to the front room, staring at each other like sex-crazed teenagers. He wonders if she wants more too.

"Aliah," he asks, his gaze sliding over her body. Look at the girl, wearing those little high-waisted shorts. She has her legs on display, just begging him to spread them and devour her again. "We're going for a ride."

She doesn't ask questions when he drops a helmet over her hair, and she climbs onto the bike first, leaving room for him to get on behind her. He slips the key in the ignition, revs his bike to life and speeds off, his engine roaring between her firm, youthful thighs.

He never feels safe with her on the back of his bike, ever since he's learned that someone's out looking her. They are like a slow moving target and she is like his life essence, trapped inside his hunched form. But the thrill of having her on his bike, wearing those tall tall shorts, is worth the risk.

It's dark and he knows just the place to settle their scandalous desires. It doesn't look like anyone is following them, but Aliah makes it difficult to stay focused. She wiggles her rear and snuggles back against him at the stoplight, like a lazy cat looking for love. He wonders if she knows what that does to him. If she hadn't, then she certainly does now, with his aroused cock stabbing her in the rear end.

With a quick change of plans, Harley makes a speedy turn and heads down the long dead-end ramp that leads to the public park. The second he cuts the engine, he feels the need to get her underneath him. He loses his helmet and flattens her on the seat. His breaths are hurried, as he divests her of her helmet. He brings his lips close to hers. He really wants to kiss her. Her lips look ruby red and silky soft. Her mouth is partially open, leaving him wanting to dive in to fill that void.

The urge to fuck her overwhelms him. He unbuttons those sexy little shorts and slips his hands inside her panties.

"You're so wet. You're always so fucking wet for me." His lips are so close to hers that he can almost taste her.

She looks up into his eyes, and in that moment it's as though she only has eyes for him. "Only for you," she whispers.

That's all it takes for him to make his decision. There's no question now. He's fucking her. Right here. Right now.

He drags down his zipper and pulls his dick through the fly of his briefs. Aliah closes her eyes and sucks in a breath, when he massages his fingers over her. He makes sure she's ready for his thickness before taking the plunge. Her chest is heaving. She's so excited. He kisses the tops of her fleshy mounds, letting his tongue dart out for a taste. Holding her panties to the side, he slides into her, and pauses when he's pressed in to the hilt.

"Oh, sweet Jesus." He lowers his head to the leather seat, over her shoulder, hissing in her ear. "I could fucking stay here, like this, all night." He keeps the pressure on her, and loves the way she wraps around him, gripping onto him from the inside out.

After kissing her neck, he lifts his head until they're nose to nose again. His lips barely kiss her, a whisper over her soft flesh. "Tell me you want this." He backs out, painfully slow, and eases back into her, burying himself again to drown in her warmth. "Tell me you need more."

Her hand hooks around his neck and she arches her back, bringing her luscious lips to his ear. She takes his lobe between her teeth and tugs on it. It has him aching inside her. "I need you."

A bullet crackles through the air and ricochets off the curb next to where they're parked. Harley instantly slides Aliah off the bike and slams down on top of her, still wrapped in her silky warmth. He reaches for the gun strapped to his ankle, hating the moment when he has to leave her body. He pulls out a gun and reaches for another one, tucked in the back of his pants.

Once Aliah tugs on her shorts, he hands her a twenty-two Mag. "Have you ever used one of these things before?"

She takes the small gun and gets a feel for it in her hands. "I've been shooting *one of these things* since I was a little girl." Rain begins to sprinkle from the sky. "Ask any of my four brothers. I've always given them a run for their money." She then glances at the smooth black gun clutched in his palm. "I prefer the Glock 40."

A sly smile touches his lips as he checks the magazine of bullets and slaps it back into the gun. "The Glock is mine."

After feigning a pout, she cocks her gun with her thumb. "So what's the plan here exactly?"

Harley wipes the rain from his forehead with the back of his hand as the droplets turn into showers. "Let's start with why you think Brandee would want you out of the picture." A rumble of thunder sets the stage for a war.

"Because she's crazy? I don't know. Why are you asking me this? You're the detective. Why don't you figure it out?" She peers around the bike carefully, but she can't see anything, between the rain and the darkness.

"I plan on it, smart mouth. But a little cooperation can go a long way in an investigation."

Aliah huffs. "Since when was I the one on trial here? Jesus! All I can think is that she's jealous of me. If I were out of the picture, then she'd have Mitchell all to herself."

Harley nods, accepting that as the truth in the matter. "Do you think she's capable of murder?" he asks, as another shot is fired.

Another miss.

He doesn't leave her time to answer. "We're not safe here. If they hit the gas tank, we're both cooked."

She crouches to her feet behind the motorcycle and aims the gun in the direction of the shots. If they only knew how good of a shot she is.

"What are you doing?" he asks.

"Saving our asses."

He puts a hand on top of the revolver and lowers it until it's pointing away from them. "This isn't like at the range, Aliah. If you pull that trigger and you hit the bull's eye, you're taking a life."

A visible tremor rocks her body, but she nods her head meekly in acknowledgement.

Now he's the one crouching, ready for a pre-emptive strike.

"What are you doing?" she snaps, with a hushed voice.

"We've nowhere left to hide. The next time a shot fires, cover me."

Another shot rings out, and she screams, "No!" as Harley makes a hunched run for the nearest picnic table. He pushes it over and flattens his back to the wood.

Aliah's outburst seems to have worked to his benefit. They're likely to believe he's been hit. He can now hear the gunmen talking. Then another shot rings out and he hears it clank off his bike. He realizes then that Aliah is a perfect target for the ricocheting bullet. Her silence is like a sudden knife in his gut.

Someone's dead now.

He's not used to having to worry about anyone but himself and Hannah. If something has happened to Aliah, the responsible gunman can only hope that Harley murders him after he's done torturing him. Then Aliah shouts out, and relief washes over him temporarily.

"Why are you hounding me?" she shouts, her voice bearing heavy emotion.

Aliah's a good actress.

Harley's shocked when the guy answers her. "We're only doing our job, Miss Brooklin. Now, if you'll let us get to it..."

Aliah looks like she's going to scream out to him, but he presses a finger to his lips and she manages to zip it like a good girl. He pulls away from the picnic table and sneaks up behind the outdoor auditorium, where the voices are coming from.

He peers around the corner. One of the gunmen are in range. He fights the urge to blast the guy's head off. One false move and Harley will have no issue with blowing his brains out.

Aliah cries out again. "Who's put you up to this?"

She's brilliant.

"Whatever they're paying you, I'll pay you double."

The distraction is just what he needs to sneak up on the criminal.

The man laughs to himself, seemingly joyous to hear the offer. "We don't want to hurt you. Only scare you a bit. If you come with us, we can get this all sorted out. Just tell your boyfriend to get out of here, and everything will be just as it should."

"How will I know you won't kill me?"

The man suddenly realizes that Harley's been awfully quiet. He looks agitated and is scouring the area for him.

"Looking for me?" Harley growls, as he clocks him over the head with the butt of his gun.

The other assailant calls out to him. "Will you shut up, Larry? I can't see Gates anymore. Can you see him?"

Before Harley can locate the other man, another shot is fired. He hangs onto his breath as pain sears his midsection. Then he hears his bike motor to life, as three distinct shots fire toward him. He can hear a man howling nearby. He's been hit too.

Harley wants to tell Aliah to stay put, but he's short on breath. When he turns toward the sound of his bike, he sees her riding through the grass with her gun drawn.

She just keeps getting sexier.

"Wipe that dumb look off your face and get on," she orders.

He's in no position to argue with her.

"Are you okay?" she asks, as she gives it gas and tears away.

The injured man emerges from the shadows. A few blasts wail through the night, but they're mere echoes passing behind them as they speed off. No one seems to have followed them, but Aliah is driving as though their life depends on it. He has no idea where she's heading, as she motors out of town. When she finally slows, she takes a turn and hits a slick of mud. He feels the bike wobbling beneath them as it tries to regain traction on the wet, country road.

It's going down.

He tries to right them, but it's too late. Aliah lets go of the steering wheel and flies off the bike into a lake of mud. Harley's motorcycle crashes on top of him, and he slides to a stop not far down the road.

Not much caring about himself or his bike at the moment, he drags himself out from under it and fumbles back toward Aliah. She's sitting in a swamp-like mud puddle, crying.

"Are you hurt?" he hollers.

She narrows her eyes, and that stops him in his tracks. "No!" she barks out.

Harley laughs at her. The happiness that wraps around his heart is a mystical force of nature.

"You are not laughing at me right now. You've been shot, dumb ass."

"I'll survive," he answers, with a chuckle.

"I have never felt so filthy in my life."

Harley secures his gun inside his pants and covers it with his jacket. He doesn't know what the hell he's thinking, but he's going to do it. "I can fix that."

He takes a running dive into the mud bath, face first. It

splatters all over his face and gets more in her hair. Not that there was an inch of her face that wasn't already covered in the dark brown muck.

"What is wrong with you?" Her voice screeches, but he can already hear the change in her tone.

He starts laughing again, and he feels more playful than he ever has, dating back to his childhood. "I thought you could use some company." His face turns more serious, but she still can't believe what he has just done.

Neither can he!

"Was that really necessary? I already look disgusting, and now you're a mess too." She lays back in the mud and he watches her hair sink in deeper. She doesn't even seem to care.

Harley crawls closer to her and leans over, resting on his good side. The moment feels surprisingly intimate. He smears a muddy finger over her right cheek. "You have never looked more beautiful than you do at this very minute."

Aliah stares at him, dumbfounded. He too wonders if he has lost his brain.

"Who told you to say that?" She looks around, as if someone is dictating his words to him.

"My heart." His answer is quick, spoken without a doubt.

Her pretty green eyes pop right out, causing him to groan. Her shock squeezes at his heart, and grips his ribs, making it difficult to breathe.

What is she so afraid of?

Harley pulls his hand away. "You're fine, Aliah. I'm not going to say it." He sounds a little disappointed. That's because he is.

"Say what?" Now she's playing stupid.

"I won't say that I'm falling in love with you. Not until you're ready to hear it."

His heart has never thudded so loud and fast in all his days. He can see that she is very uncomfortable having this conversation. But too damn bad for her.

"You've been hit," she says, noticing the way he favors

his left side. She reaches out and lifts his shirt, running a finger just above his melted flesh. "The bullet's only grazed your skin."

"Yeah, but it hurts like a mother-fucker." The flesh wound will heal. It'll take a little longer for his heart to recover from this rollercoaster ride. Harley's never felt more fear than that moment when he thought Aliah had been shot.

He instantly takes her hand and tugs her back to his motorcycle. He only hopes that it'll still run. Harley rights his bike and tries to get it started. It stalls out on the first try, but with his next attempt he finds success.

"Where are you taking me?" she shouts, over the roar of his engine.

He doesn't look at her, but then again it wasn't up for debate. "Away from here."

CHAPTER SIXTEEN

Why does he make her feel this way? She's not allowed to feel. She doesn't need something to lose. He doesn't even tell her where he's taking her. It's so infuriating, but it's of no use to fight him. Harley is a big boy. There's no winning with him. He can cheat the law and lie all he wants and he acts like there's no one he has to answer to. That attitude is going to stop today.

He drives for what seems like forever, then he turns into an average, run-of-the-mill hotel parking lot. She's sure now is as good a time as ever to ask him what the hell is going on.

"Who are we running from?" she asks him. "It's obvious that you know."

"I don't."

"Who do you *think* it is then? And why do we have goons after us?"

"Those goons you're talking about, I'm afraid to say this, but they're after you."

"What?" Her voice is shrill. What a ridiculous suggestion. She hasn't done anything wrong, unless being fabulous is a crime. "Who?"

Harley removes his key from the ignition. "Brandee Hawkins."

"I keep hearing this girl's name." She isn't very happy about it.

Aliah is reminded, with a sharp pain in her side, how Harley has been seriously lying to her all this time. First, about his name. Then, about his daughter. And now about the investigation. It's obvious there's something he's not telling her. Is the investigation truly over, or is he still pumping her for information? Their entire relationship is a sham.

"What's the first thing that comes to mind when I say the name Brandee Hawkins?"

He's tried this once before and it didn't work. Why does he think now is going to be any different? He's the one who lies.

"That bitch who hired you to stalk Mitchell? I thought that was over. You told me the case is closed."

"And it is. But I fear that she's found someone else to replace me. She doesn't believe I've done a very good job. She thinks that you've worked your wiles on me now too and, since it's true, I'd have to agree that maybe I'm a little biased in your favor."

"What do I have to do with this?" Aliah feigns a pout. "We haven't even discussed the whole of it yet. I know there's more to it. I feel unsafe in my own home. You said you'd protect me."

"You're still sitting here, aren't you?" Now he's acting smart.

She usually swoons over his confidence, but now it's just annoying.

Aliah rolls her eyes, then makes eye contact with him. "You really think it's her? I feel like there are eyes all over me. It's only gotten worse. Why would Brandee have anything to do with this?"

Harley glances around the parking lot, suddenly in a hurry to get her inside the hotel. "Let's go. We can finish this conversation inside."

He gets out, rounds the hood and is opening her door in a matter of seconds. He makes a grab for her arm, but she yanks it out of his grip and stomps off ahead of him. With his long strides, he keeps up with her rushed pace with ease.

In the lobby, they're greeted by a receptionist sitting at a computer desk. She is illuminated by a bluish light shining from her monitor, making her skin look even more pale than it already is.

"Good evening. Do you have reservations?" she asks them, ogling the filth covering their clothes, but making no comment on it.

"No," Harley answers gruffly. "Give us whatever room you got."

By the way he's acting, Aliah wonders what it is he's seen in the parking lot. They had stopped at his house to exchange his bike for an SUV, but he'd insisted there was no time for a change of clothes. Has someone followed them? She just wishes he would be honest with her.

The woman smiles at Aliah and thoughtfully poses her next question to her. "Are you looking for one bed or two, hun?"

"One," Harley answers.

"Two," Aliah insists at the same time.

Harley looks frustrated, but glances back at the woman, seemingly unprepared to argue about it at the moment. "Two."

It's really for the best. Aliah figures she's probably better protected without her silky thighs rubbing up against his hard muscular legs all night. She wouldn't be able to keep her hands off of him and he can't say no to her.

"Okay, then. Maybe I'll give you two another minute to discuss that." She turns to walk away, but Harley stops her.

"No. Just make it two. Please," he adds, making his tone sound no less urgent.

Aliah smirks. Harley's trying his hardest to remain pleasant, but both ladies can tell that it's forced.

The receptionist gets her fingers tapping away on her keyboard. "Uh, oh."

"Uh, oh? Why, uh oh?" Harley says.

"I really am sorry to say this, but we're all booked up for the queen rooms. There's only one room left this evening and it's the honeymoon suite." Her face takes on a pained expression, knowing how Aliah's going to react to that.

"That'll do," Harley answers, without turning to Aliah for her opinion.

That certainly isn't going to stop her from adding her two cents. "Whoa, wait. We are not staying in a honeymoon suite. Have you lost your mind?"

"Have you, Aliah? We've searched this City high and low. There isn't another room available for miles. We're staying here. So suck it up, buttercup."

The woman interrupts again and, by the look on her face, Aliah knows it isn't to deliver good news. "Unfortunately, this room only comes with one bed. Would you like me to send up a cot?"

"Is there a couch?" Harley barks, even less pleased with her now.

"Yes, sir. But it is no problem for me to send up a bed."

"The couch will do. Thank you." He slides his credit card toward her and she processes the transaction before handing him a key. He lifts the two black bags, one in each hand, and storms past Aliah to get onto the elevator. She puckers her lips and follows after him with a scowl plastered across her face.

Neither of them comment about the extravagant elevator or the decadent room when they enter it. In the instant that the door closes, he drops her bag to the floor with a thud and secures the room. He opens up the only closed door in the place besides the bathroom and scours it, to make sure the suite is clear. Lucky for her, he didn't find a boogie man under her bed.

Within a matter of seconds of his approval, Aliah hears water spraying behind the closed door.

Good, maybe that will get him to cool off.

While Harley showers, Aliah slips out the patio door, to check out the view from the Juliet balcony. The air is fresh and the night is quiet. The sky is decorated in a hazy collection of golden stars. She takes a deep breath when she hears the water stop. She waits for Harley to join her on the balcony, but he doesn't.

Deciding to be equally as rude, she makes a bee line for the bathroom. It's rather easy for her to slip past him unnoticed, with him pacing the living room and shouting into his cell phone. He's consumed with anger, and she's just happy not to be on the receiving end of it. The room is steamy and she locks that heat in before she removes her clothes.

Even with the water pounding against her head, she hears when Harley ends his call. She hollers out to him, to make sure he knows how it's going to be tonight. "The bed is mine! I called it," she informs him from the en suite bathroom.

After combing her fingers through her clean, wet hair, Aliah heads straight for the living room where she expects to find Harley on the couch. She denies herself the admission that she's looking for him, but he's nowhere to be found. She huffs, angered by the thought of him leaving her in this situation, and decides to call it an early night.

She retreats to the bedroom, closes the door and presses the lock so he can't try any funny business if he's feeling a little frisky later. When she spins around to approach the bed, she's faced with a minimally clothed man in an incredibly sexy pose, that seems to accentuate every agile muscle and highlight all of his tattoos.

A whimsical canopy hangs over the bed and Harley's lying inside it, like a tattooed present waiting to be unwrapped. She begins to wonder if she has died and gone to heaven. Maybe she's at home, asleep in her own bed, and she's only dreaming. Either of those scenarios would be too lucky for her. Her voice cracks when she speaks, giving away her not-so-secret delight.

"What do you think you're doing?"

"Just because you called it, doesn't mean you get to make all the rules." The slant of his lips only encourages her.

"Harley, I'm not kidding. Get out of my damn bed." She folds her arms over her breasts, which are covered only by a very small towel that refuses to cover both her chest and her thighs at once.

"Make me."

Using her powers of persuasion, she lightly parts the white, fluffy towel and lifts a knee onto the mattress, as it drops to the floor behind her. She slowly crawls toward him, leaving her resolve outside the canopy, as her legs slide over his thighs.

"What are *you* doing?" he asks, sounding very intrigued.

Even she doesn't know! She wants to be mad at him, but he looks so God-damned delicious.

"Claiming what's mine," she states, with a raspy breath. She means to claim the bed, and he knows this, but the electricity flashing between them blinds the particulars.

He taunts her as she inches closer to his lips. "Come and get it." He flashes her some teeth and she loves every quirk in his expression.

Though she wants to smack that sexy look off his face, the need to have him thrusting inside her wins out. She cups a hand around one of her breasts and swipes a thumb back and forth over a large aroused nipple to tease him. She only ends up turning herself on more.

His hand covers over her, as his gaze locks onto hers. "I'm waiting."

She watches every twitch of his lips. She wants to taste him, but it goes against everything she's promised herself. He reaches up for her face and cups her cheek to draw her closer. He leans in to kiss her and she makes to bury her face in his neck. He smells fresh and masculine, her desire only growing more impatient with her.

The pulse in his shorts isn't helping the matter, growing no less hard by her avoidance. He seems to take it more as a competition than a denial.

She reaches inside his briefs, glancing down as she does, pulling him out and wrapping her small hand around his large endowment. She wants to put that smooth thing in her mouth but she doesn't want to give him the impression that she wants to please him. She's still mad. Instead, she decides to take what she wants and please herself. She takes his full length in one slow descent. He groans, feeling how perfectly they are fitted for each other.

"So sweet," he growls, holding himself deep inside her, by clinging to her shapely hips. "Make-up sex has never felt this sweet."

Aliah covers his mouth with her hand and stifles a moan before explaining it to him. "This is not make-up sex. This is me taking what I want."

"You want me."

"I want sex," she corrects, manipulating him to move in and out of her.

"With me," he adds, not allowing her to fully immerse into her fantasy where all is good, there are no lies and loving him is okay.

She holds him deep inside her and squeezes onto him. "Just shut up; will you?"

The pressure alone has her insides twitching against his swelling cock. She squeezes onto him again. He feels so hard, and his groan is so strangled that she wonders if he's already going to blow. She wishes he will, so she can find her own relief, since his hesitation seems to keep her on the brink of ecstasy, without allowing her to find it.

Harley closes his lips and drives into her, slamming her away from reality. She moans wantonly, expressing how grateful she is for his efforts. He doesn't let up, tightening every muscle in his amazing body, holding himself there. When his finger brushes her pussy, she comes undone on top of him in a spiral of pleasure. His eyes are alight with satisfaction, as he follows seconds later, lifting upward from the magnitude of his orgasm.

After a breath is caught, Aliah opens her eyes. Harley snares her lazy gaze for an electric moment. She pulls away from him and rolls aside, pressing her eyes closed. Why does he always have to make it so personal? She feels her emotions churning, like a train chugging uphill. It's only a matter of time before she reaches the top and has nowhere left to go but crashing down.

Harley doesn't speak as he takes her hand and pulls her to the bathroom. They share a steamy hot shower that is completely functional. After smoothing the soap over his sweaty chest and between her thighs, he draws a finger up and down her spine. Harley kisses the part of her neck that becomes exposed when she rolls her head to the side.

There's something affectionate about this moment that Aliah refuses to admit. But letting Harley wash her, tenderly caressing her body out of affection rather than desire, has her head swimming. She wants to deny that she needs it, but it feels so right; much like their relationship, despite all of its setbacks.

Aliah turns her face into the water and gives it a good scrub. She opens her mouth and breathes, though fully submersed in the spray. When she opens her eyes, she notices the flesh wounds marring Harley's otherwise magnificent body. She makes to check the place where the bullet has grazed his side, but he jumps from her touch. He plays the tough guy, but she wants to see who's hiding beneath all that muscle and pride.

She leaves his war wounds alone and massages soap across his shoulders and down his back. Once they're both rinsed clean, Harley turns off the water and breaks the extended silence, as if he's just then been revived from a life-ending orgasm.

"That was unbelievable. I didn't realize I could cum like that without making a single move."

Aliah smirks, flaunting her beautifully naked form as she dries her hair with a bath towel. "Anything is possible with me, sweetheart."

Harley chuckles. "It sounds like you're stealing one of my lines."

"So you're feeding me lines, are you? What's next?" She doesn't mean for the conversation to turn serious, but he instantly closes the distance between them until they're but a breath away from each other.

If she closes her shocked lips, they'll be kissing his.

It looks like he has something important to say, but he freezes. An uncanny silence ensues. His eyes become glued to hers.

"Someone's here. Keep your mouth shut," he whispers.

He holds up a finger and listens some more, until the door handle to their suite jiggles quietly. His voice is low and raspy. "Follow me, and stay close. We're getting out of here."

He wraps himself with the towel and raises his gun as he

peers out of the bathroom door. He waves her forward and she immediately runs to the black bags he's packed for them. She forgoes panties and covers herself with a clean shirt and a pair of jeans with zippers slanting across the legs.

Harley reaches his bag, after a few quick strides, and stuffs some of her things into it, including their shoes, quietly kicking the rest of her things under the bed to rid the room of evidence from their visit.

He covers himself with a pair of jeans and high tails it out the balcony, after ushering Aliah out first. She tries not to notice the flex of his muscles as he helps her over the railing, but she can't, even in the dire circumstances. She jumps to the ground and stumbles backward when the bag lands next to her. Harley hurls himself over the edge of the railing, as a single blast shatters the glass door behind him.

"Run!" Harley shouts, as he covers her.

She races to his black SUV, as lights flash in the darkness around them. Rather than rounding the hood, Aliah opens the driver side door and dives into the passenger seat. Harley climbs in behind her and has them squealing out of the parking lot before she even has a chance to snap on her seatbelt.

They don't speak while they're on the road. Their salacious habits have obviously been getting them into trouble lately. They would be smart to keep each other's bodies off the menu from now on.

Aliah watches Harley pull out his phone and glance in his rear-view mirror. He doesn't ask for help, or look to her to explain what the hell is going on. She listens to him phone a friend. A few of the comments stick with her.

"I need a favor," he says at first.

After an extended silence on his end of the phone, he adds, "It's an emergency. Please?"

She hasn't exactly known Harley for long, but what she has noticed is that he's not one to beg. To hear him pleading makes her realize the severity of this situation. Aliah listens carefully and soon realizes it is a woman on the other end of the line. She strains to hear the woman's response.

"Well, if you're using your manners with me, it must be important. You know where the key is."

A flicker of jealousy shoots through Aliah's veins like a poisonous feed straight to her heart. She feels like a mute piece of candy, as she lets him drive her wherever he may. She has no idea where they're going and she has no idea what they're doing. She only wishes she could return to some semblance of normalcy.

If this situation, as it is, doesn't resolve itself soon, Aliah worries that there will not be a job for her back home when she returns.

Harley flashes a glance at Aliah, as he turns down a long gravel road that seems to go on forever before it takes a bend and trails perpendicular to the shore of the lake in a narrow, single lane. There are ditches on either side of them; ditches much too deep to drop off and survive.

On one side of the road, all you see is cornfields. The stalks are already battling her for height. The other side of the road is covered in brush, except for a random clearing to expose the beauty of the lake hiding behind it.

As Harley pulls up to the house at the end of the lane, he glances at her again, suddenly feeling the need to explain himself. She had been too scared to ask.

"A friend owes me a favor. This is her vacation home."

Her.

Aliah's jealousy doesn't fade. If anything, it hacks at her chest harder. She swallows her breath, trying not to feel the wariness seeping into her veins. A cold sweat sweeps across her entire body. Her limbs are limp, but she has to pull it together if she's going to stand her ground. She doesn't respond to him, but he keeps on talking.

"If someone has followed us, we will know it."

But there is no one coming up behind them and even if someone has, the sight of Harley's oversized shotgun will be enough to scare any man away. The yard is eerily silent, except for the waves crashing violently against the break wall and splattering everywhere.

Harley opens up the house and refuses her entry until he's searched the darkness for intruders. Then he orders her to come in and takes another survey of the yard surrounding the house. He secures the door and drops their things to the floor, now jammed into the one bag. He rummages through the cupboards looking for something edible and sighs. There's nothing. He turns to look at Aliah with raised brows.

"I have to go into town. There's nothing here."

"I'll come with you." She already feels a sharp tension in the air. She doesn't want to be alone.

"It's not safe. You'll stay here."

"I don't feel safe here, Harley. Please don't do this. Forget about the food for now. Just stay," she pleads.

"You're starving and dehydrated. I should have never invaded your privacy. You could have used the rest."

"Don't say that. If you hadn't joined me, there's no saying what could have happened back at the hotel." Her voice is now soft and helpless.

When he cups her face, she closes her eyes and he strokes her cheek with his thumb. "I promised I would keep you safe, right? No one will find you here. Will you stay? Please?"

As if he isn't already pushing all of her buttons, he adds, "For me?"

CHAPTER SEVENTEEN

Harley makes it to the grocery store in record time, but something nags at him the entire way there. Aliah had agreed to stay back, but her pleading had very nearly killed him. She needs food. There's no doubt about that. He feels responsible to keep her safe, but he can't bear to watch her starve.

Although he is certain she'll be safe at the beach house, he relies on his sharp instincts and only picks up the bare minimum. The late-night patrons are in his way and the cashier takes much too long, stopping to chat about stupid shit he obviously could care less about.

After he loads up his trunk, he checks his phone. Aliah hasn't tried to contact him. Figuring she isn't too interested in talking to him right now, he pulls out his laptop. Every time he's pulled out the thing, Aliah's gotten all fidgety and nervous. But there is some serious work that needs done, and he can't live another minute until he's got something.

He returns to the hotel parking lot to collect evidence, not expecting the gang of police officers to hassle him with questions when he gets there. He feeds them a story that he and his lady friend were out when the shooting took place and, lucky for him, the intruders had taken care of the security cameras to corroborate his fictional story.

Harley doesn't like the way Spencer Caldwell watches him, brooding from afar. He wonders if Caldwell too has a thing for Aliah. Focusing on the task at hand, Harley glances casually at the ground. Fresh tire tracks show that there were two vehicles there. One set looks bolder than the other. They look awfully familiar, but he doesn't tell the cops that.

He's certain the new set of tracks come from a GMC pickup truck. He's seen those very same tracks printed across his office parking lot over the past few years.

"Jillian."

Harley rushes back to his vehicle and makes a call to a buddy who works in a similar field. He asks him to look up his assistant at this ungodly hour to see if there's any way he can make the connection between her and Brandee Hawkins. Harley recalls the time Jillian first met Ms. Hawkins. Jillian knows the girl, there's no doubt about that. But he doesn't expect what he finds out, while sitting in the hotel parking lot.

There are no birth records in the name of Brandee Hawkins. Harley's always known the police have been monitoring Brandee, but he didn't know she is living under an alias. He opens the library's records online and searches the local high school's annual year books, dating back to when Aliah was attending there. Once he narrows the search, he scrolls through the pages for something to catch his attention. His eyes grow wide when he finds a single photo that puts it all together.

Without a doubt, this girl is a murderer. A quick Google search of Brandee's maiden name brings up horrendous results. Though never convicted, it is a fact that three of her boyfriends have strangely gone missing, only to be found murdered under mysterious circumstances shortly thereafter. It's all there in the newspaper articles. He reads one himself, as vomit pools in his throat.

He's been so wound up with his desire to claim Aliah that he's dropped the ball on this retainer. He always does a background check on his clients before taking on a case. But this one seemed so simple and Aliah was a case he didn't want to give up for extenuating circumstances.

He skims to the bottom of the article to find out the result of the heinous accusations. The families have all pointed fingers, but no one has been able to prove her guilt... And now she has an unhealthy obsession with Aliah.

Aliah!

This is all his fault. He's put her in danger and now he's left her all alone when she'd felt the threat and begged for nothing but his company. Even she felt the need to follow her hunch. She wanted him to stay; even while he was probably the last asshole she wanted to look at right then.

A bad feeling has him glancing at his phone a few more times, as he races back to their hideout. When he reaches a red light, he makes a grab for his phone. He dials up his voicemail to check the message that appears once he returns to an area with good service. Call display tells him the missed caller was Jillian.

Hey Harley. You've been busy, I suppose. You didn't make it in today. I'm kind of getting worried. I haven't checked your line for messages, but I know there are a few on there. You might want to check them when you have a minute. Anyways, I hope things are going okay and I hope to see you real soon.

Something about the change in her tone has him hanging up and dialing his office in an instant. He blasts through a red light and picks up speed, until he's driving like a maniac to get back to the beach house.

He skips past the first few messages. Two are from clients and one is an old one from Hannah. The next one has him reeling.

The woman's voice is disguised, and to the untrained ear it might have even sounded normal, but he knows better.

After the woman retraces his footsteps from the day, she gives him the threat he has been avoiding.

"Stay away from Aliah. That is a threat. If you don't, I will kill her myself. Oh, and *David*? Or Harley. Whatever name it is you're calling yourself today. Don't go to the police. I will know if you do, and it'll be like you're pulling that trigger yourself."

He tries to call Aliah, to warn her, but the landline is dead. He tries the spare phone he'd given her, but it goes straight to voicemail.

Why didn't she keep the cell on like I'd instructed her to?

As he speeds back to the beach house as fast as his

vehicle will carry him, he considers how much this unstable woman knows. She knows where he's been all day. He was careful to check all of their luggage and everything was clean. He recalls standing at the bar the other night, and placing his phone on the counter for all of one minute, while he tried to seduce Aliah.

When he slams on his brakes, his beast of an SUV slides down the gravel road. Before it even comes to a stop, he pries open his cell and nearly crashes when he focuses on the chip tagged onto it, for one second too long. It feels like someone has made a grab for his heart. The painful squeeze has him gasping for a breath.

He's been bugged, and no doubt tracked by his cell phone. He digs his foot into the gas pedal, but feels no comfort from the rev of his engine. He quickly pockets his SIM card and wheels the damn phone out his window, watching it break into a million pieces on the road behind him. Then he takes the corner on two tires, nearly rolling his high-end machine into a bottomless black ditch.

Aliah had better be okay, or he'll never forgive himself.

CHAPTER EIGHTEEN

Harley leaves her all alone. What was he thinking? There are men after them, and they have guns. All Aliah can think about is the lengths to which Harley has gone to bring her to safety and then he just takes off without her. *What the hell?*

She supposes she hadn't told him, and he couldn't possibly know, how scared she is. She likes to keep up a stony front, after all. But she is downright terrified and she wishes she'd had the guts to share that with Harley. Instead, now she finds herself swimming in her deranged thoughts, alone in this woman's beach house, who's likely Harley's ex-lover.

So now, not only is she worried for her life, but she's fuming with jealousy.

Aliah searches the flat surfaces for something – anything – to show Harley's involvement in this woman's life. She finds but one picture that says it all. At least he hadn't lied about one thing. He has a sister. One of the women in the picture looks like an older, more mature version of Hannah, with softer eyes and a deeper smile. But put her next to Harley, and you can see the resemblance.

Everything in the place screams femininity; from the softness of the drapes, to the blanket thrown across the sofa. It's well-kept and well-decorated, clearly a home of wealth. Why wouldn't he just tell her that it's his sister's place and save her the agony? Clueless, that man is.

Aliah, now satisfied that her jealousy is unwarranted, still cannot shake the eerie feeling in her blood. She had hoped finding her answer would put her mind at ease, but the hairs on the back of her neck still stand on end. She shrugs it off, and chalks it up to aftershock from the unexpected attack at the hotel.

Her stomach growls, while she notes her surroundings. It's a nice place. Quiet. But nice. Though the rumors seem to indicate that David H. Gates is a self-made millionaire, it is clear that he comes from a family of wealth.

Family. When Aliah starts to think about Harley's daughter, she gets a little worried. Don't get her wrong, she's always liked how she can just up and do whatever she wants as a single girl, but she's starting to understand what it's like to care about people other than herself.

She hurries to the bag of things Harley has left her with and digs out his phone. She searches the call log and finds the number she's looking for. She picks at her fingernails as she waits for the girl to answer her phone.

"Dad?" Hannah answers.

"No. It's me. Aliah."

"Oh, no. Now I know something's wrong, if he's given you his spare phone. What's going on?"

Aliah tries to clear the fear from her voice. "What do you mean? I was just calling to see how you're doing."

"You lie like a rug. No one abandons such a mint car with a teenager and takes off like that. My dad isn't that careless, though he might lead you to believe that. You'll be happy to hear that I locked your car up in my dad's garage."

"Thank you," Aliah says, stunned that she hasn't thought twice about the state of her most prized possession. When you're running for your life, possessions don't seem to have the same importance.

"Now tell me the truth. What kind of shit has my dad gotten into now?"

Aliah can't believe the mouth on this girl, but it makes her trust that she can handle the truth. "I don't know. I just know that it's bad. Like guns and knives bad." She hears Hannah's voice change.

Shit. She's just a kid. Maybe telling her that wasn't the brightest idea.

"I'm sorry. I shouldn't have said that."

"No. I need to know these things. My dad doesn't tell me shit. He treats me like a child. I need to know these things," she repeats. "I wouldn't have snuck out tonight without telling him if I'd known. Looks like tomorrow night's going to be a Twilight marathon for me."

Hannah sounds a little disappointed, but mostly because she'll have to sit through the marathon alone. It sounds like their conversation is over, but Aliah waits quietly to see if Hannah's already hung up the phone.

She takes a moment to glance at the clock. It's after two o'clock in the morning. She starts to feel guilty for dragging Hannah into this at such a ridiculous hour.

"Aliah?" Hannah asks, out of the silence.

"Yeah?"

"Thanks for being real with me. Please take care of my dad."

"Okay," Aliah answers, not knowing whether she can even do that.

"Promise?" Hannah asks.

Aliah licks her lips and swallows the lump from the back of her throat. "I promise."

When Aliah ends the call moments later, she feels significantly worse. Now she's made a promise that she's afraid she can't keep. Unlike Harley, Aliah doesn't lie. She is now going to make it her full time job to cover Harley's ass. She powers down his phone and peers outside. He doesn't appear from the shadows, like she's been dreaming of all night.

Her stomach growls again, and it sounds like it's going to start gobbling up the rest of her insides if she doesn't find something edible real soon. She slides open the back patio door and slips outside. The waves are loud and the wind is harsh. A storm seems to be brewing.

She scoops the hair out of her face and hurries down the steps to take a walk through the dying garden. It's the end of the season, but there are a couple of blobs of color that catch her eye. She has to get on her knees and squint just to see in the dark, but it's not until she's getting back up that her nerves catch up with her. A chill skips across her skin. Why hadn't she thought to bring a flashlight?

Aliah swiftly plucks a bright red pepper from a plant and hightails it inside.

Her thoughts start reeling, but she welcomes anything over the dose of anxiety that has just began to plague her. She still can't believe how she'd forgotten about her car. Her car! Her pride and joy. What else is she forgetting?

Whoa. She hasn't seen her massage therapist in weeks. *What is up with that?*

She certainly prefers Harley's type of massage over Michael's any day, but the fact that she's skipped the spa entirely has her shaking. She pops a slice of red pepper into her mouth and tosses the rest into the garbage. She can't eat. Not until Harley steps foot back in that door.

Aliah stands there silently for a moment and refocuses on the unfamiliar beach house, now eerily quiet. The tree branches cast shadows across the room and appear to be clawing at her with long scratchy nails and a black foggy night. The night seems to come alive around her. Every creek in the house has her glaring in its direction.

She can't manage anything better than a grimace. She decides a bath is what she needs to settle her shaky muscles and overactive imagination. She heads straight for the bathroom, locates a towel, then gives the door a shove until it clicks shut. It takes a second, but before she knows it, light is flooding the room.

Aliah checks the shelves and finds a small cylinder of bath oils there. She starts up the water, plugs the bottom of the tub and drops in a few pink balls of oil.

After placing a clean towel on the counter, she drops her clothes to the floor and slips inside of the small claw foot tub. She has to whip the curtain around it, to keep in the heat. After a few steady breaths, she finally feels herself relaxing, letting the steam calm her nerves and the hot water to work away her aches. She closes her eyes and slips beneath the water completely.

When she resurfaces, she thinks about the man who has saved her life on countless occasions in a matter of days. Harley can still make her smile. Just the image of him diving head first into a mud puddle has her mouth widening across her face. With a little added imagination, she pictures what would have happened if she wasn't completely mortified and he hadn't just been shot.

Aliah falls into a much needed slumber until Harley has her moaning in her dreams. She has no idea how much time has passed when her eyes suddenly flash open. She hears a thump in the next room over. She hadn't heard the door open, or Harley's imposing boot steps, so her nerves have officially sky-rocketed again.

Deciding to err on the side of caution, she escapes the tub and wraps herself in a towel without making to dry herself. The room has lost its steam and the water has cooled, so there's no telling how long she's been asleep; though the deep wrinkles on her fingers and toes suggest it was for a while.

When she inspects the door, she notices how it creeks open and remains held ajar, just a crack. She hears the front door click shut and a wave of air opens hers even further yet. She listens carefully, but she can't hear anything until heavy boots step slowly across the wooden floor.

Someone is in the house!

Biting a lip, she turns the door handle and closes the door, without pressing the lock. She doesn't want anyone to know that she's onto them. She rushes across the room, on tip toe, and is startled by her discovery. She covers her mouth to muffle her shriek.

Any thought of Harley being the person in the other room is immediately stifled by the greasy handprint pressed onto the other side of the window. Lucky for her the window was locked. There's no saying what might of happened if it hadn't been.

Aliah presses her lips together, trying to calm her trembling limbs, that shake partly from the cold but mostly because she's terrified for her life. She eases the window open, pausing half way to take a breath and listen whether anyone has heard her. Satisfied that no one has, she peers out the window, praying that she doesn't have any company.

The back yard is dark, but there's no one there. She looks down. The ground has got to be a good ten feet from where she is, and there's a good sized rose bush decorating the house beneath her. There's a trellis on the wall, a mere five feet away, and it has crushed roses and broken stems hanging from it. That only confirms her theory that the man inside the house didn't enter under lawful circumstances.

This is the only way out.

Aliah lifts herself into the smallish window and sits on the sill. She decides that taking a leap feet-first would be smart, since she doesn't think hurdling herself at the thorny trellis is much of an improvement. But when the bathroom door swings open, her plans are made for her.

A lanky man is standing there, with a snarky smile on his face. He appears to take pleasure in the fact that he's found her naked beneath her parted towel. He makes a dash toward her, and Aliah takes a dive head-first out the window.

She crashes into the bushes, soiling her now bloody hands and rolling onto her back. Her towel does little to save her flesh from the prickly thorns. She cries out as she crawls away from the house and takes the millisecond to retrieve her towel from the shrubs.

She considers going to the lake, but the dark murky waters don't look very inviting. She huffs on the air that's rushing into her lungs and forces it back out, to the beat of her heart. She doesn't have time to think on it. The man follows her out the window.

What a dumb ass.

Hoping he's there alone, she runs around the house, clutching the towel in a bloody palm. His partner is standing on the doorstep. She hangs onto the corner of the house, calculating how much time she needs to get to the vehicle left parked in the driveway. She is closer to it than him. He is a fatty, but she is barefoot.

She hikes up her towel and clutches it to her chest, knowing that if she worries about it for one second too long, it could be the death of her.

Aliah doesn't need told what they want. Clearly it's her. And everything she has seems to be free agent at the moment. She drops the towel and takes a deep breath, as the scrawny goon reaches out for her.

She takes off in a sprint toward the car, completely naked. The guy standing at the doorstep, just watches for a second, enjoying the view, as her breasts bounce freely. Then he quickly snaps out of it, when he realizes that she's making a run for their car.

Aliah gets in the car and hits the lock, forgetting about one important thing. A key. The ignition is empty, so she flaps down the visor to look for one. Papers fall onto her uncovered lap, but there's no key. The skinny guy starts knocking on the window and hollering at her. The other guy rounds the car and stares at her from the passenger window.

"Come on, lady. We aren't going to hurt you."

"Yeah," the skinny one agrees, with a cackling laugh that no one trusts. "We aren't going to hurt you." He waggles a long, slimy tongue at her. "The boss lady wants to do that."

With a pained look on her face, she whips open the glove box.

Please... please be in here.

Again, more papers. And whoa! A gun. She takes it and immediately releases the safety. Both of the men jump back from the car when she checks to see whether it's loaded.

"You left the gun loaded? You dumbass!" the big guy shouts.

"At least she hasn't found the key."

Aliah glances out at the skinny guy and smiles. His eyes show his fear. He's in trouble now. He'll get a beating later for sure. But she doesn't care about him. She still has to find the damn key if she's going to save herself from the wrath of fat-ass and slimy tongue.

The car is surprisingly clean, but she doesn't waste time thinking about it. She opens the compartment between the two seats and instantly finds what she's looking for. She digs out the big key and drives it into the ignition. The expensive car purrs to life.

"You're not going anywhere, doll," the big guy shouts, as he pulls out a handgun and points it right at her.

The dumb one manages to stop him from pulling the trigger. It gives her the second she needs to slam the car into reverse.

"But she said she wants her alive!"

Aliah puts the pedal to the metal, shooting stones at the two men standing there. She thinks she's home free, as she cranks the wheel and whips the car around, until it's facing the open road. She starts hollering in triumph as she heads forward again, but screams when the back window shatters from a bullet. It's hard to drive when you're ducking, but the bullets continue to fly.

Still terrified, long after she's out of range to be hit, she stays hunched in the front seat, until she sees headlights approaching. It could be Harley! It could also be backup coming to murder her good this time.

She reaches for the gun, with tears in her eyes, and releases the steering wheel to cock it. The SUV that's coming looks like Harley's, but her eyes are too watery to tell for sure. She squints her eyes and slams her breaks, willing to take the chance. She can't let Harley walk in on an attack.

As the vehicle passes, its brake lights instantly flash red. She jumps out of the car and points the gun directly at the driver's door. Harley flies out of the vehicle and sprints to her side. Aliah's crying when he rips the gun out of her hand and drops the mag of bullets into his pocket.

"It was loaded," she gasps. "They were trying to kill me. I thought they would get you too."

He pulls her into his arms, crushes her against his chest and kisses her forehead. "You take the SUV. I'll take care of this one."

"I'm not leaving you again." She's putting her foot down this time.

"That's good. I need you to follow me."

She nods and turns to run for his SUV, knowing that time is of the essence.

"Aliah?"

She turns back to him and glances at him with wide, wet eyes. "Yeah?"

"Where are your clothes?"

"Oh my God!" she shouts, just then realizing that she is stark naked. She covers her breasts and crosses her thighs, but it doesn't help the exposed feeling she suffers from.

Harley peels off his shirt and pulls it over her head. It's big enough to cover her ass, and that will have to do.

"My jacket's in the back seat if you're cold." He drops a kiss on her lips and stares right through her, with his thumb hanging onto her chin. "If they did anything to hurt you, I'll kill them."

"I'm okay," she admits, though her voice defies her. It's shaky and soft and breathy.

He kisses her again, and she lets him. She's too shaken to fight his chaste acts of affection. "Can you pop the trunk for me?"

When he paces around the car and leaves her standing there, she shivers. Then she dutifully crawls back into the car, pulls open the glove box and pops open the trunk. She slides back out of the driver's door, and when she turns around is slammed with the sexiest image of Harley holding a machine gun. His gaze is deathly and he's surrounded by night. Every muscle in his body looks tense, sweat glistening over his large arms and across his firm chest.

"You say you're alright, but these guns aren't for a small time investigation. Brandee's hired a fucking hitman."

The look on his face is puckered, like he's just barely hanging onto his last shred of willpower to not go back and kill those two guys with their own weapons.

"No. The guy said I shouldn't be killed."

She says it fast – too fast. She's afraid it might be the last straw that will send Harley over the edge.

To her surprise, Harley sighs and lowers the loaded gun to his side. "Let's go. We'd better get out of here."

Harley lifts his trunk and hides the machine gun under a heavy blanket, together with a few smaller weapons he finds in the car. She doesn't ask any questions.

He walks her to the driver's side door of his SUV and helps her up into the seat. "You stay right behind me, you hear? Right on my ass. I don't care what you have to do. You understand?"

She nods and he kisses her again. She closes her eyes, unable to stop the onslaught of relief, even in the circumstances. She has never found such comfort in a kiss, but the touch of his lips gives her a false sense of security.

"Let's move, before someone else comes out this way." He states it like an order, but she can't help herself.

"Like, your friend maybe? The one who lives on the beach?"

"You mean my sister's girlfriend? She won't be coming out here for a while. It's only a vacation home. I'll have her place fixed up before she ever knows that anything's happened." He grabs onto Aliah's chin and presses a kiss against her lips. Then he hurries to the running car.

She closes the door to his SUV and snaps on her seatbelt. It takes a four point turn to get the beast turned in the other direction down such a narrow road, but she isn't taking any chances of putting it into the ditches, that line either side of the road. The car in front of her doesn't move until she's inches from rear-ending it. Then Harley steps on the gas, knowing that she can handle a little speed.

Aliah follows him, having no clue what he's thinking. A few minutes pass before more distance is put between them. She can't seem to keep up. Then they reach the end of the gravel road, where Harley slams his breaks and veers right. He opens the passenger window and indicates that she is not to follow him, with a vicious point of his finger.

She watches the car tires spin and then gasps when Harley dives out of the driver's side door. Aliah's car now barely moves, but she slams her breaks, kicking up dust not far from where she has just watched her man expel himself from a moving vehicle. Are her eyes working right? *Is that man crazy?*

The car heads downhill, speeding toward the cliff. When she comes to a full stop, she watches the car climb over the edge of the bank and disappear down the bluff. A few seconds pass and a horrid feeling creeps its way into her gut.

"Come on, Harley. Where the hell are you?"

He needs to be okay right now. She doesn't know what she'll do if he doesn't make it out of this alive.

Suddenly, Harley appears from the forest looking like a dark angel. He's gazing directly at her, dimly lit by the headlights and surrounded by a cloak of darkness.

He opens the driver's door and she quickly shoves over to let him take charge. He has them flying out of there and far away, without either of them feeling it necessary for words. His hand is gripped around hers like she is his lifeline, when really he is the only thing keeping her from the edge. If it weren't for him, she would have jumped already.

CHAPTER NINETEEN

It feels odd being in her own home again. It has been trashed and everything that she has appears to be torn apart or missing. Harley doesn't think they'll come looking for them back there for a while, and she trusts his judgment.

They bathe together, but it's completely out of necessity. She doesn't want to be alone. He washes her and she rests against his chest, but their touch is not provocative or sexual in any way. She seems as upset with herself as he is with himself. She lets the tears flow, thinking he can't see them mingling with the spray of water. But it's like a stream of red from her eyes, spiking his adrenaline and making his alpha core flood with anger. Though he tries to hide it, there's no more hiding from her.

After towel drying her hair, Aliah slides onto the bed next to where he has stretched out his muscular frame. She smiles, when she notices how he takes up the whole damn thing. Her bed is not nearly big enough for the two of them. She has never found a good use for a queen sized bed in the past.

She outright giggles, and that seems to capture Harley's undivided attention.

"What are you laughing at?" He looks amazed by the fact that she is able to laugh after what she has been through.

She was nearly killed.

"You. You look like the Big Bad Wolf."

He is both too tired and too troubled to follow up with her in an instant. But then she winks at him and it seems to draw out the molten lava from his veins.

He lets out a smile of his own and leans over her, trapping her beneath him. "Did you just call me hairy?"

"Maybe. It looks like you haven't shaved in a few days. It's okay though. I think a little hair on you is incredibly sexy." She draws her hand over the soft hair covering his chest.

Harley smirks. "It's funny. Even when you're being a controlling witch, I'm still attracted to you."

"Oh, Harley. You're such a sweetheart," she teases playfully.

He locks onto her wrist, and draws her hand to his pants. "This is no joke."

She gasps for a breath when he presses her hand against his oversized erection. Then she takes a gulp in anticipation of what he might do next. He's always surprising her with the magnitude of his desire. He wouldn't have it any other way.

He releases her hand, but only long enough to pull her flat against him. Then he takes back her hand and slides it in between them, until she's massaging both of them at once. Even though it's her fingers touching him, the knowledge that it's his guidance and pressure is a heady cocktail. She lets him control the pace. He loves when she gives in to him.

"Get naked," he says.

And though Aliah nearly belts out laughing, she saves it when she feels the swell of that monstrous thing against her. She rolls off the bed and, by the time she loses her clothes, she finds him lying there, wearing nothing but a pair of super short fitted boxers that cling to a pair of massive thighs.

As she drops her own panties, the last scrap of fabric from her body, she notices that his boxers can't even contain his length, the smooth head peeking out the top of the black elastic band. She swallows again, her mouth feeling suddenly dry.

She has to taste him.

He smiles, and his eyes connect with hers, but when he pulls down those underwear, she can't remove her eyes from *it*. It springs free, launching itself from his body.

"Come and get it," he says, the anticipation only growing between them as they take in each other's naked bodies.

She climbs onto the foot of the bed, crawls over him and slides her hands over a rock hard body. She traces the path of her hands with her tongue, discovering every solid inch of his chest and torso. When her hand grabs onto his steely length, she shudders from the sheer size of the thing. She slowly strokes him from the head to the base, with a twist of her hand. Harley groans and licks at his bottom lip.

"You like that?" she asks, with a smile.

He doesn't open his eyes, but he answers with a sinful smile, patiently waiting for her to continue with the sensual assault. Aliah gladly continues and drags her tongue across his body, until her mouth is only a few teasing inches from his cock.

She gives him a gentle twist again, as a pair of soft full lips close around the head. She slides her mouth down the length of him, until he's puncturing the back of her throat and groaning with pleasure. Then she draws her mouth back to the top. Her lips makes a loud kissing sound when she sucks on the end of it. Every time she does, Harley groans.

He clearly likes that. And apparently the louder the better.

"Do that again," he begs.

His pleading only encourages her, as she takes him deep into her mouth again. This time, she finds his fingers lacing into her hair and holding her where he likes it most. Regaining control, she moves her mouth up and down, switching between an airless suck and a lick of his shaft. She bobs her head up and down with his hand as her guide. She brings him close to the edge, but she knows he's not ready to go there just yet.

Harley releases her hair as she repeatedly kisses his body. She crawls over top of him, sitting on a pair of strong, large thighs. He cups her breasts, and squeezes them, his eyes flickering with a want so sexy she can barely contain her cheer. Then he lifts his legs to bump her higher, making his point with body language.

She smiles and rips open the small packet he hands to

her, then rolls the condom over his magnificent cock. She wraps her small hand around him and squeezes. When she slowly pumps her hand up and down, his hand comes down and stops her.

"Drop it," he groans. "I want you on there before I blow my load."

He keeps his fingers pinned at the base of his cock, waiting for her to impale herself. His other hand reaches out to find her wetness and smoothes up and down a few times before spreading her open. She lifts herself onto her knees and nudges at where he wants to be.

"Do it," he groans, as she eases onto his head. He urges her forward, but she doesn't give in.

"More," he begs, but she only eases him back out, toying with both of their sanities.

With each penetration, she grants him deeper access, until he is buried as deep as he can go. She settles down on top of him and slowly rolls her hips, gyrating against him and stimulating herself immensely in the process. He grips onto her hips, but allows her to continue to control the speed, a slow, sensual assault that drives their arousal to new heights.

The length of his cock becomes close to unbearable for her to accept so deeply, causing Aliah to lean forward to catch her bearings. Even after she's stopped the motion, Harley's hardness continues to stoke the fire. She begins to move again, a longer stroke, but not much faster than before.

"Aw, fuck," he moans, telling her that he likes it.

She maintains the excruciating pace, as he senses her orgasm mounting. Her speed hastens as she strives to hit the right spot. She mounts higher and higher, until her shaking arms can't hold her up any longer. She crashes on top of him prematurely, but he continues to spike her, taking her to the verge of epiphany.

Her eyes are only partially open, so he nudges her cheek, until she's staring him right in the eye. She's ready to cry out, but he can tell she doesn't want her orgasm to send him over the edge until he's ready for it. Unable to take any more of it, he flips her over and buries her into the bed. She grits her teeth together as his lips close in on hers. She turns her head, pulling her mouth away from his. He catches her cheek in his hand and holds it there, as he stops all motion from his hips.

That gets her attention.

"No," she screams, as he cuts off her climax. She's feeling so confused, wanting him to take her there.

"Kiss me," he demands, giving her a little pressure. But not quite enough.

"No," she gasps, needing to feel him move inside her. She struggles beneath him for motion, but he doesn't allow it.

"Kiss me," he orders again.

Without giving her the option, he takes her mouth against his, and knots a hand in her hair, just like the first time they'd ever kissed.

Her mouth softens against his, as he pumps inside her, giving her the pleasure she has been working for. As her muscles tighten and spasm around him, he stabs her again and finds his own release. She has given him a kiss, but it is half hearted. That clearly isn't enough for him.

Even after they both have finished, he holds her mouth against his and spikes her with his warm tongue. He kisses her. He makes love to her mouth. But all he finds on the other end is cold, hard lips.

He sighs, sounding defeated. But he doesn't give up that easily. "Kiss me, God damn it! I just want to kiss you. Is that too much to ask?"

It is amazing how he invokes such passion and depth in his tone. Though whispered, Aliah feels like she has been struck by the baritone sound. She closes her eyes and allows herself to feel for what seems like the first time since forever.

She lifts her lips, until they melt against his. But he doesn't let her in. She works her mouth over his, and tugs on his lower lip until he smiles. She needs him to know that she has feelings for him; that it's more than just the sex for her, no matter how scary that may seem.

He suddenly regains his erection and he allows her to sweep her tongue into his mouth, but now he is the hesitant one. She doesn't stop kissing him and he finally joins in for a passionate kiss that threatens her footing, as she elevates beyond cloud nine.

She kisses him for a long while, showing him how much she feels for him, until his cock is throbbing and twitching for round two. When she finally pulls away from his mouth, he instantly pins her with a breathtaking smile.

"You see? That is called love." Then he pauses, before stabbing back inside of her. "This is called sex."

He fucks her so hard and fast, that she is screaming out, stuck somewhere between pleasure and pain. He presses her ankles forward until they're resting beside her head, then he continues to pump into her at a ravenous pace, skin slapping, mouths gaping, curses ringing through the night. When he is done, he rolls aside, flings the overused condom into the wastebasket and passes out.

For a change, Aliah falls asleep smiling.

CHAPTER TWENTY

After scanning the perimeter of Aliah's yard, Harley eases up a little and takes a deep breath of early morning air. The sun is warm and the neighborhood is quiet. There doesn't appear to be anyone watching them.

He has a beautiful woman inside, passed out from contentment. He forgets about the investigation for just a minute. Life can't get much better than this. Then he returns inside and is reminded that the thieves have destroyed Aliah's home. He tidies the living room as best he can and fills another trash bag with broken furniture that is beyond repair. He doesn't want her to wake to such a mess and, though he tries to be quiet, he makes a lot of noise.

Harley is shocked by what that woman can sleep through. Smiling, he makes his way back to the bedroom. He removes his jacket first, then slowly undoes his shirt, one button at a time. When he gets the last one free, his shirt flags open and Aliah's mouth curls up in a smile.

"You're awake."

She gapes at him through squinted eyes. "I thought you'd left."

"Do you want me to leave?"

She's afraid to answer that question. She *doesn't* want him to. Ever. That's what scares her most.

It's like he's listening in on her innermost thoughts. "It's okay to love."

Why does he have to bring that up now?

She immediately replaces her smile with a frown. "Leave it alone."

"It is, Aliah. It doesn't have to hurt."

"Easy for you to say. Your boyfriend didn't cheat on you with another woman, and then choose her when she gave birth to their love child."

Harley's eyebrows pop up and stay up there.

"Oh, wait. There's more," she adds, as if he isn't already shell shocked by her sudden outburst. "I work with the witch, and guess what? It's twins!"

"Wow."

That's all he has to say?

"Tell me about it. Could it have been any worse?"

"Yes."

Aliah rolls her eyes. "That was a rhetorical question."

Harley's face remains serious. "It could have been worse." When he doesn't elaborate, she considers whether she's prepared to hear his story.

"Tell me then."

When he sighs, she wonders whether he's actually going to tell her. Then he gazes into her eyes. "You could have been the one with a loveless family. Bear a child who doesn't even know her father's name until she's forced to move in with him after your lonely death. You lie on your death bed knowing the man doesn't want her, because he'd abandoned you when you needed him most and never looked back."

"Jeesh. Yeah. That is worse."

"That's me, Aliah. That's what I've done to my family. It's no wonder you don't want me." He turns his head to the floor and closes his eyes. "You're smart to guard your heart from me. I take what I want without looking back."

"You don't mean that."

Harley's gaze scalds her, as the heat radiates from his skin and glimmers in his eyes. "I knocked up my girlfriend when I was young. She was a year younger than me. Sixteen."

"Oh."

"Exactly." He sighs, but finds the strength to continue. "Her family disowned her when she decided to keep the baby. So did I. We were both so young. She was my first."

"You knocked her up on your first try?"

Harley chuckles. "You have confidence in my skill." Then he outright laughs. "No. It wasn't my first try." He scrubs at his face and looks Aliah in the eye. "But it was just plain stupid of me. It was an accidental pregnancy. Neither of us were ready to have a baby, but she shouldn't have had to go through that alone. Unfortunately, I didn't hang around to regret it. Now I'll spend a lifetime making up for it."

"You left her?" Aliah chews on her lip anxiously. She wonders how he still feels about *her*.

"In the worst kind of way. I was a coward."

"I don't understand."

"I didn't love *her*." Their gazes lock and a breath catches in Aliah's throat from the force of the meaning in that look. "Even after our daughter was born, I refused to see her. I left her all of my savings from working two part-time jobs and then I enlisted in the army."

"What happened to Hannah's mother?" Aliah just has to know; the curiosity pecks away at her insides.

"While I was dicking around on the other side of the world, she was over here fighting for her life. After I served my time, I came back to check up on her and to apologize, but I was too late."

"What do you mean, *too late*?"

"She died." Harley seems a little choked up, so he clears his throat. "I'm a rotten person. Hannah was dealt a raw deal. Her mother became terminally ill and her father was M.I.A. She had no one. Her grandparents refused to come to her rescue and my sister was too young to get involved. Hannah deserves a better father and you deserve a better man. Maybe I'm just not cut out for the job."

"Last I checked, *my man* didn't come with a job description. But that can be arranged," she teases, trying to lighten the situation.

Harley finally smiles, and it eases the tension squeezing at her heart.

She thinks better than to delve any deeper into his past, but she just has to know. "How did you get your daughter back?"

"That's the funny thing. I didn't plan to get her back. But

I just had to know that she was okay. When I finally found her, and I saw Hannah for the first time, all that changed. I couldn't leave her in the foster system; not when she is my blood."

Aliah rests her hand on top of his, to show she understands. She brushes her thumb over the veins in his hand and smiles into his eyes. "You're not all bad."

He nods, but it's not to agree. It's clear he's done with his story and she worries when he finally reconnects with her eyes.

"Why do you find it so hard to love?"

Aliah tries to act like that question hasn't thrown her for a loop, but she's dizzy like she's just been spinning on a merry-go-round. "Who said I don't know how to love?"

"I didn't say you don't *know* how. I said that you find it hard."

"No, I don't," she snaps. "Loving you has been much too easy." Aliah slaps her hand over her mouth, choking on a strangled cry.

Harley smiles, taking a lot of pride in her response. "Does it really kill you that much to admit it out loud?"

Her hand slips to the floor and he collects it in his. She gulps, not one hundred percent sure that she's ready to repeat it.

"Tell me. What happened to you?"

Aliah sighs, but decides it's about time she get it off her chest. She can't seem to face him though, so she looks away. He squeezes her hand ever so slightly, and it gives her the push she needs to admit it.

"The day those babies were born was the day I officially retreated from the idea of a relationship. I was ruined. Jealous. Callous. Even I hated being around me. I told myself... No man, means no problems. No kids, means no stretch marks. And no love, means no heart break. The plan *was* foolproof."

"*Was?*"

She tries to hide the terror in her eyes, when he catches the slip of her tongue that describes exactly how she feels without a need for further explanation.

He's blown her plan out of the water.

She swallows, but it does nothing to retrieve the ball of cotton from her throat. Aliah licks at her lips, and that will have to do. "I only wish I could find a man to hold up his end of the bargain. But they always press for more."

"They?" he asks.

"You."

Harley's done beating around the bush. "Why won't you kiss me? I want to understand."

Aliah pauses, drumming up the courage to tell him how she truly feels. She awkwardly clears her throat, but he turns her chin toward him.

"Why won't you kiss me?" he repeats, his lips as soft as his eyes.

"Because I can't," she whispers.

"But you can, Aliah. It hurts me to know that you don't want to feel my lips moving against yours. It's the most intimate way to show someone you..." He's almost said it, but he fills the blank with the next best thing. "...care about them."

Aliah gulps, knowing exactly what he was going to say. It is too soon to be throwing around that four letter word. Aliah starts back stepping, not knowing any other way to escape the feelings exploding from her body.

"Maybe we've taken this too far already." She turns and walks away.

"That's B.S. I know you love me. Don't say it. Fine. But don't stand there and act like you didn't know it was coming to this."

Even though she has put a lot of distance between them, it feels as though she's run away from her heart; having left it clutched in his hands. Harley's voice is no less painful, but she can't possibly respond to that.

"I might as well come clean, while we're pouring our hearts out," he adds. "I'm an investigator. I investigate people. I was hired to look into you."

There it is – the lie that has been tagging along this entire time.

She can't even think of the words to say and she doesn't have to, because Harley keeps talking.

"The night we met was completely concocted to see if I could earn your trust. I attracted your eye. I ignored you, knowing it would only gain your interest. Then I kissed you."

I'm not going to cry.

"The guns," she recalls out loud, mostly to herself. *That explains that.* "The number you gave me?"

"My cell. The message is depersonalized."

She narrows her eyes at him, to give him her full reaction. "You fucking prick."

He lifts a hand, in an attempt to explain. "I decided to turn in your case. I didn't give her any info on you. Except that I thought you were innocent."

Aliah hears what he's saying but she refuses to believe another word from that filthy, lying, no-good mouth. "Was that before or after you fucked me with your tongue?"

"Before... After..." He's clearly torn. "I honestly don't know anymore."

"You don't know? Or you don't have the balls to admit that you duped me? You tricked me and you fucked me, like a recycled piece of trash. You stole my information, and you took advantage of me after I let my guard down." She brings her hand to her forehead and shakes it side to side. "Stupid, stupid girl."

"You were always willing." His words only make it hurt that much more.

"Don't use that sexy voice on me." She huffs. "I trusted you." And his deceit only seems to cast a shadow over everything he's ever said or done.

Harley takes a deep breath. "I know. And I'm sorry. But you weren't exactly forthcoming about your work."

"I guess I was right to trust my instincts. I knew something wasn't quite right about you."

He smirks, trying to lighten up the conversation. "I'm not a serial killer."

She doesn't respond. It's like he's stuffed her heart back in her chest cavity, but he's already stabbed what is left of it, leaving the other half flagging from its mass.

He can see that she's not handling this very well. "You continued to see me after you learned about my investigation into Cavanagh."

Is that supposed to make it all okay?

She shakes her head and stares up at the ceiling. "Gah!" *Why is she making excuses for him?* "The sex is good," she admits.

She makes him smile. Even in this situation. "That is true."

"Just because I'm educated, doesn't mean I'm all that smart."

He tilts his head, not for one second buying into what she's selling. He doesn't' want her to go. "Stay with me."

Oh, she's tempted. So she can use his face as a punching bag. "You must think I'm really stupid." A tear slips down her cheek, as she rushes out her front door and drops into the driver's seat of her car. She admits she doesn't want Harley to follow her, but she's surprised when he doesn't.

CHAPTER TWENTY ONE

Four long weeks later.

Harley stumbles into the living room, where Hannah's on her tablet watching her favorite music videos on YouTube.

"Hannah, I think we need to talk."

She acts like she hasn't heard him, when he knows that she has.

"Hannah!" The force of his voice catches Hannah's attention in an instant.

"Really, dad? Do we have to?" she moans, like a typical teenager.

"Quit with that. It's important, okay?"

Hannah flops back onto the sofa and kicks up her feet, making herself comfortable. Does she really think this is going to take that long?

"I just wanted to ask how things have been going." Harley struggles to say the right thing.

Hannah shrugs her shoulders. She doesn't even give a peep.

"Nothing, Hannah? Work with me here, please. I'm trying."

She props herself up on her elbows and glances at him. Her facial expression changes, when she realizes that he's being serious. "You're going to have to think of a better question, unless you want my one word answer."

Now she's got him curious. "What's the one word?"

She smiles, loving how he can't escape his child-like inquisitiveness. "Good."

Harley's smile grows equally as fast. "That's good."

"Okay, dad. I get it. You want to talk about Aliah. You don't have to beat around the bush. I know you like her. Is that all?"

He can't even keep the stunned expression from his face.

He hadn't realized Hannah has been paying that close of attention to him. Apparently she has.

"I know a lot has changed in a pretty short period of time. These past few weeks I've been around a lot more than I used to be. Aliah had been taking away my evenings and stealing most of our weekends together. How does that make you feel?"

"How does that make you feel?" she mocks, in her best tight-wad psychiatrist voice. After giggling, she answers him. "It's okay, dad. I'm happy for you. You should do what makes *you* happy."

"You make me happy," he admits, wanting to make sure she knows that.

"Yeah, but that's not the only kind of happy I'm talking about. You've been stodgy and miserable without Aliah in your life. I like Aliah. I'm glad she's your first."

"My first?"

Hannah smiles really big. "The first girl you've brought home to me. I feel like I have a new girlfriend, or something. She's really cool."

Harley shakes his head. "I cannot believe it," he pauses, thoughtfully. "Thank you."

Hannah swings her feet to the floor. "You hardly need to be thanking me. I should be thanking her. You were in such a good mood when you two were hanging out and it's amazing what Aliah has done for my social life."

"Is that right?"

"Yes. Aliah might appear all hard and cruel on the outside, but I think she's like a Cadbury egg. She's sweet."

He wants to agree with her, but he doesn't dare with the lewd comparisons he wants to make. Harley clears his voice, growing uncomfortable in his own head.

"Like, when we were chatting the other night..." Hannah starts.

"You were chatting with Aliah?"

"Yeah. Just because you dumped her, doesn't mean we can't still be friends."

Harley mumbles. "I never dumped her. She ran from

me."

"As I was saying!" Hannah interrupts dramatically. "When we were chatting, your name came up."

Harley closes his eyes and keeps them squeezed shut. "Did the conversation involve Aliah's fists and my face?"

"Ha ha, dad. That's none of your business. But I did tell her that she shouldn't take you so seriously. You get like this all the time when you get into an investigation. You'll lie, cheat and steal to get to the bottom of it. But I also told her that if you said that you love her then she should believe it, because that's the one thing I know for a fact that you would never lie about."

Harley reopens his eyes to connect with his daughter. "You said that?"

She looks so grown up right now. "I did."

"Thank you."

Hannah just smiles through the thoughtful silence. "I've been working on her for you. I think she's ready to see you again. I think you should make your move already. That is, if you still want her."

Hah! Dumb question. But not something he's likely ever to discuss with Hannah.

"I'm going out tonight. Is everything okay here then?"

"Yes, dad. Everything's fine. Go. Get your girl back." She smiles at him and his heart clenches in his chest.

He can't believe she's taking this so well. "You're sure you're okay with me seeing this girl."

"Do you like her?" Hannah asks frankly.

He tilts his head to the side, suddenly uncomfortable sharing his emotions by voice. He starts to mumble, but he can't lie to his daughter. "I like her a lot."

"Then go."

"I want you to be happy though."

"If you're happy, I'm happy." Hannah's voice tightens up and she swallows before making her next statement. "Mom isn't coming back. I know you didn't love her. It's okay. I understand. She explained it to me a long time ago."

"You were only little."

"Yeah, but her diary doesn't lie."

"I should have never given that to you."

"I'm glad you did."

Harley gathers his daughter in his arms and they share a moment of forgiveness. He wants to explore this conversation further, but he can see that Hannah has already made peace with it.

"Here goes nothing."

Hannah smiles and gives him a shove. "Good luck."

"Thanks. I have a feeling I'm going to need it."

Harley leaves the room and plucks his keys from his pants pocket. He kicks his bike off its stand and settles on the seat as it rumbles to life beneath him. If Hannah thinks he stands a chance at reconciliation with Aliah, then he has to give it a good shot. He only has one chance left. He's not going to mess it up this time.

After running a few quick errands, to procrastinate, Harley pulls up to Aliah's short paved driveway. He feels his palms growing sweaty and loses his nerve. David H. Gates *never* loses his nerve. But he still finds himself pulling back on the accelerator, shooting himself down the road in a flurry of speed. He only hopes she hasn't caught a glimpse of his embarrassing attempt, as he passes by her house.

He rounds the corner, but knows he has to do this. Swallowing his nerve, he takes his final approach. He forgets about thinking altogether, as he marches up to her front door. The doorbell is right there, but he decides to put his fisted hand to the door instead.

She appears in the doorway instantly, like she's been waiting for him to arrive.

"What?" She peers around the door, as if he's an annoying solicitor and she can't be bothered to open it up for him.

He sighs, disappointed by her reception. "I need to make things right, Ally. Can I come in?"

"No."

"Will you come out with me?" His voice pleads his case rather effectively.

"I really shouldn't." But she looks like she might actually say yes.

"I'd like to take you somewhere." He raises his eyebrows to her in apology.

"Why? So you can get me alone and strangle me with your charm?"

"Yes, Aliah. That's it, exactly. Now, do you have a blanket? And grab a jacket. We're taking my bike."

He turns away before she can tell him no. It's a beautiful sunny afternoon made even more memorable when Aliah appears in the doorway behind him with a blanket tucked under her arm. The early autumn breeze sends her dark hair passing over her face. He watches the way she pulls a hair from that mouth and smiles. He still can't believe she's said yes.

He silently follows her to the motorcycle and pulls on his helmet. He starts it up, as she slips behind him. She rests her forehead on his shoulder, making him wonder if she knows how wretched he still feels. He's sure she feels awful too, but he doesn't breathe a word of it. He's just happy to have her next to him.

Harley has a destination in mind, but he takes the scenic route, steering them where he wants to go. They take an extended cruise, with her clutched around him, until it feels like they are isolated from reality, surrounded by the sights and sounds of nature. Despite her hesitance, he can still feel the magic shimmering in the atmosphere between them.

He turns down a long, dirt drive, and veers around the barricade with the sign marked, "Private property. Keep out."

The worn path seems to indicate that few others have made the trip before them. He travels farther up the property until he can see the berm separating the land from the water. He pulls his bike over, where the land's still flat, and parks on a small patch of gravel. The grass is tall and the land is overridden with weeds, but Aliah seems to see past all that, as her eyes train in on the pathway leading to an old, oversized barn. The breeze gently rustles the grass to the north, as he drops the kickstand and waits for Aliah to unwrap herself from his waist.

"We're stopping? Here?" She looks confused, and it only makes him smile harder.

He reaches for the blanket and retrieves the chilled bottle of wine he has packed as a surprise. Then he takes her hand and pulls her around the rustic, old barn. The look on her face when she sees the field of dandelions out back is priceless. She even stops moving and covers her mouth with her free hand.

"Oh my gosh!"

"You like it?"

"It's beautiful." She peeks up at him, smiling between the cracks of her fingers.

He smiles too, appreciating the whimsical feeling in the air as they transcend the patch of dandelions and leave any reservations about their relationship behind. Aliah lets go of his hand and runs into the field. She kicks at the dandelions, like a carefree child. Some of the older ones blast their seeds into the wind, making it look like Aliah's trapped in a magical snow globe.

She lifts her hands in the air and closes her eyes, smiling up at the sun.

Harley comes up behind her, and brings his chin over her shoulder to drop a wet kiss on her cheek. He nuzzles his nose behind her ear, and then whispers to her. "You're beautiful."

She presses her butt backwards, to knock him away from her. "You don't have to say shit like that." Aliah tries to muddle the moment, acknowledging how intimate it is, but he won't let her.

"It's okay to take a compliment, Ally."

"I know. But I don't want you saying things just because you think you're supposed to. You know?"

"Yeah, I do. But do *you* think I actually do what I'm supposed to do?"

Aliah's smile grows three sizes.

"I say what I want to say. And right now, I want to say

that you look beautiful. Is that okay with you?"

She presses her lips together, but she can't supress her grin. "I guess so."

"Good." He lifts up the blanket and a breeze catches it, throwing it in his face.

Aliah starts laughing, but she's wearing a friendly smile. "Need a hand, honey?" she teases.

"I might be a little out of practice here. I can't say I've ever had to lay out a blanket before. Is that a bad thing?"

"It's okay. You're making up for lost time."

The cheesy smile on her face makes him feel good. "I try." He sits on the blanket and leans over, until he's on his side, resting on an elbow.

Aliah drops to her knees in front of him and leans forward, on all fours. He can see right down her shirt, but he forces himself to keep his eyes off.

"You really are trying, aren't you?" She cups his cheek and he closes his eyes. Aliah has never been so soft with him. Though he enjoys her snappy comebacks, he's really liking this side of her.

Her thumb brushes over his lips, so he kisses it. He's shocked when she brings her lips to his and initiates a kiss. *She* kissed *him*! And it's not just any kiss. It's the most amazing kiss he's ever had. The kind where you have to stop because you can't help but smile.

After taking what he can, he cups her face with a palm.

"You're kissing me now?"

She shrugs her shoulders. "If you're going to such an effort, I thought I should give it a try too. Is that okay with you?" she mocks.

"Come here," he says, not letting her go. He pulls her over top of him, until he's on his back and she's straddling his hips. Their lips are attached, in a slow, sensual kiss that he feels in his gut.

She parts those beautiful lips for him, so he can sink is lower lip in between them. When he does, she grinds her lower body against him and flattens her breasts against his chest. He weaves his fingers into her hair, his other hand skimming over her hip to stroke her behind. The way she delivers a provocative lick with each smooch, he knows she's thinking what he is.

Time seems to stand still. Then when he speaks, it's like he's trying to verbally seduce her all over again. He plans to keep on doing that too, until she believes every last word of it.

CHAPTER TWENTY TWO

Two weeks pass and not a single night goes by that they don't spend together. Harley will not let anything happen to her, but he thinks it's safe to spring a surprise on her.

"I'm taking you out tonight."

Aliah hands Harley her helmet and smiles. "You don't have to do that."

When she opens the front door of her house and turns back to him, he mesmerizes her with a glance. "I want to. So quit acting like you aren't worth it and go throw something nice on. I've already made the reservations."

"What if I'd said no?" Aliah can't help but smirk as she closes the door behind him.

"You didn't. Now go."

She hurries ahead of him and rushes up her stairs with a smile gracing her lips. It hasn't taken them very long at all to get back on good terms. After weeks of Harley begging her for forgiveness, and showering her with love and honesty, she's finally given it to him. But she doesn't plan to tell him that. She likes this new thing they have going on. Harley aims to please her. She's been enjoying that very much.

Aliah's already smiled more today than she has in the past four weeks combined. She peers back at the man who is responsible for her upturned lips. "Where in this City are you taking me that requires reservations?"

"Armandos," he states. "And you're not getting out of it this time, so don't even try."

She spins away and slips into her bedroom. She doesn't realize Harley's kept up with her, but when she goes to close her door, his hand grabs onto it.

"Don't even think about closing that door. I plan to watch this time; make sure you don't stand me up again."

Aliah lifts her brows. She finds the idea of him watching her dress rather intriguing. "I'm not going anywhere. What about you? You can't go dressed like that," she says, as she shrugs off her top.

She loves the way he looks in those jeans with a simple t-shirt strapped across his chest, but they'll throw him out looking like that. At least they can try.

"Don't you worry about me." His eyes remain locked in place, taking in every naked inch of flesh as she removes her clothes and replaces them with a sophisticated pair of slacks and a feminine top. He watches her choose her sexiest black heels that hike her a good five inches off the floor. At first glance, the shoes look a simple black, but the blood red soles make her feel like a sexy deviant.

She touches up her makeup and returns to the bedroom. "Now you," she says, then dashes for the front door before he rids her of her freshly pressed clothes and decides to dine in for the evening. He chuckles as he slowly follows her out the door.

Harley is ready within minutes after pulling into his driveway. Despite the length of time it has taken him to dress, he still looks stunning. This man's body sure knows how to wear a suit. He looks perfect, from his angled smile to his shiny black shoes. He drops a kiss on her lips and then takes her hand. He opens the door for her, like a complete gentleman, and escorts her to the restaurant.

Dinner is amazing. And Aliah spends the comfortable silences wondering why she'd ever stood Harley up in the first place. She never had a really good reason, except that she was scared of what might come of it.

Although he'd lied in to her in the beginning, she if anyone can understand the importance of client confidentiality. Her heart does not lie. Their desire is not something that can be imitated. It has taken her this long to recognize that her greatest fears have been realized.

Despite her best efforts to avoid love and all the other emotions that go along with it, she knows she's toast. Not only has she fallen, but it's like she's been slammed over the head with it. She wouldn't be surprised if others could see little cupids spinning around her head or little heart-shaped bubbles bursting from her eyes every time she glances at Harley.

She chews on her lip after dinner, wondering if he has it half as bad for her. Harley rescues her battered lip, by leaning in close and softly tugging it into a kiss.

"Thank you for coming to dinner with me," he growls.

The entire night has felt incredibly intimate, but that moment trumps it all. He doesn't wait for her to respond and, since he's already paid, he pulls her to the exit. While walking down the sidewalk back toward his SUV, Harley has her giggling, and she allows her her mind to drift from any serious conversation.

She doesn't even notice that there's anyone behind them, until she sees the look on Harley's face. He doesn't seem to know who it is, just that maybe he should. It feels like someone knifes her in the stomach. Has Brandie come back to finish her off? She spins around and finds Hunter and Maddie standing there.

Yes, cheating ex-boyfriend, Hunter, and slutty bitch-who-stole-him, Maddie; each of them with a snot-nosed kid in their arms.

"Oh, it's just you." A breath of air releases from her lungs.

"Hey, Aliah. How are you doing?" Hunter looks really interested in the subject.

The stabbing pain in her gut eases slightly. "Really good, actually," she answers, surprised by how true it is. She glances up at Harley and smiles.

"You look good," Hunter admits.

Maddie's elbow comes jabbing out and lands against Hunter's side. She tries to keep a straight face, but fails miserably. Her eyes bug out of her head and her lips pucker in distress.

"Thanks," Aliah answers.

Harley smirks and covers his mouth with a hand, trying to hide his amusement. His forehead wrinkles as he glances at the ground. He looks incredibly sexy.

Maddie huffs as she puts her squirming little girl down. The toddler instantly takes off toward the street. "Oh!"

Aliah grabs onto the little girl's hand before she makes it two steps away. Then she crouches close to the ground to pay her a visit on her level. "Careful, sweetheart."

"Melody Rae," Maddie snaps. "Her name is Melody Rae."

"Ah, yes. How could I forget," Aliah mumbles, remembering how painful it was the day they'd named their children.

Maddie scoops her troublemaking child away from Aliah, who manages to smile softly at the overreaction.

"And this is Darien," Hunter informs her.

The introduction seems to upset the boy. He instantly starts to whine and throws his toy phone onto the ground. Hunter tries to rock him, but he looks very sleepy and refuses to stop crying. His wails grow more impatient by the second.

When Maddie doesn't move to pick up the toy, Aliah does, crouching down at the same time as Harley. Their eyes meet and he holds her gaze.

"I've got it." Harley takes the toy phone from Aliah's hand and flashes it to the little boy, effectively stealing Darien's attention.

Harley hands the phone to Hunter's boy. The little guy promptly throws it back on the ground wearing an oversized smile.

"Oh, I see how this goes," Harley says with a chuckle, as he retrieves the phone again. This time, after he hands it to the boy, he finds a smiling Darien reaching the colorful toy back out to him.

"Is it for me?" Harley asks him.

The boy's smile is adorable.

Harley glances at Aliah, then shrugs a shoulder, taking the toy phone from the kid. No matter how big and bad Harley looks, even this little dude can see how sweet he is under that hard exterior.

"Hello?" he answers.

The kid is pleased. His father? Not so much. Hunter rips the phone out of Harley's hand and forces it into Darien's. It's promptly tossed onto the ground and the boy resumes screaming.

When Darien is handed to his mother, he quiets down oh so slightly, but starts to make an attempt to wiggle out of Maddie's arms. With her arms now full, she struggles to keep them from poking each other's eyes out.

"It's past their bed time," Hunter says, trying to explain their bad behavior.

Darien breaks free from his mother's arms and runs for the street.

"Darien," Maddie shrieks.

Aliah swiftly scoops the boy into her arms, just sparing him from the curb. The boy looks her right in the eye, shocked by her closeness. It stuns her too, when she notices the dark hair and hazel eyes. There is no doubt that this little boy is Hunter's kid.

Hunter instantly grabs Darien and lifts him onto his hip. "Since when did you like kids?" He looks suddenly angry with her, even though she's done nothing wrong.

Darien instantly starts screaming again, sparing her a response.

Aliah presses her lips together. "He wants to go, I think."

Maddie lowers her wiggly daughter to the ground again, but refuses to release her hand. Neither of them look very happy at the moment.

"Yes. Go. We should," Hunter admits, looking awkwardly between Aliah and his baby momma.

Aliah nods, feeling only half as awkward as him. She watches Hunter lift his daughter onto his only free hip and smirks when she notices how Hunter lifts his chin in an attempt to match the height of Aliah's bigger, buffer new man when he passes him. As he walks off, both of his kids start wailing.

Maddie looks exhausted, but she doesn't speak a word of it. Nor does she follow after Hunter to give him a hand.

"Aliah? Can I ask you something?" Maddie starts.

"Go for it."

Maddie delivers a pointed glare and her tone turns glacial. "Alone."

Aliah glances at Harley, who's now a spectacle among them.

"I'll just be over here if you need me," he says, without needing to be told. He strolls farther down the sidewalk, glad to put some distance between him and the noisy kids.

"Who's your new friend?" she asks expectantly.

Now Aliah feels incredibly rude. "Oh! This is my... Harley," she says, stumbling over her words. She still hasn't said it, even though they've played around with words all day.

"Oh. I thought he looked like someone else I know." Maddie points at the nearest bus stop where Harley's service guarantee is plastered next to his handsome face."

"Oh. Right. Yeah, that's him. Harley is his middle name," she admits, not even a little embarrassed by the size of his advertisement.

"I'm being serious here," Maddie says, leaning into Aliah to keep their conversation somewhat private. "Tell me why you would want to date a manipulative old man like him when you're still young and beautiful."

Funny. She had never looked at him that way. Harley has never made her do anything she didn't want to and, to be frank, he takes quite good care of himself. Hunter has put a little weight on himself, and she'd wager that Harley is a good deal more buff than him, with a strong angular jaw and a face that oozes masculinity. She thinks of Harley like a fine wine. He only seems to get better with age.

Maddie must be jealous!

Aliah can't help but smirk, as Maddie tries to hide her assessment of Harley's fine ass. Aliah checks it out too. She really loves his ass; two round globes of muscle that look even better naked. She can't wait to get him naked.

"I've always had a thing for older men," Aliah admits, with a smirk. It's more of a joke than anything. There is no excuse necessary. Harley is an incredibly attractive man.

He exudes sex appeal and even his gaze is dangerously sexy. He's like sex on a stick. A really tall, handsome, dangerous stick.

Just as she says it, Harley turns and meets her eyes, scorching her with a glance. She can't stop smiling, but just as quickly, he glances down at the ground. He's trying really hard to mind his own business.

"He makes me happy," Aliah admits softly, still staring at him with a smile covering her face.

Aliah can't believe she's just said that out loud, let alone to big-mouthed Maddie. The two of them lock eyes. Maddie looks just as surprised as her. She hopes no one else has heard her. With another glance at Harley, she can tell that he hasn't.

Maddie smiles. "Your secret is safe with me."

That would be a first.

CHAPTER TWENTY THREE

As the days pass, Harley grows more frustrated by the fact that he can't solve the mystery of who is following Aliah and why. He's slowed down and cut back his efforts on Aliah's case so he can work on others, but he's afraid it's only giving the criminals a chance to regroup.

No concrete evidence has surfaced and the crazy lady has outright denied it was her. Brandee Hawkins now claims that her problem was solved the day Harley pulled Aliah away from Cavanagh's bar. Harley isn't too quick to believe such nonsense.

He takes a drink from his mug, as the front door chimes at the Thorncliffe Café. Aliah is late. She must have had a busy day at work. She hurries to where he's sitting and leans into him for a kiss.

"Hey. Sorry I'm late. What is it you wanted to talk to me about?"

Harley scratches at his head. "I've been thinking about what you said about Jillian."

"You mean, how I think she's a total nut job?"

"You never said that."

"Oh, right." Aliah smiles.

"I have noticed she's been acting kind of odd ever since I've taken on your case. When I told her that we're – you know – together, she didn't seem very happy about it." Harley pauses, in thought. "Maybe I should see what she's up to."

"I like the sound of that idea. Thank you."

"What did you just say?" The shock on his face is priceless.

"Thank you," she mumbles, again.

He's not going to let this one pass so easily. "I didn't quite hear you. You're going to have to speak up."

"I said thank you. I'm not as heartless as you let on. Thank you for trusting me. Thank you, Harley. Is that good? Thank you."

"Okay, okay," he says with a laugh. "You're welcome."

He denies the satisfaction he feels when she opens up to him. But it's true; they've formed a bond of trust in what little time they've share together. He only hopes it'll hold against the dangers that lie ahead.

Later that night, he puts his plan into action. But not before finding a little surprise text from Aliah that makes for damn sure that he doesn't pull an all-nighter this night. It has him looking forward to their *stay-in* plans for the evening. He doesn't remove his eyes from her provocative photo, until his phone starts ringing.

"David here," he answers.

"She's just exited the building," the man voices.

Harley had hired a fellow detective to keep an eye on his *dear friend,* Jillian. "I'm just around the block. I can take it from here, thanks." He ends the call and pulls his motorcycle around the block, until Jillian pulls out of his parking lot well past closing time.

What the hell is she doing at work afterhours?

He keeps his distance, with his headlights turned low, but follows close enough behind her to know that it's Brandee Hawkins she runs into outside the mall entrance.

Coincidence? *I think not.* His lead was good, even though Harley was hoping it wasn't.

The way she keeps looking over her shoulder tells him it's not an unexpected friendly meeting. Harley turns off his headlights and rolls forward until he has an unobstructed view of them. They chat for a minute and then enter the mall together. He parks his bike and walks quickly toward the entrance, seeing nothing but red.

Harley's so enveloped in deceit that he doesn't notice the two men making a dash for him. The scrawny one hollers out, but not until the other has his big fat arms wrapped around his neck. He's yanked aside, and feels his faced being crushed against the brick wall. He can feel the blood trickling from his nose, but he's far from giving up.

David H. Gates never gives up.

"Your girl thinks she's so smart," the skinny guy cackles.

Harley stands still for a minute, ready to strike, as he considers the safety of his *girl*. Are they talking about his daughter or his woman? He doesn't even know. Before he bashes their heads in, he's going to have to hang onto his temper and bleed a little information out of them. He has a couple of ideas in mind.

Without a second thought, he opts for plan B, head butting the big guy behind him. As the man stumbles backward, Harley knocks him out cold with a right hook. The big guy drops to the cement with a sickening thud. The scrawny man is so caught up in the moment, he forgets to run.

His head-start is nothing a few paces won't fix. Harley runs after him and quickly reaches out. He grabs onto the back of his jacket and yanks him backward. "Where do you think you're going?"

The man is close to crying, a dirty, wily man who he won't give a smidgen of trust to. Harley readjusts his grip on the front of his shirt and gives it a twist before he lifts him up to make his threat. His fisted hand presses against the man's throat, pinning him to the brick wall of the building.

"You're going to tell me what *girl* you're referring to, or I'm going to beat you within an inch of your life. I might just do that anyway."

"I can't. If I tell you, I don't get paid. I have a family to feed," the man whines.

Harley doesn't believe him. From the stench of body odor, combined with the the stale splash of beer on his breath, he knows no woman in her right mind would let that man into her home; especially a house with children.

"Wrong answer." Harley drops a heavy fist, connecting with his face.

The man is dazed for a second. He doesn't even put any effort into it and still the man nearly passes out. "Tell me what girl you're looking for. I'll give you five seconds. Four. Three. Two…"

"Aliah Brooklin!" he shouts, as the sound of scurried footsteps sounds behind him.

Harley drops the useless shell of a man to the ground and spins around to find the big guy coming at him with a knife. His reflexes aren't fast enough, and the man takes a slice out of his face. Blood spills instantly downs his flesh, but he's already thrown two fists. They connect with the big man's midsection and he folds in half, crumbling back to the ground. The knife clanks on the sidewalk, falling a few feet away from his hand.

Harley rushes to grab it, but no one is going for the knife but him. The wily sidekick has already made a run for it. When Harley leans over to retrieve the knife, he can see the splattered blood pooling on the ground. He grabs at his face, only then realizing that it's his blood decorating the parking lot.

The gash is bigger than he'd realized. He has already lost some blood from his nose, but he has been so concerned with getting information that he doesn't notice exactly how much, until he finds the evidence on the pavement. He gets a little lightheaded but grabs at his injury and heads for his bike anyway.

I have to get to Aliah.

As he reaches his motorcycle, he drops to his knees, barely able to maintain consciousness. He hears screaming behind him, but it's no one he recognizes. His body decides for him that he has to lay down and take a nap. When his eyes blink open, there are flashing lights and an ambulance attendant is hovering over him. He's still outside, because he can feel the cool night air rushing over his skin.

He's bandaged up and he notices the moment when they enter the hospital, because it's bright. So bright. It feels like he's entered a tunnel of white light with a collection of men and woman dressed in white chattering over top of him. He's ready to take another nap now.

Then he hears a familiar scream.

"Nooo!" she cries out.

Aliah appears over him, and slides a cold hand over his good cheek. "Oh my God. Harley. What have you gotten yourself into?"

"Excuse me, ma'am, but you're not allowed in here," says a woman dressed in blue.

"Like fuck, I'm not," Aliah announces, with a scowl.

He wants to smile, but realizes he can't. His face feels frozen and his eyes are so heavy he can't open them. He wants to tell the staff to let her stay, but his lips won't move. The harder he tries, the worse he feels. He starts to panic, as the reality of the situation sinks in.

Alarms on the machines he's hooked to start beeping off the charts. "You have to leave," the doctor shouts. "Now."

"He's flat lining," a nurse shouts.

"I'm not going anywhere. Now shut the fuck up and save him," Aliah screams.

Another nurse is already connecting him to yet another machine, while the other rubs two pads together. "Clear!" she shouts.

They all back off and the pads latch onto him. The jolt stimulates his body, lifting it from the table, and the machine bleeps for a second, but he flat lines a breath later.

"You have to save him," Aliah cries hysterically.

"Get her out of here," the doctor shouts irately.

A male nurse appears behind her and tears her from the room, escorting her to the waiting room. Aliah's so shaky, she can barely stay on her feet let alone fight to stay there.

Harley knows she's missing from the room when her crying voice leaves him, but he doesn't want her to go. He tries to keep a clear head, but he swears his mind is playing tricks on him when Aliah suddenly returns to him.

"Here I am, Harley. I'm here," she says, standing at the end of the white tunnel.

He shakes his head, not believing it for one second. She looks so beautiful, dressed in a fitted dress of white that slices up her leg exposing an extremely tall shoe. "Come, David. Come and play with me."

David?

Aliah has never called him David. She despises his name. That can't possibly be her. She's alive and well. Unless...

No. It's not Aliah.

"I'm not going with you," he states, even though she's exactly what he needs right now.

The image of Aliah darkens. Her hair. Her eyes. "Come with me," she demands, in a demonic voice. Her hair snakes around her head by some invisible force and light behind her fades to black. It still looks like his Aliah, a beautiful depiction of her, but her eyes flicker like globes of fiery coal and she sounds like death. "I need you, David. Come."

He wants to laugh, but he can't. "Like hell, lady. I have too much to live for. I'll catch you later."

He closes his eyes and relaxes, remembering Aliah the way he wants to. She's on the blanket beneath him. Her hair is splayed out over her head, tangling in the dandelions. She's smiling and so is he.

"I'm here," she says. "Come back to me, Harley."

He's confused. He is right here with her.

Why would she say that?

"Come back to me, Harley," she repeats.

He now realizes she's crying again. He can hear it in her voice. He tries to open his eyes, but he can't, and it feels like he's stuck in some underwater paradise between fantasy and reality. With a deep gasp for air, his eyes shoot open.

"He's awake!" Aliah screams. And he means screams. If he weren't half deaf from too many years of loud music, then he is now.

She kisses him silly. "Oh, Harley." Kiss. "I thought..." Kiss. "I would never..." Kiss. "See you again." Kiss.

He wishes she would never stop kissing him.

She closes her eyes and angles her head. She steals another long kiss that he doesn't want to end.

"Aliah," he croaks.

She freezes in place to hear him speak, with her hands cupping the unbandaged portion of his head and face.

"I can't breathe."

Her eyes bulge from their sockets. "Do you need a nurse?"

"No." He smiles. "I need you to quit stealing my breath."

She retrieves her hands and smiles, but a tear still sneaks out. He likes this side of her. It shows that she cares. She presses her head to his chest and teases a finger over him.

"Harley Gates, you bastard. Promise to never scare me like that again."

"I wish I could."

She looks up at him and scowls, but it's half-hearted. "You're lucky you woke up before your daughter got here. It's a horrible thing to find you here like that."

He looks down at himself and sees he's wearing a blue night gown about ten sizes too small. He makes to sit up and his monitors all start to go wild.

Aliah presses a hand against his chest. "Just rest. For me?"

He takes another breath and relaxes his muscles. "For you."

CHAPTER TWENTY FOUR

It's not long before Harley's back on track. One of the goons were caught, thanks to Harley's heavy hands, and the guy had given the name of his accomplice to the police. The only missing link is their employer, whom they claim they've never met in person. He's convinced it's Brandee Hawkins.

Jillian finally admits to him that Brandee is an old friend, but she claims it was mere coincidence that they ran into each other at the mall that night. Harley hasn't been able to find any proof to the contrary and the fact that Jillian looked horrified when she learned about Harley's attack, seemed to tie up her end of the story. Aliah's not so quick to accept Jillian's *story*.

Aliah can see that Harley's growing tired of this investigation and she knows just the fix for his problem. No matter how long a day or how hard a night, Aliah can fix it. After helping Hannah with the dishes, Aliah asks her if it's okay to steal her dad away for the evening.

With Hannah's blessing, Aliah swoops into Harley's home office and grabs him by the shirt. "Let's go. You're coming with me."

"Where are you taking me?" Harley's smirking now.

But when Aliah waggles her eyebrows, suddenly he's the one with the sense of urgency. He tugs her the rest of the way to her car, tucks her into the passenger seat and slams the car into reverse. He has them racing out of town like they have somewhere important to be.

When Harley's not watching, Aliah slips her hand into his. He smiles over at her.

"How did you know?" she asks, lifting his hand to her mouth. She drags her bottom lip over his knuckle, then sucks on it.

Harley groans and swerves off the side of the road, deciding that they've driven long enough. "Men just know these things." He slides the car into park and unlatches his seat belt. Then he leans over to kiss her.

She backs away and smiles, with the memory of how he's urged her to trust him with her life and with her kisses.

His hand reaches out for her face and he smoothes a thumb over her cheek before swooping in again. She doesn't stop him this time and he wastes no time sharing how hot just the idea of making love to her in her car has made him. The constant press of his lips and lick of his tongue has her sweltering within seconds. His hands grow more daring, as his tongue discovers her mouth.

Harley stops for a breath and steals her gaze. "Backseat. Now," he orders.

The deep baritone sound has her body humming, as she wiggles into the backseat. Harley slaps her ass and escapes from the car, since his body is much too large to maneuver around the interior of it. When the door closes behind him, his lips crash into hers. She can feel the hard lines of his muscles raping her clothed body. It has her tugging at his shirt, as he divests her of her clothes.

He flings away everything but her skirt. "Not the skirt." He hangs onto it, to make sure she doesn't tear it off in a fit of excitement. He toys with the short frilly thing. "You look so God damn sexy tonight. Do you have any idea how bad I need this right now?"

He slides a hand up her leg, until her skirt is flipped up and she is completely exposed to him. "How bad I need you?" he adds.

Their eyes meet for a moment of intense connection. She's unsure what it's supposed to mean, but it's exhilarating and makes her smile. She's never felt anything so real in all her life... except for that. He sinks into her with a slow flex of his pelvis.

"Yes. That's what I'm talking about."

He sinks into her again.

"Mmm, Harley," she moans, sensation spilling from her

body.

Before long, he's pounding her into the backseat and she squealing with an orgasm that has her losing sight of reality. The way he slides into her repeatedly has her moaning out loud, like she's in heat and she's trying to attract a troop of male foxes. It only encourages him to lunge faster and pump harder.

She ignores the headlights passing by and enjoys the heated kiss matched with Harley's strong hands touching her body. The faster he pumps, the closer he gets and she's squeezing around him finding a fast second release.

Suddenly she notices a silhouette in the window, but she can't make out who it is through the fogged glass. It's especially difficult with Harley bouncing her around erratically on the seat. The window is a little more than a crack open, so it's not like their visitor can't hear them loud and clear.

How long have they had a spectator?

She makes to laugh, but then the person taps on the window with something hard and heavy. Surely that person can see Harley's ass bobbing up and down.

Really?

Harley growls. "Just a minute."

Aliah breaks out laughing, as he finds his release and grips onto her with a furious grunt.

She slaps his ass and he lifts up so he can pull her skirt down. He yanks on his underwear and turns around to face the authorities.

Phew! It's only Spencer.

Aliah crawls across the seat and eases the window down a little farther, clutching at her breasts. The provocative display is unintended, but both men seem to be enjoying the view.

"Can I help you, officer?" she inquires.

"Why do I keep running into you? I don't even do road stops, except I keep finding you breaking the law. You have to know this is illegal. You work in law and he's a P.I. for Pete's sake."

"It's all good, Spence. We were just leaving."

"Not just yet." He finishes scribbling on his pad of paper, as Harley readjusts his shirt and climbs into the front seat. He turns on her car and puts his window down, allowing some fresh air to flood the cabin.

Spencer slaps him with a ticket.

"You have got to be kidding me." Harley is smirking though.

Aliah's smirking too, as she pulls a shirt over her head. When she reaches her arms up, she regains the attention of both men. She doesn't realize it, until she pokes her head out the top. She freezes in place, but neither man removes his eyes from her chest. Her nipples harden from the sensual scrutiny, gearing her body up for another round. She covers her breasts with an arm, still shocked by the invasion.

"I can't believe you! You're actually writing me up?" she balks.

"No. I'm writing *him* up. Have a good night." He salutes them and walks away from the car, making a quick adjustment of his pants. His sexy accent did nothing to ease her disbelief.

The pair look up at each other at the same time and burst into laughter.

"We're fighting this one. Even if I have to go flash your abs to the judge," Aliah jokes. "No one will call my man's ass indecent and get away with it."

Aliah's overreaction has Harley howling with laughter.

"We do have some pretty bad luck when it comes to cops." He slaps the ticket across his opposite hand, then tosses it into the backseat.

"I would have to agree with you there." Aliah leans over the seat for a kiss, no less provocative than before, and crawls into the front with him. He gropes her braless breasts, appreciating what God gave her.

Harley kisses her too, ready to get back inside her. She can tell by the pressure of his tongue and the length of his cock. He looks out the rearview mirror but it doesn't look like Spencer's going anywhere.

"I can fix that," Harley says, as he puts the window up.

He pulls the gear into drive and signals like a law abiding citizen. He drives down the road at a granny's pace, until Spencer finally gives up and passes them. As soon as the SUV is out of their sight, Harley pulls the car back over and pins her against him, his tongue showing her how much he wants her.

They're getting hot and heavy across the front console, when lights flash in their back window. Aliah pulls away and turns back to see if the car is stopping and instantly ducks, with a scream, as the car rearends them at full speed. The impact alone sends Aliah's head cracking against the passenger window.

The car backs away, dragging Aliah's car a few feet with it. Then it spins around and squeals off. It looks like it's leaving. But then it spins back around and starts coming for them again.

"Harley!" Aliah cries out.

He's already one step ahead of her. With the car slammed into drive, he drops a heavy foot on the accelerator, as if he knows exactly what is going to happen next. "Are you okay?"

Aliah feels herself growing tired, dizziness causing her brain to falter. She can't answer him.

"Aliah, stay with me."

She touches her hand to her forehead. She finds a handful of blood. She takes a deep breath. "Oh God," she whispers. It's barely audible against the noise of her whining engine.

Within seconds, their playful night has turned into a high speed chase. She looks in the side mirror through the now speckled glass.

"Recognize that car?" he asks.

"Brandee." Without a doubt, that nut bag has come to finish her off once and for all.

Aliah snaps on her seatbelt. "I hope you know what you're doing."

He digs his phone out of his pocket and dials up his assistant. "Jillian. Call 911. Tell them Brandee's lost her marbles. She's trying to run me off the road, most likely with the intent to commit murder. We're heading east on Highway 42, just before the Rouge river, and she's right on our tail."

"I've already got the police on the other line. They're dispatching an officer as we speak."

Aliah feels some relief, but as Brandee starts to gain on them, that feeling quickly passes. Her car has taken the hit pretty hard, and the side panel is rubbing against one of the back tires. The scent of burning rubber hangs in her nose and the tang of blood is apparent in her mouth.

"Ask them to send an ambulance too. Aliah's hurt pretty bad."

"Okay," Jillian answers, and even Aliah can hear the fear in her voice. "David?"

"Yeah," he says, leaving it on speakerphone.

"Be safe."

Just as he goes to end the call, Brandee pulls up next to them.

"Harley!" Aliah screeches. But it's too late.

As he looks toward Aliah, their gazes collide, and Brandee rams into them, sending their car ramping up the river bank. She would never forget that penetrating stare that lasts a mere millisecond but burns into her brain for all eternity.

That one hit sends her car sailing into the water.

The force of the crash locks her seatbelt and bruises her neck. Harley's head smashes off the windshield, as her airbag deploys in her face. She's stunned for a minute, but she recalls the severity of the situation. She pushes the airbag out of her way, to catch a breath, while it tries to suffocate her. When she finally makes contact with Harley's slumped form, she knows that he is unconscious.

Aliah's freaks, but she doesn't cry. She can't cry. She's his only hope.

The car teeters on the surface of the water, but she's

read about this a million times before. The likelihood of them both escaping this accident alive is not good. One of them might be lucky to live.

She crawls on top of him and fumbles with his seatbelt. His arm is bleeding pretty bad and his recent facial wound appears to be seeping red. With the sharp edge of her battered car door still piercing his skin, Aliah doesn't know how she's going to free him.

Aliah gets Harley's seatbelt off of him, but he feels like dead weight. The car starts to sink and she starts to panic. The longer the car sits there, the more water seeps in through the cracked windshield and demolished rear-end. She doesn't dare try to escape, until she has a plan on how to get Harley out. They're both running out of time.

"Harley!"

She screams and shakes him, but he's not responding. She yanks off her jacket and rips it in two. She ties off his arm and presses the other scrap against his bloody face. He's losing a lot of blood.

"Oh, God. We're going to die in this car. Please, Harley. You have to wake up." She holds her fingers against his throat and finds a very weak pulse.

Suddenly, like an angel, Jillian's voice comes from out of nowhere. Aliah wonders if she is dead. Then she hears it again.

"Aliah, where are you? You have to tell me where you are."

Shaking out of her dizzy spell, Aliah presses the airbag away and scours the floor for the phone. "Jillian!" she shouts. "We're in the river at the Anderson crossing. Please send help. We don't have much time," she cries.

"David?"

"He's out cold. I can barely move him."

"They're already on their way, hun. They shouldn't be long now."

"Jillian. Please tell Hannah I'm so sorry. This is all my fault. I'm taking her dad away from her. I'm sorry for you too."

"No. I'm the sorry one," Jillian answers. "I never meant for David to get hurt. He wasn't supposed to be driving."

Aliah is stunned by her confession, but a throb in her head won't allow her to think on it.

"You listen to me, you hear?" Jillian states. "Don't give up. You're David's only shot. I need you to save him. Get yourself out of there and scream for help. That's the best you can do for him right now."

"I can't leave him," Aliah whispers, feeling selfish for wanting to share these last few minutes with him alone.

"You must! He would be so irate right now if he knew you were risking your life for him like this. Don't be stupid. Stay calm. You can do this."

Her words ring in Aliah's ears. A nervous laugh trembles from her lips. That is exactly what Harley would have said to her. She can't give up. She has faith in the emergency response team.

"What do I do?" She pants, as the emergency vehicle lights appear from up above like a white flash from the sky. "Another minute and we're going under."

"Get out," Jillian answers.

Aliah refuses to listen to her. "I have to get him out first."

"Get yourself out, Aliah. Listen to me. Harley would never forgive himself if anything ever happened to you." There's a slight spark of jealousy that seems to lighten her words.

The tears start crashing down Aliah's cheeks and mingle with the water splashing in through the dashboard. "I can't leave him. Oh, God. I don't know what to do." She tries again to move him, as the cabin begins to flood with water.

The cold tenses her already petrified muscles. She tries the door, but the pressure is too strong. She starts kicking at the cracked windshield, screaming, in an attempt to flag down some help. It takes all the energy she has, to break a small hole through the glass.

She cranks her head around when she sees someone next to the car, yanking on the door. But he's not having any luck either. With another kick at the windshield, it breaks open, letting the water rush inside. She covers her head with an arm and passes through the broken glass. It claws across her skin, as she crawls out of the sinking car. She gasps for air, kneeling on the hood of the car, surrounded by water to her waist.

Forgetting about the glass, Aliah reaches back inside the car and tries again to pull Harley from his seat. He's easier to move now, with the water flowing freely around his body, but he's pinned somehow, or he's too heavy. She doesn't know.

"I can't get him," she screams, her heart seizing in her chest. "Help me, God damn it. Please, Harley. I love you. You can't die on me."

She's so blind with fear that she doesn't notice Spencer's the one dropping in the water and swimming toward her.

"I'm going to help you, Ally. Grab onto this."

When he offers her a buoyant object, she tosses it away and screams at him.

"Don't worry about me! Save Harley! I need you to help me save him. Please!" she screams, as she feels the dizzy spell take her.

She chokes on some water and feels her muscles seizing up. She feels herself going under the water, and she can't bring herself back to the surface. She feels like she's thrashing for help, but her body is completely limp and she submerges with her eyes wide open.

She turns her head under the water and sees a blurry version of Harley, still stuck in the driver's seat, as the car begins to sink to the bottom of the riverbed. She squints at him, lost between dream and reality. Harley opens his eyes and smiles at her.

"I love you," he mouths, as his eyes close again.

She closes her eyes, and slips completely unconscious, not much caring about her own life anymore, since she can sense that Harley will no longer be in it.

CHAPTER TWENTY FIVE

If Hannah Gates knows one thing, it's that her father is a fighter. She sits by his bedside in tears. He's all she has left. If he leaves her, she has no one. She just finally started to feel like they had moved toward a new step in their life, with the addition of Aliah in his. And then this has to happen.

Is she doomed to a life without a parent? It's bad enough God had to take her mother's life too early. She intends to put up a fight of her own, if he thinks her dad's time is up now.

Hannah watches the way her dad's chest rises and falls, the only thing maintaining her sanity. The machines are constantly beeping, but she has no idea what that's supposed to mean. She still welcomes the noise to douse the horrible sound of him sucking on that oxygen mask. A tear slips from her eye as Jillian bursts into the room, unannounced.

"I came here as soon as I could!"

Was she supposed to care?

"Is he going to be okay?" Jillian asks her.

Hannah tries to keep a straight face, but the scowl is unavoidable. She has never liked her dad's flirty blonde assistant with long legs and an even longer nose. That bitch lies. She trusts her as far as she can throw her, which isn't very far at all.

"Hannah?" Jillian demands, dragging her out of her reverie and back into her nightmare. Jillian looks perturbed by her ignorance.

Give me a God-damned break. My father is dying.

"He'll be fine, as soon as he wakes up," Hannah spits out, unsure how else she can word it.

Jillian gathers that Hannah doesn't like her very much.

"Is that what the doctors are saying?"

"How did you even get in here?"

Jillian doesn't trust her. Hannah finds that laughable. Leave it up to a liar to have trust issues.

"Let's drop the act," Jillian croaks. "Just tell me that he's going to be okay."

Hannah shrugs her shoulders indifferently. "You've never listened to me before. Why start now?"

"Don't get sassy with me, young lady."

"Young lady? Really? What are you, twenty? Get over yourself. My dad has a girlfriend now. It's safe to say you need to back the fuck off. He doesn't want you."

"You don't think I know that?" Jillian's voice screeches to an almost unbearable tone.

"Why are you here, Jillian?"

Jillian looks stunned, and is stumbling over her words. "I-j-just..."

"Just get the hell out of here. We don't want you..."

"Shut your mouth, you stupid little bitch. I should have ridded David of your big mouth when I had the chance two years ago."

Hannah's eyes grow wide, as realization dawns on her. "That was you!"

Before she can form another word, Jillian has the door closed and has hands reaching out for her throat. Hannah chokes on a breath and claws at the psycho lady's face, breaking her skin with her long nails.

"You crazy bitch!" Hannah screeches, fighting for a breath.

A nurse pushes the door and props it open, not realizing Hannah is fighting for her life.

"I'd appreciate if you would leave this door open," the nurse says, paying them no attention.

When she glances up, she's horrified by what she sees, next to the unconscious patient.

Jillian has Hannah on the floor, with her thumbs digging into her throat, shaking her neck like a rubber chicken. She's snapping her head, like she's trying to break a wishbone and starts bouncing it off the floor. The nurse charges them and bangs the crazy lady's head off the hospital bed. She then reaches for the red button, knocking the mask off Harley's face in the process.

Security has Jillian in cuffs, leading her kicking and screaming to meet up with the police on the main floor in a matter of minutes. Hannah is sitting there with security, her hands shaking with a potent mix of adrenaline and fear. She starts telling them what has happened, just as her father's eyes open.

Harley opens a pair of dry, cracked lips, but no words come out.

Hannah can't stop shaking, even with the thick blanket drawn over her shoulders. Her knee bounces the entire time she talks to the police, even though she has done nothing wrong. She's relieved when the old man with the horrifying questions leaves her alone.

Suddenly, she catches a handsome young man with an attractive English accent asking about her. With but a glance in her direction, he makes his way toward her, smiling at her as if they are long-time friends.

"Are you okay?" he asks, kneeling next to her, gazing up into her eyes.

The colorlessness in his irises hit her like a blast of fresh air. She nods her head, finding it difficult to speak after Jillian's had her fingers digging into her throat.

The man turns away. "Get this poor girl a glass of water," he orders. A glass materializes in his hand mere seconds later.

"Here. This might help your sore throat." He watches her sip from the glass. "They're treating you alright, yes?"

"Yes," she sputters, taken aback by her attraction to this older man. But he's charming and well-dressed and really cute.

"I'm Sergeant Caldwell. But you can call me Spencer, if

you like."

She nods yes, hiding her smile behind her jittery nerves.

"You've done well. We've been trying to catch this woman for years," he explains, in the sexiest accent that has ever graced her ears. "When she became employed by your father, we knew it would only be a matter of time before she reverted to her old ways."

"My dad knew?" she asks, finally regaining her voice.

"He knew."

"Who are you?"

"The fuzz," he says, with a wink.

"But you're not dressed in blue."

"Would you like it better if I was?"

She shivers from his intimate suggestion. She'll deny it if she's ever asked, but she'd like very much to see that ass in uniform.

"I apologize. You've been through enough. You don't need me harassing you. How's your father doing?"

Hannah wishes he'd return to their other conversation. It had taken her mind away from the series of stressful events that had just occurred, if only for a moment. "Not good at all."

"I'm sorry to hear that. He's a good man. But if he's with my girl, Aliah, then he's got his work cut out for himself. Even if he thinks he's ready to die, Aliah isn't going to let him call the shots that easily."

Hannah smiles softly. "You know Aliah?"

"Ah, yes. I've had the pleasure of dealing with her on many occasions. I admit most of late have involved cherries flashing and a high-speed chase to the fitness club."

Hannah loves how the words roll right off his sexy tongue. "She does have a fast ride." Her eyes grow wide, as she slaps her hand over her mouth.

I can't believe I just admitted that to him!

His smile is slanted and mischievous. "It sounds like I'll be having to add you to my watch list, Miss Gates."

Her heart flutters at the thought.

CHAPTER TWENTY SIX

"Harley. Harley," Aliah cries. "I can't get you! I'm sorry."

Abigail Santora leaps to Aliah's bedside, as fast as a pregnant woman can. "Ally, I'm here. It's Abby. You're okay." She grabs Aliah's hand and squeezes it, hoping Aliah awakens with a clear head.

Aliah's eyes flash open, and she looks like she's returned from the dead. "Where am I?" Her question is borderline hysterical.

"You're at the hospital. Don't worry. You're going to be okay. Just relax."

"Harley?" she screeches. Her eyes scatter around the room looking for someone else; for any indication that he is with them.

"Don't worry about that. You have to concentrate on you right now. You scared us all with that bump on your head."

"Abby, I swear to God, you're going to tell me right now, or I'm going to rip these machines off of me and go on a rampage tearing up every room until I get answers. If he's dead, just say it. Have the decency to just tell me."

Aliah closes her eyes, keeping her tears locked inside her eyelids. She knows that Abby is going to tell her, but she's not sure she's prepared to hear the news. If he has died, she'll never be able to live with herself. They might as well pull the plug on her now.

"He didn't die," Abby says, clearly leaving something out.

"But... Abby, don't bull shit me right now."

Abby sighs and rubs her swelling belly that is pretty-near ready to burst. "You're not well enough to be dealing with this right now."

"If it was Edwin, wouldn't you want to know?"

"Edwin's my husband. Of course I'd want to know."

"Oh no," Aliah states. "You're not playing that card on

me." Then she delivers Abby an emotional plea, acting totally out of character. "I love him, Abby. Please. I have to know."

Abby nods, disbelief marring her worried features, as she carefully regards the scared tears in Aliah's eyes.

"He's not in the clear just yet. They got him out of the car, but he took in a lot of water before they got him on land. They've had to revive him twice already. It's a good sign. He's fighting."

Aliah shakes her head, as the tears come pouring out of her eyes.

"The doctors wanted to run some tests, to figure out why he's not waking up."

"I have to see him," Aliah states. When she stands from her bed, her knees fail her. She drops to the floor, plucking the intravenous from her wrist. She wants to cry some more. Everything is so out of control. She takes a deep breath and stands on shaky legs.

"At least let me help you," Abby says, grabbing onto her elbow.

Abby helps her walk down the hall and stops at the double doors that lead to the intensive care rooms. "I just need to use the restroom. The baby's been putting so must pressure on my bladder these days. Wait for me?"

Aliah nods, but she has no intention of waiting for her. The second Abigail disappears into the bathroom, Aliah squirts the hand sanitizer into her palm and waves at the nurse on the other side of the glass who has just started her shift. Aliah quickly hides her bloody wrist and smiles at the woman, who watches her as she passes. Aliah walks quickly past her and ignores the other severely injured patients and their traumatized family members, searching for the room bearing Harley's name.

When she turns the corner and stops at the room where Harley's expected to be, she holds her breath and covers her mouth. She wonders if she'll ever breathe again. It's his room, according to the white marker board with his full name plastered across it.

David H. Gates.

But there's no Harley there.

Tears flood her cheeks, as she assesses the room with a blood splattered floor and an empty bed. "No!"

Aliah means to scream, but it comes out as a heartbreaking whisper. Then she falls back down to weakened knees. The worst of all feelings balls in the pit of her stomach, squeezing on her insides with a death grip. She swallows to moisten her dry throat, but she is too terrified to speak. Does she want to know how he died? Was he in pain?

A nurse approaches her and shoves her aside, causing her to get to her feet. The woman pulls the curtains closed with a huff.

"You aren't supposed to be in here. Please go back to your room, Miss."

Bitch.

As if Aliah weren't already cool from the slit in the back of her pale blue hospital gown, a chill overtakes her body, making her tremble violently. Abby comes running and grabs onto her arm.

"What's wrong? You said you would wait."

"I lied. Please take me to my room." The breathless request causes Abby concern. Aliah can see it in her eyes.

Aliah mopes back to her room, preparing herself to ask Abby for the truth. She hopes the stitch in her side is not a sign of the truth. She crawls into her bed, ready to cry the rest of her life away, but tears don't come.

"What is it, Ally? What did you see?"

"Blood. He's gone."

"What? Are you sure?"

Aliah turns away, to grieve in silence, but when she glances towards the door, Hannah's standing there. She looks completely lost. Aliah smears her tears away and holds her hands out to her.

Hannah comes running into the room and latches onto Aliah with a hug that is so real. "I'm scared, Ally."

Aliah closes her eyes, pinching her tears off. She

smoothes her hand over Hannah's hair. "I'm scared too," she whispers.

Abby steps toward the door, instantly picking up on the connection. "I'll give you two a minute."

"I'm so sorry, Hannah. It's all my fault. He's dead and it's all my fault."

"What?" Hannah's eyes light up. "No! He's not dead. He's awake!"

Aliah sits there in shock for a few seconds, taking in Hannah's smiling face. "But the blood. The floor was covered in it." As she inspects Hannah's expression, she notices a few scratches on her face and a dark bruise forming on her neck.

"It was my blood," she admits, looking horrified.

"Who? Abby told me the police had caught Brandee up the road."

"Jillian."

That name echoes through Aliah's head for what seems like an eternity.

"It was Jillian all along," Hannah explains.

Aliah becomes very confused. "I want to see him. I have to see him." She moves the blankets aside, and drops her feet to the cold floor. "Where is he? Can you take me to him? Please?" she begs.

"Uh..." The smile leaves Hannah's face in an instant. She doesn't know what to say.

"What is it, Hannah? What's wrong?"

When she doesn't answer, Aliah pulls on a robe and heads for the nurses' station. The woman there recognizes her, but she doesn't look real impressed by the intrusion.

"I understand Harley, I mean David Gates, has been moved out of intensive care. You can tell him I'm ready to see him now."

The nurse mulls over that information for a minute. "I'm sorry," she pauses, choosing her words wisely. "You can't go in there."

Like hell!

"Then I'll wait."

"I'm sorry, but you'll be waiting a while." She is only being honest. "I really am sorry. But his visitors are restricted to immediate family only."

Aliah hears the words, but it's not computing. "Tell him I'm here. I need to see him." Aliah moves to shove the nurse aside, but the woman plants herself firmly in front of her and softly clutches her wrist.

"Please don't make a scene, Miss Brooklin. I need you to take a seat."

"Why won't you people just let me see my man?" Aliah throws up her hands and takes the first seat at the edge of the waiting room. If it means seeing Harley sooner, then she will suck it up and do it.

The nurse takes her hand this time, crouching down next to her. Aliah shifts with discomfort, but lets the nurse keep her hand. This can't be good.

"I know how anxious you must feel. I can see how much you love him. But I have strict orders to keep you out of there. I'm so sorry, but he doesn't want to see you."

Aliah is flabbergasted, a blank expression coloring her canvass. That is the last thing she expects to hear. "That's B.S. I'm going to see him. She rips her hand away and takes three fast steps in the direction Hannah had come.

"He's suffered a serious trauma," the nurse shouts after her. "Any distress will cause a serious setback."

Aliah stops in her tracks and closes her eyes. She knows she's a selfish person. She wants to ignore the woman and be selfish. She wants to run into Harley's arms and tell him how much she loves him, but she can't do that to him. She can't hurt him anymore.

She can't believe this is happening. This is all her fault. Maybe that's why he doesn't want to see her. She's caused him too much pain. She's pushed him too far. It's over for her.

Aliah tries to open her eyes, but she feels like she's floating underwater. She hears Hannah's voice approaching her, but she can't respond and it sounds so distant.

"Are you okay, Ally? My dad doesn't know what he's

thinking."

Those are the last words she hears before she collapses onto the floor.

Hannah manages to just barely break her fall, as a nurse rushes toward her with a wheelchair. Aliah is immediately returned to a hospital bed.

This time, when Aliah's eyes reopen, he's there. She must be dreaming. Maybe she's dead.

"Am I in heaven?" she asks softly.

Harley chuckles, and it tugs at her heart.

She didn't think she was ever going to hear that handsome voice again. She waits for him to say something, but he doesn't speak and he doesn't move.

"Maybe this is hell," Aliah says aloud, not quite trusting her eyes. "You don't want to see me. You don't care to talk to me." She starts crying, having lost all her hardness over the past 24 hours. She hates being so weak.

Harley brings his hand to his chin, his finger pressing over his lips when he finally speaks. "I didn't think it would land you back in a hospital bed."

Was he talking to her?

Her spine stiffens, but she ignores him, and continues to talk to herself. "I can see why he wouldn't want to ever see me again." She clears her throat and smears away the tears. "I'd hate me too."

He wheels closer to her. Her eyes flash forward and meet his.

She doesn't know what is real anymore. Harley's in a wheelchair?

"I don't hate you, Aliah." His voice is gruff. "Now quit talking like that."

"But... you..." She can't even spit out the words.

He doesn't hate me!

"I thought it'd be best if I stayed away from you for a while. I damn near killed you. Someone else can do better by you."

Aliah scowls at him fiercely. "I don't want someone else. I want you, Harley. Don't you get it?"

Harley looks stunned. "After how I've hurt you? I can't be trusted."

"That's it?" She tries to make eye contact with him, but her eyes don't quite reach his. "You just expect me to turn my back and walk away? What, you don't want me anymore?"

"I never said that." He answers as if Aliah has accused him of something horrible.

"No, you said *you* don't want to see *me*. *You* want to stay away from *me*. But here you are."

"Here I am."

Aliah presses her hand against her forehead and instantly regrets it. There's a rather large bump there and what feels like a handful of stitches. She drops her hand to the bed, leaving her tired eyes shut.

"What are we doing here? It started out all in good fun, and I've tried hard – really hard – to stay detached. But I think it's clear that we've gotten a little closer than either of us ever planned," she admits.

"Maybe a little," he teases, with a growly voice.

"I'm glad you find this so funny. That sound you just heard is my heart breaking. This, after I promised I wouldn't do *this*."

Harley smiles, but his face turns serious as he lifts his body out of the wheelchair and moves closer to her. "You don't find love, Aliah."

She looks away, terrified to see the heat in his eyes, but he lifts her chin with his index finger until her eyes meet his.

"It finds you."

His mouth looks warm and inviting, and when he touches his lips to hers, she confirms that it is. She tries to erect a hard expression on her face, but she finds herself softening beneath him as he touches his tongue to hers. The more his mouth moves, the harder her heart hurts. She can't possibly live without this.

Depression tugs at her hospital gown. What she really needs is a stiff drink and a drunk Harley moving inside her. There's no insecurity when she finds that place.

A nurse enters the door and starts shouting at them, as their kiss grows more emotional and demanding.

"Mr. Gates! You're in no condition to be standing." The nurse rushes to the bedside and pulls him back, parting their lips, as she helps him into the seat of his wheelchair. She gently rolls him away from the bed like a scorned elderly man. His angled smile is breathtaking.

"Miss Brooklin can really use the rest. She can't handle what you have to offer her right now," the nurse insists. "If it's a matter of the heart, then it will wait."

Aliah presses her lips together, not quite allowing her smile to show through, as her man is escorted out of the room. She's almost afraid to be left alone, not knowing how many more crazy bastards are out there to harm her. Who else is in on this conspiracy to get her and everyone she loves?

When Mitchell knocks quietly at the door, she gladly welcomes him.

"What was that all about?" he asks.

Aliah shakes her head. "Don't ask."

Mitchell comes right up to her bedside and takes a seat on the edge. He's so heavy she feels the bed slant toward him. "I think I need a break from all of the drama in Rose Arbour. Do you want to come with me?"

Aliah smiles. The idea sounds great, but the thought of moving away from Harley rips at her heart. "What do you have in mind?"

Mitchell smiles, loving that she's considering it, even if only to appease him. "I've been thinking about opening a new night club in Collingwood. I'd have to spend some time there to get it up and running anyway. Now's probably as good a time as ever to do that."

"That's where Abby's ex is moving. You must know Cameron Clarke. It's definitely a nice place."

"So, you'll come with me?" He sounds wistful, but he already knows her answer.

"I think I have some unfinished business here that needs attended to."

Mitchell sighs, admitting to himself that she's taken. "I figured as much."

"We'll miss you here," Aliah insists.

He smirks. "I really don't think Harley will miss me at all."

He's got that right!

"Okay, then *I'll* miss you." She really will. Who will be there to give her free drinks and a friendly ear when he's gone?

Mitchell shares a really big smile with her. "I'll miss you too, Ally. What are you going to do without me?"

"I really don't know."

"This thing you have going on with David Gates, is that something you see turning more serious? You two have been seeing each other for a while now. I'm sure you've thought about it."

Aliah smiles softly. "I try not to. I'm afraid I've jumped a little too high, too fast."

"Jumped? Or fell?"

She shoves at him. "You know what I'm saying."

"What you're saying isn't jiving with what's in your heart. I hope for his sake that you can overcome it."

"I don't know if Harley's looking to settle down. It's been fun, but maybe that's all he was meant to be for me. A fun little detour in my life."

"You don't mean that."

"But I do. This is probably just a sign to remind me that my life is a train wreck. There's no need for anyone else to crash and burn with me."

Mitchell looks thoughtful. But he really does care. "I hope it works out for you, chicka. But can I give you a suggestion?"

"Give 'er."

"If you're all in, tell him so. No man takes well to being

strung along."

She nods, but her breath is cut off. She finds it difficult to speak. "Thank you," she whispers.

Why do I think it's such a bad thing to fall in love with Harley?

Mitchell collects her in his arms, and she sheds a tear that she flicks away with a laugh.

"Look what you've got me doing, Mitchell!"

He smoothes his hand over her hair. "It's going to work out for you. I just know it. It has to."

CHAPTER TWENTY SEVEN

Jillian enters the courtroom, dressed in a blue jail-issue jumpsuit, with a white t-shirt underneath. She fidgets during the entire bail hearing, keeping her eyes glued to the floor, not even glancing up at duty counsel when he whispers in her ear.

Harley's leg is bouncing, as they await the decision, having left the hospital against the doctor's orders to make this trip.

"Bail is denied," the judge announces, granting her no leeway for the heinous crimes she has committed.

Hannah turns her head and buries her face in her father's shoulder. Even after begging her to stay away, she'd insisted that she be there to hear the verdict. Harley gently pats her back in an attempt to calm her.

"The Order is to go as asked by the prosecution," the judge announces. "Miss Briscoe, you are a danger to the public and I question whether you are fit to stand trial. Do you understand the serious nature of your charges?"

"I haven't done anything wrong," she screeches. Her voice echoes across the otherwise silent room, as she picks Hannah out of the crowd and points at her. "Her! She is the one that should be sitting here."

"That is enough, Miss Briscoe. Counsel is ordered to arrange for a psychological assessment forthwith."

Wesley Carver, the newest recruit to the prosecutor's department nods his head and takes note of it.

"Miss Briscoe shall abstain from communication directly or indirectly with Miss Aliah Brooklin, Miss Hannah Gates and Ms. Brandee Hawkins while awaiting trial. Bail is denied," the judge repeats.

The judge slams his gavel and Jillian responds hysterically. She immediately flashes a glance at Harley. He scowls at her, causing her to shout out to him.

"I never wanted you to get hurt, David! Please don't let them do this to me. I love you!"

Her hysteria has the entire crowd stirring in their seats, mumbling their disapproval to each other. When the bailiff seizes her, she starts to kick and scratch at him.

"Get her out of here," the judge insists, as the bailiff takes her forcefully by the elbow and escorts her to the door in a very unfriendly manner.

When Harley grimaces, Aliah squeezes onto his arm. He presses his forehead against hers. "At least we know she's in pre-trial detention. She's in the custody of the court now. That alone should have you rest better at night."

"Next on the docket is Brandee Hawkins."

The bailiff continues to speak, but Harley drowns it out with his thoughts. Aliah can't take her eyes off of Joshua Bailey, who stands and takes his place at the table next to his scumbag client.

"I still can't believe he's taken this case," Harley grumbles, while scowling at Aliah's ass-hole boss. "Bailey deserves to be shot."

Harley scrubs his hand over his five o'clock shadow, knowing the police weren't able to get a confession out of her. The prosecution relies on Aliah's testimony, but he knows Bailey will tear that apart. Wesley Carver, an old co-worker of Aliah's, had told them in preparation that her word alone is hardly enough when her boss is sitting on the other side of the table rooting for the Defendant.

After the prosecutor reads out the allegations, defence counsel responds. Before long, the judge is perusing the documents before him. Every one sits very quietly awaiting his decision. Aliah seems to be fidgeting a little more than the rest.

"Miss Hawkins. You shall not associate or communicate directly or indirectly with Miss Aliah Brooklin or Mr. David H. Gates. You shall abstain from possessing a firearm until a decision has been rendered. The restraining order stands. You shall report to an officer at the specified times. If you violate the terms, you will be right back in here so fast it will make your head spin. Do you understand, Ms. Hawkins?"

Brandee nods her head repeatedly, putting on a good show.

"Bail is set at sixty-five thousand dollars."

"I object," Wesley shouts.

"You cannot object to my ruling, Mr. Carver. Sixty-five thousand dollars it is."

Harley feels like he's frozen in place, waiting for the Order to issue. When the gavel drops, so does his heart. Aliah crashes into his chest and his daughter's tears finally break free. With an arm around each of his girls, he glares in the the direction of the accused and her counsel. Both of them turn to glance at Harley at the same time.

Harley snarls and shoots them the finger, not caring if the local paper plasters it among its front page highlights. Brandee's composure slips for a mere second, but he recognizes the depraved smirk well.

The evil woman walks, but there is no way he's going to let her harm the ones he loves.

It's a month before there's even a semblance of normalcy in the Gates house. Jillian is set up for definite jail time and Brandee isn't about to walk away unscathed. Together with Wesley Carver, he will ensure that Brandee pays for her crime.

With Jillian locked away, Harley has had to pick up the slack at the office. Aliah helps out where she can, but he doesn't want her working her life away. Despite Aliah's insistence that he hire an assistant, he doesn't have the nerve to hire a new one. He has other plans anyway.

Aliah manages to go back and work for that prick, Joshua Bailey, even after he backstabs her like he did. A conflict of interest has her taken off the case, to the point where Bailey can't even meet with his client at the office. That's just the way Harley likes it.

It's true, he's been so busy, he hasn't had a chance to tell Aliah a few things that have been weighing heavily on his mind lately. He's now ready to make that his priority.

With Hannah's permission, Harley takes Aliah out for a ride on his motorcycle. It's their first ride on his new Harley since the insurance claim has processed, and it'll be their last ride before the snow flies. He wants to celebrate their clean bills of health. They could use a reason to celebrate.

"Are you ready?" Harley asks Aliah, handing her a helmet.

She smiles and nods and then follows him outside.

As Harley pulls out of Aliah's driveway, he notices an unfamiliar van parked on the street a few houses down. He watches the suspicious driver from the corner of his eye. The female driver crouches down to hide from them, but no amount of headdress and makeup can disguise Brandee Hawkins from David H. Gates.

At the next street, Harley makes a right turn. She doesn't appear to be following them. He pulls his bike over on the side of the residential road and turns it off. Before he can even think to grab his cell phone, he notices how Aliah already has her phone to her ear.

"Did you see that?" he asks.

"ADNL 971," she quotes. "The license plate."

Harley smiles as she is connected with the lead detective on the case. She asks Spencer Caldwell to run the plates. Sure enough, they belong to Brandee, but under another alias the cops have been trying to pin on her.

"Spencer insists that he and his team are maybe five minutes away from making the arrest," Aliah tells him, with a saucy smile.

Harley lifts his brow in question. "What do you say we pay Ms. Hawkins a visit in the meantime?"

Aliah seems just as eager to confront the psycho. "Let's go."

They hustle through the neighborhood on foot, sneaking down driveways, cutting through backyards and hopping a fence. Harley glances over his shoulder at Aliah and presses a finger to his lips. He bends down and pulls a .357 Bulldog from his pant leg. Then he hands it to Aliah, as he pulls out his Glock.

When he peers in the mirror of the van, he can see Brandee staring at the phone in her hand, oblivious to the pair of them coming up next to her. Harley kicks the passenger mirror right of its mount, then bangs on the door with the butt of his Glock.

"Open up, Hawkins. You have company."

When he nods at Aliah to take cover behind him, she does as he silently asks. Psycho bitch does the unbelievable. Brandee propels herself from the driver's side door and whips out an oversized handgun. Aliah runs for cover behind her neighbor's car. Harley stays plastered to the side of the van. A shot is fired. Harley instantly glances to where Aliah has run.

"I'm okay," Aliah hollers out.

A depraved laugh rings from Brandee's throat. "You make this too easy. I was only doing a bit of recon, but if this is how you want it to go down, then so be it."

"We don't want any trouble," Harley shouts at her. "We just want you to fuck off already."

"Really. Is that it? And let this bitch get away with everything?" she chants.

Harley watches Aliah peer over the roof of the car. He hears Brandee tisk tisking, using her own gun as a dramatic prop, waving it side to side like an inverted pendulum.

"It's bad enough that my dear friend Jillian has to do jail time. And for what, David? Loving you? That's hardly a crime. She was only trying to help out a friend. Unfortunately, my girl is a little cuckoo," she admits, making her gun revolve in circles next to her head.

Who is the cuckoo one?

"Drop the act," Aliah hollers. "I know it was Jillian calling the shots. It was her all along, wasn't it? Just like in high school, *Lori*."

"Aliah, what are you doing?" Harley shouts, not liking

where she's taking this. Egging on the psycho holding a gun is never smart.

Aliah had explained to him how Brandee looked strikingly similar to Jillian's best friend in high school. But they weren't able to find any hard evidence to make the connection, until Spencer ran the van plates. Facial reconstructive surgery and a little hair dye can go a long way. Harley had never once doubted Aliah's hunch. Fact: Brandee Hawkins and Lori Eagleton are one and the same person.

"No!" Brandee shouts. "It was me. It was all me. I had planned everything myself. I even had to take things into my own hands, but that bitch didn't drown," she screams toward Harley. Then she glances back at Aliah and blurts her threat, pointing her gun right at her. "You were lucky then. You won't be so lucky this time."

"Bull shit!" Aliah hollers, trying Harley's patience. "You don't have what it takes to take me out."

"You wanna bet? Remember Casey Jacob's trial last year? You should; you worked the case with Bailey. Even he couldn't get his guy off. And he's supposed to be the best. That's how good I am. The dumb ass cops can't seem to pin anything on me. I don't know how anyone in Rose Arbour can sleep at night, when killers like me can get away with murder time and time again."

Aliah lets out a sigh of relief. "It's over now, Brandee. Drop your weapon. We've got all the evidence we need to drop you in that cell right next to your *dear friend*."

Brandee laughs again, a long hearty laugh that has her exposing her chest to the sky. "In your dreams, lady. There's no way they're going to trace any of that shit to me. You think I haven't thought this through? There are no links to me to be found. The guns have been disposed of. And I've *taken care of* those useless doofuses who couldn't get the job done. There's no one left to testify against me. Except for you."

She points her gun at Aliah.

Aliah stays crouched behind the car with her gun aimed

at Brandee's heart.

"Put the gun down, Brandee," Harley threatens. "Or I will shoot you."

"I dare you to try," Brandee states.

"Do it," Aliah hollers, heating Harley's blood to a boiling point.

"Why should I surrender to you?" Brandee screams. "So you can have me arrested? So you can go back to my Mitchell and fuck him some more behind my back?"

"You don't really believe that," Harley says, trying to regain her attention and redirect it from Aliah.

"I sure as fuck do. Just because she's screwing around with you, doesn't mean she isn't playing my man too," she barks, growing more agitated the closer Harley gets to her.

She backs away, until she's standing in the middle of the street, scratching her head with her revolver. "She's an evil seductress. She must be stopped." Brandee laughs again, aiming her firearm at Aliah. "I might not have succeeded before, but that won't stop me from finishing the job now."

She fires the gun at Aliah. She shoots to kill.

Harley takes a shot of his own. Time seems to stand still as the bullets sail through air.

The first shot shatters the windshield of the car and lodges in the passenger door, only inches from Aliah's chest. Harley's aim isn't quite as unpracticed. It catches Brandee in the left shoulder, tearing into her flesh and knocking the gun from her hand. She cries out in pain, as three police cars, two marked ones, one dressed in black, come racing up the street behind her.

"You fucking shot me," she screams in disbelief, as blood begins to drain from her gunshot wound. She clutches the injury with her other hand, the injured arm gone limp.

Aliah steps out from behind the car, with a gun raised to Brandee's face. She walks straight toward her with a steely glint in her eye. The police have now exited their vehicles and are hollering at Brandee to get down on her knees. But Aliah knows her loaded gun is right there on the ground.

Brandee's eyes grow wide when she realizes that she is

in danger, but Aliah moves quickly.

She kicks at the gun and it scatters toward the police. "Nice try, Brandee, but your luck has run out."

Aliah points her gun at Brandee's face, positioning the muzzle some three inches from her forehead.

"Don't do it, Ally. She's not worth it," Harley rasps.

The bitch smiles, believing that the cops will save her from Aliah. No one speaks, except Brandee. "I dare you to shoot me."

Aliah presses the revolver against Brandee's skin and cocks it. She can now see the fear in her eyes.

"That," Aliah states, showing Brandee exactly how it feels.

Harley too fears what is going to happen next, seeing the determined look in Aliah's eyes. Aliah pauses, lowers her hands, and then whips out her pistol. It slaps across the girl's face, knocking her to the ground. Aliah promptly drops the gun and puts her hands up over her head.

"That was worth it," she announces to Brandee's bloody face, then waits for the police to cuff her.

To Harley's surprise, they push her aside and collect the woman off the ground, reading Brandee her rights as the ambulance tend to her life threatening wounds. It takes a moment for it to sink in, but eventually Aliah puts her hands down, once she realizes she's off the hook. She turns to face Harley. He hands his gun to a police officer and holds his arms out to her.

Aliah runs to him, crashing into his chest. She squeezes him so hard that he wonders if she's trying to make his head pop off.

After the ambulance tear off for the hospital, and Spencer shares the story of today's events with his fellow detectives, he comes to speak with them.

"That was a dumb move you made there, missy. Entertaining - but stupid. Are you looking to put yourself in jail?"

"No. But don't ask, because I'd do it again if given the opportunity."

Spencer chuckles. "I'm sure you would, love. Lucky for you, my team's been gunning for this girl for a long time. I can pull a few strings to make sure you never see the inside of a cell. I can only hope we have enough on her to keep her locked up this time."

"She's violated the restraining order. That'll at least keep her off the streets," Harley tells him.

"Yeah, but for how long?"

"Spencer's right," Aliah admits. "You'll need video evidence to put this one away. Good thing I got it then, eh?"

Both of the men stare at her.

"Come again," Spencer says, then chews on his lower lip.

She pulls her phone from her pocket and clicks on the video she's taken. "This should come in handy at trial, wouldn't you agree, Sergeant?"

Spencer takes the phone from her hand and watches her homemade video with disbelief written across his brow. "In all my years..."

"I know, Spence. I'm that good."

Harley's smile is enormous.

"May I?" Spencer asks.

"It's all yours, *love*," she teases.

Spencer nods at her. "I guess there's no reason for you two to hang around here anymore. I think we have everything we need right here."

How convenient is it that the video ends when the bullet lodges in the door right in front of her face?

Harley wraps his arms around his hotshot woman and squeezes her close. "Let's get out of here."

Aliah curls into his arms and hugs around his waist. Together, they walk around the block, and manage to avoid the herd of onlookers.

Harley remounts his bike. "Are you ready now?" he asks her, as she snaps up her helmet.

She climbs onto the bike behind him. "I've never felt more ready than I do right now."

With a smile, Harley turns forward. Then he pulls away from the curb and they motor off into the sunset.

CHAPTER TWENTY EIGHT

Aliah doesn't ask questions when he speeds out of town and she even keeps her face clear of emotion as he turns down the familiar dirt road. She looks surprised when he takes her back to the farmhouse he'd shown her before, because this time there's a SOLD sign tagged to the large tree out front.

After rolling to a stop, he turns off his bike and tugs her back to their field of dandelions, now covered in tall dry grass and fallen leaves. Her smile is a picture of ultimate beauty. The atmosphere remains unchanged since their last visit. There's a serenity in the air that you just don't find in the City.

The air is fresh and he's glad he has a blanket, so he can wrap it around Aliah. Even with her jacket on, she shakes for the entire walk; her nerves a little shot from the day's events.

He pulls the blanket over her shoulders, and glances down into her eyes, hanging onto the edges. He smiles, appreciating how she's let him capture her between him and the blanket. After a pleasant silence, Harley sucks in a breath. He's prepared to take the next step in their relationship. He only hopes that Aliah is prepared to make that move.

His gut instinct has been off ever since she's come around, and he hopes he's not misreading how she feels about him. He needs her to say yes. If she doesn't, then he knows what it will mean for them. And it won't be good.

Harley clears his throat and takes a leap of faith. "You know how I've been looking to expand my business?"

"Right." Aliah smiles up at him, respect glimmering from the emerald depths of her eyes.

"I wonder whether you would ever consider joining me."

He smiles. "I could use a mouthpiece."

Aliah slaps at his chest. "Oh, you're so kind."

Harley turns more serious. "I like having you around."

Her smile is out of control. "I know."

He swallows the lump from the back of his throat, but it doesn't clear the obstruction. "I know you have a secure job, and that you like it. But Bailey's an ass. He doesn't deserve to have you."

Harley pauses and scrubs a hand across the back of his neck. "I think you'd like it with me too." He glances down at her. "What do you think?"

When she hesitates, his heart seizes in his chest.

"Can I think about it?"

He nods, not at all satisfied with her answer. She hasn't said anything about how big of a douche Bailey is and she's barely responding to him at all. Something is up.

What is she not telling him?

Aliah's smile looks coy; a look he never expects to appear on her face.

"That's a major commitment," she answers, with an anxious laugh. "Michael, my massage therapist, is already jealous. You've stolen me away from him. How do I know you won't fling me aside for the next girl in line who turns your crank?"

Is she being serious?

An all-over ache consumes him. "I'm not about to push you into anything you don't want to do. But if that's your only concern..."

Does she want him to beg?

Aliah looks upset by his reaction. "I didn't say no." When she swallows and turns her head down, he feels like a jerk. She's acting so standoffish.

He really shouldn't push her, but Harley feels like a bull. He has to plow on. "Look at me," he orders, softly lifting her chin. "If you'll consider it, then that will have to be good enough for me."

Her blackened lashes flutter open, so she can look into his eyes. "I can put you out of your misery now, if you like.

I have thought about it," she whispers.

When the words come from those beautiful ruby lips, his heart takes a full stop. "Already?"

Once she regains her nerve, she says, "I'm one step ahead of you, Harley." Then she smiles. "I would love nothing more than to join you." Her smile lights up her beautiful features, as she turns to teasing. "Of course, *I* would have to be the boss."

"Of course," he agrees. "In the bedroom, anyway."

She outright laughs this time, readjusting the blanket over her shoulders.

"I was hoping you'd say yes." He tugs her back toward the old barn that appears to be sealed up by tree roots and weeds, but he's already had it stocked and secured. "So I could give you this."

He smiles, loving the look of the wonder on her face. "Are you ready for it?"

She flashes a look at him that has him laughing.

"I got you something."

"What is it?" She sounds almost scared to find out.

"We'll call it a signing bonus." He unlatches the lock and pulls open the old wooden door. He turns his attention back to the woman standing there with two hands covering her mouth. She's shell-shocked. Stunning. He's suddenly certain he's made the right decision.

"Harley... it's gorgeous."

"It's yours."

She shakes her head side to side, then moves closer to him, leaving the blanket disposed of on the ground. She flattens her hands on his chest. "What?"

He licks his lip and then presses a kiss to her mouth. "It's yours," he repeats.

She eyes up the brand spanking new motorcycle that he's purchased just for her. She doesn't move from his arms, until he nudges her forward.

"I know you already have a motorcycle at your dad's..."

"Is this a Harley?" she interrupts, sliding her fingertips over the leather seat.

"In matte yellow. I'm told it's a perfect match to your car."

Tears are in her eyes, but she doesn't admit that she's emotional about it. "You're crazy."

Feeling confident in his progress, he decides to push it one step farther. "I'm not done yet."

Her eyes widen. She has absolutely no clue where he's going with this.

After retrieving the blanket, and returning it to Aliah's shoulders, he pulls her back to the yard, until they're surrounded by whispering trees and fresh air. It's just like he'd imagined.

"You know how I told you I bought this place because I've always dreamt of living out here?"

"Yes." Aliah's stare is burning right through him. She knows something's up, but she's not saying anything. That's unlike her.

He clears his throat again, afraid to see how she's going to react, and even more terrified to compare that reaction to the gift of the bike. "That wasn't exactly one hundred percent true."

Her eyes fall shut, and she instantly grows distant, erecting an imaginary wall between them. "You said no more lies. I thought we'd gotten past all that. How am I supposed to trust you with all these lies?" The words whisper from her trembling lips.

He now realizes he's going to have to put up a fight if he's going to get her back on his side. "It's true that owning this land was a dream of mine. That's no lie. But since a certain someone's come barrelling into my life unannounced, all of my old priorities have been knocked aside."

Aliah looks back up into his eyes. She's listening again, and it's as though her wall has come crashing down.

"They told me to chase my passions."

Harley pauses. Aliah's swooning.

"You're it, Aliah. You're my priority now. No more lies. Only promises that I intend to keep."

The look in her eye scares him.

Has he blown it again?

It is far too late to turn back now. "I used to want to come out here to get away from people. Now it's so I can have you to myself." He pauses, letting what he's said sink it. "You're the reason I bought this place."

She stares at him through squinted eyes, while she tries to put it all together. "I don't understand." The look on her face seems to indicate that she's telling the truth.

He doesn't know if she's ready for it, but he certainly is. He knows this will straighten out any confusion in an instant. He stuffs his hand into his pocket and pulls out a diamond.

The blanket drops to the grass behind her and her mouth turns into a pleasant O shape.

He swallows the lump from the back of his throat. "I've been putting a lot of thought into this…"

"What do you think you're doing?" she interrupts.

There is no mistaking the reason for the rock.

"Will you let me finish?" He asks nicely, and can't help but let an anxious smile sneak out.

She nods her head, too shocked to say anything else. That's what he banks on. He can't help but smile at her reaction.

But damn, he's nervous.

"As I was saying. I've put a lot of thought into this, and I've been hanging onto this ring for the right opportunity to present it to you. Hannah thought it would be best this way. I've taken her advice. I didn't actually think there'd be such a time, but here we are.

"Here we are," she echoes softly.

He's surprised she's being so soft. He half expected her to slap him and leave in a rampage on her new bike. He laughs inappropriately. Nothing's come this close to important to him in many many years.

"It's no secret that I love you," he blurts.

He expects her to roll her eyes, but she just continues to stare, all wide-eyed, at him. That only makes him smile wider. His hands are sweating. This is a new feeling for him.

"I'd like to prove that love to you now." He drops down to one knee, too scared to scan her for a response. When she begins to cry, he glances up immediately and returns to his feet equally as fast.

"Please don't cry. I'm sorry." He bows his head until their foreheads are pressed together.

She shakes her head side to side, garnering his attention. "It's just too sweet for my Harley," she whispers, and takes a sharp intake of breath.

My Harley?

He then realizes it's a happy sob coming from her throat. He proudly returns to a jean-clad knee. He takes her small hand in his and gazes into her wide, expressive eyes. "Aliah Brooklin. Will you promise to kiss me and only me, David H. Gates, for the rest of your days?"

"Yes," she answers, without question.

He's stunned. Elated... but stunned. "You'll marry me?"

She presses her lips together in a smile and nods her head with certainty. Her answer is neither too brash, nor too slow. It's *just right.* Just the way their life will be together.

He lifts himself back to his feet and crashes into her lips, smearing her tears with his hands, as he kisses his fiancée. He takes her hand and slips the dainty ring on her finger. Her eyes turn wide again. That look will never get old.

"I love you," he tells her again, his voice brimming with affection. He intends to tell her that for the rest of his life.

Finally taking her eyes off her new addition, she glances up at him with a soft green gaze, her lips moving before she can even think to stop them. "I love you too, David."

He seals her mouth with another kiss, stunned by her confession. He's never felt this relieved and euphoric in all his life. He plans to make many more days just like this one. With Aliah by his side, anything is possible.

SUPPORT THIS AUTHOR!

LEAVE A REVIEW!

GOODREADS
www.goodreads.com/christasimpson

AMAZON
http://amazon.com/author/christasmipson

SMASHWORDS
www.smashwords.com/profile/view/christasimpson

ABOUT THE AUTHOR

Christa Simpson is a Romance Author who enjoys entertaining her readers with sexy alpha males and sassy heroines. She writes sexy new adult and steamy adult romances loaded with passion, suspense and sarcasm. In her "free time", she loves reading, writing, music, movies and dancing. She likes her men muscled, her music loud and her kids happy.

She's a small town girl, living in Southwestern Ontario with her husband and two beautiful daughters. She's a legal assistant by day, wielding a sexy imagination by night. She's a dreamer and has always believed that you can do anything you set your mind to.

Please visit her website:
http://christasimpson.com

www.twitter.com/_christasimpson
www.pinterest.com/christamsimpson
http://plus.google.com/+christasimpson
www.facebook.com/authorchristasimpson

Author of...
THE TWISTED TRILOGY
Book 1: Twisted
Book 2: Twist & Turn
Book 3: A Twist of Fate
Book 4: Twisted Desire

THE DESTINY SERIES
Book 1: Finding Destiny

The Twisted cast returns in TAINTED LOVE, releasing 2015.

TAINTED LOVE

http://christasimpson.com/tainted-love

THE TWISTED TRILOGY: BOOK 1

TWISTED

Can a man and woman be just friends?

In case you've skipped ahead in the series, here's a look at what you've missed!

Excerpt – Edwin and Abigail:

I carefully unclipped a long black pencil skirt from a hanger and slipped the fitted skirt over my hips. Before I topped it with a flirty blouse, I decided I should've probably brushed my teeth first. There's nothing worse on a Monday morning than tooth paste splatter on your white shirt. Acting quick and careless, I headed for my door, and when I stepped out into the hallway, I bumped right into Edwin.

"Whoa!" He seemed equally as stunned by the imposition, but he didn't budge an inch.

Being inside his personal space was incredibly awkward. It wasn't exactly the place I had expected to be this morning. But there I was, wearing nothing but a barely-there bra.

My eyes flashed away from his glimmering aqua glance and landed on his luscious smiling lips. Lower yet, my eyes focused in on his smooth chest peeking out of his crisp white, mostly unbuttoned shirt. *Damn it.* He looked like a tasty morning treat, his shirt fully tucked into those black slacks hung handsomely from his masculine hips.

I swallowed the lusty lump from the back of my throat. "Sorry," I said, softly. I didn't even know whether I was apologizing for getting in his face or eyeing his body like a piece of man candy.

It didn't seem to matter to him. He took my chin in his hand and looked right through me with a piercing gaze. "You can feel sorry for a lot of things, but this shouldn't ever be one of them."

His lips covered mine, his drugging kiss long and slow, as I struggled with myself to make him stop. I should have. I could have. But I didn't.

Edwin stopped first and smiled at my carelessness. I stood there a little stunned and a lot disappointed with my lack of judgment. With fists bunched at my sides, I forced a stern look to make its appearance. It was hard to keep it together.

"What do you think you're doing, Eddie?"

"I couldn't help myself, and you didn't stop me. What do you expect? I'm only a man."

How can I argue with that? I loosened my fists and took a deep breath, in an attempt to relax my tense muscles. "Well, maybe you can give me a little notice next time."

"I didn't plan for this. It just happened," he insisted.

"I'm sure. You're lips just bumped into mine."

"Like you just happened to rush out of your door at the exact time I was passing," he challenged. His arrogance was starting to make me angry, but I was relieved to feel any emotion other than sadness and despair.

"Wait a minute: that really happened! Don't try and turn this on me."

"Mmm, hmm," he replied, pressing my every button.

"Well, I hope you enjoyed yourself, because I'm not going to let you take advantage of me like that again." I backed away, more for me than for him. He smelled so good.

He laughed and just stood there, shaking his head, staring at me. His fresh aftershave and fragrant cologne mixed with his arousal in an enticing aroma. It had a terrifying effect on me, heightening my senses and messing with my mind. After being so dangerously close to him, I was desperate for some privacy to regain my composure. But his eyes never left mine and I worried that he was magically deciphering my thoughts.

With my nerves getting the best of me, I did what any reasonable woman would have done in the circumstances: I bolted for the washroom.

"I was just going to brush my teeth," I announced, trying to prove my innocence. I ducked into the washroom, feeling safe once I was out of the fathomless aqua force field he was wielding.

"Oh, really?" he replied, following after me. "Funny. Because that's exactly what I was coming to do."

My eyes grew wide with anxiety and as soon as I noticed, I glared at myself in the mirror. *Time. Space. I need...*

Edwin appeared nonchalantly in the reflection behind me. I tore my eyes from his firm chest and confident stare, and fixed them on my toothbrush, as I shakily applied the paste. I put the tube down and pressed both of my hands against the cold marble countertop to support my weight, stop the shaking and avoid his mystical eyes.

Continuing with his casual lack of concern, Edwin reached around me and under my outstretched arms to retrieve the toothpaste and his brush. I closed my eyes and inhaled his scent, totally disarming my anger and arousing my budding curiosity.

I took a deep breath, as I ran my toothbrush under the water. "What are you doing?"

"Brushing my teeth. Obviously."

"Hah!" I replied, with a mouthful of paste.

Edwin began to fight me for the sink bowl, playfully hip checking and trying to shove me out of the way. I defended better than a seasoned veteran, boxing him out with my hips and rear-end.

"I'd better warn you," Edwin mumbled, with paste foaming around his lips. He nudged me aside and emptied his mouth into the sink. "I may try and kiss you again when you're done brushing."

I sputtered into the sink, reacting to his terrifying words. "Don't even think about it!" I was feeling extremely uncomfortable with the notion.

"You asked for notice and service is effective," he taunted, dipping his mouth to the tap. He slurped up some water and swished it around in his mouth as I took a mouthful of water myself.

I rinsed out my mouth and dried it on the towel as Edwin spewed out the last of his mouthwash. I wanted to be mad. I tried to be mad. But how could you be mad at that handsome face?

"Don't say I didn't warn you," he said, winking.

There was no denying that spending time like this with Edwin made me feel a lot better about everything. Playful was doable, and I was pleasantly surprised that he was being so good about it so soon. Taking my good old time, I flossed every tooth and gargled with mouthwash. Edwin watched me intently.

I acknowledged his presence, but tried to act emotionless. It was extremely difficult. An overpowering inquisitiveness hung thick in the air between us as I dried the wetness from my mouth. I found myself in desperate need of oxygen, the room entirely starved of it as Edwin stepped up beside me.

"We're going to be okay," he said, his low, sexy growl cutting through the hazy air.

I reached past him to put the bottle of mouthwash back where it belonged, and he didn't move out of my way. My sensitive sniffer caught a whiff of him again, as I nudged him aside to open the vanity door. *Mmm. That scent.*

Edwin stood, unmoved, blocking my path to the door, making me brush past him to make my exit. As I walked away, he slowly followed, but stopped when he reached the hall. I pretended not to notice.

"You are pretty messed up," he said, stopping me in my tracks.

"Excuse me?" I spun around to face him, my expression cold and conceited.

"Did you forget already?" He hoped for a stunned response and so I acted clueless, as my eyes locked onto his heated gaze.

"I have no idea what you're talking about." If he only knew, I wanted him to try me on for size, something fierce. But I knew what was good for me.

I should stick to my original plan: evade, retreat and regroup. If I stayed away from Edwin I could move on a lot faster.

So, why won't my feet move?

"Oh, you know exactly what I'm talking about," he growled. His arousal swarmed the air around me, like a group of angry bees, and burned, fiery hot, through my lungs.

He took two long deliberate steps toward me, as I took one hesitant step backward. "I told you I would try again," he said, his voice sounding smooth and sexy, as he progressively got closer.

I should have turned and ran screaming for the stairs, but I could hardly make a peep. "I thought I had some time," I breathed, as his face drew near mine.

He brushed past my cheek, his breath on my neck and his lips against my ear. "You thought wrong."

My lashes fluttered shut, as Edwin slowly pulled away from my neck, his hand gently skimming across my cheek. I waited for his sensual attack, but it never came. I slowly opened my anxious, emerald eyes and looked up into his. His smile was soft and tantalizing, and his lips parted as he closed his eyes and titled his head for a kiss.

I gasped for air and pulled back, stunning myself with my own willpower. "I can't, Eddie. We can't do this anymore." *Though I so wish we could.*

"I realize we can't do this as a couple. But we're both single, consenting adults. We're free to do whatever we want."

I cocked an eyebrow at him, preparing to playfully test his crisis negotiation skills. "Do I look like that kind of girl to you? I don't just sleep around with random men like that."

He returned inside my zone, his lips delivering an enticingly cunning smile, shaking my confidence. "I'm hardly some random guy."

Yes! Yes! I thought, as Edwin's cologne doused my senses. At that moment, with my own hormones raging, I was unable to formulate a sentence, let alone verbalize one.

"It'd be just this once," he insisted. "No one even knows that we've split. I want to... no I need to feel you, Abs. One last time. Admit it. You need it too."

Just the fact that I was thinking about it was stressful enough, and Edwin thought that was his answer.

"What's the big deal?" he asked, smirking.

"It's not healthy!" I stammered.

"Get over it."

"But I have to go to work." I partly hoped he would give up, so I could stick to my guns.

"We don't usually leave for another half hour, at least. You know there's plenty of time for what I have in mind. Now quit with the excuses."

On a harsh exhale, I let my guard down only for a second, and Edwin didn't waste the opportunity. He kissed me, his hot lips on mine. He kissed me again, his icy cool breath in my mouth.

Stunned, I accepted the string of tantalising nibbles and devouring mouthfuls. Just last night I was worrying to myself that I may never find myself in this place ever again, and here I am the very next day wrapped in his amazing arms; his thorough hands exploring me with unguarded enthusiasm.

My mind was done fighting, my body begged me to stop fighting and I couldn't fight Edwin off anymore, even if I wanted to. Did I want to? *Hell no.*

I pushed Edwin off of me and he froze in confusion, until I started to slowly, seductively, unzip the back of my long, fitted skirt. After it slipped to the floor, I kicked it aside. I was standing there in the hallway, with my breasts bursting from my lacy push up bra and my g-string barely covering anything, and yet Edwin's gaze was still locked on my face. He was speechless.

I knew this would be my last opportunity to touch him

and so did my body. Together we intended to take full advantage of him.

A devious giggle tickled my throat, as I stepped toward him. His eyes grew wide with excitement as I yanked his pressed shirt from his pants and tore open the rest of his carefully buttoned shirt. The buttons sprinkled onto the floor like candy, as I stared up at him through dark lashes.

My hands smoothed over the rise and fall of his chest. They were cold compared to the heat radiating from his firm skin.

Edwin's lips turned up into a smile, finally revealing his arousal and forgetting about his surprise. I grinned back, provocatively, all anxiety piled back with my skirt on the floor. My hands scoured his bulky physique and my tongue found his hard nipple.

His eyes closed and his pants tented, as my aggression made him thicker and harder. Edwin licked his lips and gripped onto my behind with his large hands, letting out an excited moan as I nibbled at him.

My fingers skimmed over his rock hard abs, and then deftly unclipped his leather belt. Dropping to my knees, my lips trailed down his body to where my fingers left off. Being slow and sensual, I trimmed the band of his fitted briefs with kisses and then pulled his belt off with a snap.

"Hey, I didn't say you could rip all of my clothes off," he said, his wicked grin being his demise.

Channeling all control, "Oh, are you making the rules now?" I stopped, acting like I could actually control my sexual rage. "Suit yourself." Yanking on his pants, I lifted myself to my feet and spun away from him. With one dainty step, my body trembled with an all-consuming ache for Edwin.

"No more playing, Abs. I need you."

I froze in place trying to shake the delicious chill chasing up my body. His serious response made my anxiety return full force though none of the excitement dwindled.

Stealing a few more steps away from him, I was met with the top of the stairs. I glanced down to our front foyer, reason returning to me, as I frantically reconsidered my options: fight or flight.

"Oh, no you don't," Edwin said, reading my mind. Then, out of nowhere, he was just there; pulling me back and lifting me in the air like a doll. "You're mine," he ordered, looking up at me through deep, dark eyes.

Breathless, I wrapped my dangling legs around his waist, as he pressed me against the wall. He slowly drew my lips into his mouth, but when he grinded against me, we both became instantly frantic and obsessive.

We moaned in unison, desperate to fulfill our own fanatical desires. Edwin pulled me off the wall and turned for my room, his fly open and ready, his business attire flagging loosely from his hips.

"No! Take me now."

Edwin obeyed. He dropped his pants to the floor, laid me where he stood and boldly took me right in the hall. Arousal, pleasure, love and passion were among the many feelings blasting around me like a violent whirlpool as I quickly found my climax.

"Oh, Edwin. Oh God!" I wailed, as he thrust deep and exploded inside me, rocking me in a glorious second wave of pleasure.

He crashed on top of me, breathless and amused, his heavy chest driving the air from my lungs. Noticing my silent discomfort he lifted himself with a push up and kissed me gratefully on my lips. My head still swirled with ignorance and harmony.

"Now that's what I'm talking about," he growled, sensually. "We couldn't have done that if we had kids."

Can a man and woman be just friends?

CHRISTA SIMPSON

TWISTED

THE TWISTED TRILOGY

Available now!

http://christasimpson.com